THOU SHELL OF DEATH

THOU SHELL OF DEATH

NICHOLAS BLAKE

ISIS

LARGE PRINT

Oxford

First published in Great Britain 1936
by
Collins Crime Club

Published in Large Print 2013 by ISIS Publishing Ltd.,
7 Centremead, Osney Mead, Oxford OX2 0ES
by arrangement with
The Random House Publishing Group Limited

British Library Cataloguing in Publication Data
Blake, Nicholas, 1904–1972.
 Thou shell of death.
 1. Strangeways, Nigel (Fictitious character) - -
 Fiction.
 2. Detective and mystery stories.
 3. Large type books.
 I. Title
 823.9'12–dc23

ISBN 978–0–7531–9118–7 (hb)
ISBN 978–0–7531–9119–4 (pb)

Printed and bound in Great Britain by
T. J. International Ltd., Padstow, Cornwall

CHAPTER
ONE

The Assistant Commissioner's Tale

A winter afternoon in London. Twilight is descending with the same swift and noiseless efficiency as the lifts in a thousand hotels and stores and offices. Electric signs, winking, shifting, unrolling, flaring and blaring, announce the varied blessings of twentieth-century civilisation, proclaim the divinity of this port and that actress: a few stars, which have had the temerity to appear, seem to have quickly retired from the competition into higher air. In the streets a preponderance of children and brown paper parcels shows that Christmas is near. The shop windows, too, are piled with that diversity of obscene knick-knacks which nothing but the spirit of universal goodwill could surely tolerate — calendars to suit every bad taste or every degree of personal animosity, chromium-plated cigar cutters, sets of ivory toothpicks, nameless articles in fancy leather, illuminated and perhaps illuminating texts, bogus jewels and synthetic foods — an orgy of the superfluous. Men and money circulate with feverish activity. Even the traffic seems to pulse with greater din and violence through the main arteries, as though the whole city was sprinting desperately down a last lap.

Vavasour Square lay out of the main currents of this Christmas spate. Its superb eighteenth-century houses stood aloof amidst the gathering darkness, like aristocrats deprecating the gaudy, loud-voiced spirit of the times. The clamour of the big streets reached them subdued to a whisper, abashed by the chill hauteur of their facades. In the garden of the square, plane trees sketched leisurely and consummate gestures against the sky, like the arms of noble ladies in brocade, and the grass held all the suavity of old tradition. Even the dogs that had the privilege of inhabiting this exclusive neighborhood seemed to address their friends or their lampposts with the courtly grace of Beaus and Corinthians. Nigel Strangeways, looking out of the window of No. 28, muttered to himself a couplet from Pope. He looked down at his waistcoat and was vaguely astonished to find it West-of-England cloth, not flowered silk. He would have been far more astonished had he been told that out of this backwater he was shortly to be swirled into the strangest, the most complicated and the most melodramatic case in all his career.

Nigel, after a brief stay at Oxford, in the course of which he had neglected Demosthenes in favour of Freud, had turned to the profession of criminal investigator — the only profession left, he was wont to remark, which gave scope for good manners and scientific curiosity. His aunt, Lady Marlinworth, with whom he was having tea this afternoon, took good manners for granted. As to scientific curiosity she was more doubtful: it had a flavour of the banausic, the not-quite-quite. There were other things about Nigel that made here uneasy; such as his habit of taking his teacup for walks with him round the room and leaving it on the very edge of whatever article of furniture happened to be handy.

"Nigel," she said, "there is a little table beside you; it would be more suitable than the seat of that chair."

Nigel hastily removed the offending object and placed it on the table. He looked at his aunt. She was fragile and delicately tinted as one of her own teacups, perfect in this other-worldly setting. He wondered what would happen if she were to be dropped suddenly into the middle of a violent, vulgar situation — a murder, for instance. Would she just smash into a hundred delicate fragments?

"Well, Nigel, I haven't seen you for a long time. I hope you haven't been overworking. Your — er — profession must be very exacting. Still, it has compensations, no doubt. You must come into contact with a number of interesting persons."

"Certainly not overworking. I haven't had a case worth mentioning since that affair down at Sudeley Hall."

Lord Marlinworth laid down a sandwich with some deliberation and tapped delicately with two fingers on the rosewood table before him. His appearance was so identical with that of the earl in a musical comedy, that Nigel could never look at him for long without pinching himself.

"Ter-tum," said Lord Marlinworth, "that was the affair at the preparatory school, if my memory serves me. The newspapers made considerable stir about it. I have not had the acquaintance of any schoolmasters, not since my salad days. Excellent fellows, no doubt. Though I can only deprecate the effeminacy which I see creeping into education today. 'Spare the rod', you know, 'spare the rod'. I believe a connection of ours is engaged in the teaching profession, headmaster of some quite reputable school — Winchester, is it? or Rugby? The name escapes my memory for the moment."

Nigel escaped any further memories of Lord Marlinworth, for at this moment his uncle, Sir John Strangeways, was shown in. Sir John had been the favourite brother of Nigel's father, and on the latter's death Sir John had become the boy's guardian. In a few years a bond of the deepest attachment had grown up between the two. Sir John was a man of rather less than medium height: he had a thick sandy moustache and large hands, and his clothing gave one always the impression that he had just changed, hastily and unwillingly, out of an old gardening coat. His bearing, on the other hand, was brisk, compact, self-assured and somehow invigorating, like that of a family doctor or a competent psychiatrist: contrasting in turn with this were his eyes, which held the remote horizon look of the dreamer. Whatever deduction as to his calling one might have made from these contradictory characteristics, one would almost certainly not have hit on the correct one. Sir John was neither a landscape gardener, a poet, or a physician: he was, in actual fact, Assistant Commissioner of Police.

4

He stumped briskly into the room, kissed Lady Marlinworth, clapped her husband on the back, and cocked his head at Nigel.

"Well, Elizabeth! Well, Herbert! Been looking for you, Nigel. Rang up your flat, and they told me you were over here. Got a job for you. Ah, a cup of tea. Thanks, Elizabeth. So you've not got into the habit of cocktails at teatime yet." His eyes twinkled quizzically at the old lady. He was in some ways a simple soul, and could never deny himself the pleasure of a leg-pull.

"Cocktails at teatime! My dear John! What a horrible idea! Cocktails, indeed! Why, I remember my dear father practically turning a young man out of the house because he asked for one before dinner. My father's sherry, of course, was famous all over the country, which made it still worse. I'm afraid Scotland Yard is getting you into bad habits, John."

The old lady bridled, secretly delighted to be thought capable of the excesses of fast young things. Lord Marlinworth tapped discreetly upon the table and spoke with the air of one who understands all and can pardon all.

"Ah, yes; cocktails. A drink imported, I am told, from America. The custom of drinking cocktails at all hours of the day is on the increase, undoubtedly, amongst certain sections of society. I have always found a good sherry sufficient for my needs, but I dare say these American beverages are not unpalatable. *Tempora mutantur*. We live in times of rapid change. In my young days a man had time to savour life, to roll it round his tongue, like an old brandy. But now these

5

bright young people take it in gulps. Well, well. We must not stand in the way of Progress."

Lord Marlinworth sat back again and made a benign gesture with his right hand, as though permitting Progress to resume its advance.

"Are you going down to Chatcombe for Christmas?" asked Sir John.

"Yes, we are leaving town tomorrow. We think of going in the car: the trains are so disagreeably full at this time of the year."

"Come across your new tenant at the Dower House yet?"

"We have not had the pleasure of meeting him personally yet," replied Elizabeth Marlinworth. "He had unexceptionable references, of course; but, really, he is quite an embarrassingly famous young man. We seem to have done nothing but answer questions about him since he took the house. Don't we, Herbert? It quite taxes my powers of invention."

"And who is this famous young man?" asked Nigel.

"Not so young as all that. Famous, if you like. Fergus O'Brien," said Sir John.

Nigel whistled. "Great Scott! *The* Fergus O'Brien? The legendary airman. The Mystery Man who Retired from Life of Daredevil Adventure to Seclusion of English Countryside. I'd no idea that he'd made the Dower House his hermitage —"

"If you had come to visit your aunt lately, you would have heard," Lady Marlinworth rebuked mildly.

6

"But how wasn't it in the papers? They generally follow him about like a private detective. All they said was that he'd retired somewhere into the country."

"Oh, they were squared," said Sir John. "There were reasons. Well, you two," he continued, "if you'll excuse us. I'll take Nigel into the study. We've got to confabulate."

Lady Marlinworth gave a gracious consent, and Nigel and his uncle were soon ensconced in huge leather armchairs, Sir John smoking the foul cherry-wood pipe which was the bane and embarrassment of his official colleagues.

The two made an odd contrast. Sir John sat solid and upright in his chair, dwarfed by it, economical of phrase and gesture, looking now rather like an extraordinarily intelligent, tow-haired little terrier, except for that impressive longsightedness in his blue eyes. Nigel's six feet sprawled all over the place; his gestures were nervous and a little uncouth; a lock of sandy-coloured hair drooping over his forehead, and the deceptive naïveté of his face in repose gave him a resemblance to an overgrown prep schoolboy. His eyes were the same pale blue as his uncle's, but shortsighted and noncommittal. Yet there was an underlying similarity between the two. A latent, sardonic humour in their conversation, a friendlines and simple generosity in their smiles, and that impression of energy in reserve which is always given by those who possess an abundance of life directed towards consciously realised aims.

"Well, now, Nigel," said Sir John, "I've got a job for you. Curiously enough, it's to do with the new tenant of the Dower House. He wrote up to us about a week ago; forwarded some threatening letters he'd received lately — three of them — at intervals of a month each. Typewritten. I put a man on to them, but they don't give any lead. Here are copies. Read 'em carefully and tell me if they suggest anything — anything, that is, except the obvious conclusion that someone is out for his blood."

Nigel took the carbon copies. They were numbered 1, 2 and 3, presumably the order in which they had been received.

No. 1 read: "No, Fergus O'Brien, there's no use trying to hide yourself in Somerset. Not even if you had the wings of a dove would you escape me, my bold aviator. I shall get you, and YOU WILL KNOW WHY."

"Hm," said Nigel, "all very melodramatic: author seems to have confused himself with Lord God Almighty. And what a literary touch the fellow has!'

Sir John came over and sat on the arm of his chair. "There was no signature," he said. "Envelopes were typewritten also; a Kensington postmark."

Nigel took up the second note: "Beginning to feel a little apprehensive, are you? That iron nerve wobbling a bit? I don't blame you. However, I shall not keep Hell waiting for you much longer."

"Coo!" exclaimed Nigel. "Fellow getting all sinister. And what does this month's bulletin say?" He read out the third note aloud:

"I think we'd better arrange the fixture — I refer, of course, to your demise — for this month. My plans are all completed, but I feel it would be improper for me to kill you till your festive party is over. That will give you over three weeks to settle your affairs, say your prayers, and eat a hearty Christmas dinner. I shall kill you, most probably, on Boxing Day. Like Good King Wenceslas, you will go out on the Feast of Stephen. And please, my dear Fergus, however shattered your nerves may be by then, don't go committing suicide. After all the trouble I have taken, I should hate to be balked of the pleasure of telling you, before you die, just how much I hate you, you tin-pot hero, you bloody white-faced devil."

"Well?" enquired Sir John, after rather a long silence.

Nigel shook himself, blinked in a puzzled way at the notes, then said: "I don't understand it. There's something unreal about the whole thing. It's too like an old-fashioned melodrama rewritten by Noel Coward. Have you ever known a murderer with a sense of humour? That crack about Good King Wenceslas is really most pleasing. I feel I could take to the fellow who wrote it. I suppose it isn't, by any chance, a hoax?"

"May very well be, for all I know. But O'Brien must have thought there might be something in it, or why should he send the letters to us?"

"What are the bold aviator's reactions, by the way?" Nigel asked.

His uncle produced another carbon copy and handed it over in silence. It ran as follows:

Dear Strangeways,

I am taking our slight acquaintanceship as an excuse for troublng you with what may very likely be a mare's nest. I have received the enclosed letters, in the numbered order, on the 2nd of each month since October. It may be a lunatic, and it may be some friend of mine having his little joke. On the other hand, there's just a chance that it may not. As you know, I've had a rackety life, and I've no doubt there are a number of people who would like to see me go down in a spin. Perhaps your experts will be able to gather something from the letters themselves. But it seems unlikely. Now I *don't* want police protection. I haven't settled down in the depths of the country in order to be surrounded by a phalanx of policemen. But if you know some really intelligent and reasonably amiable private investigator, who would come down and hold my hand, could you get me in touch with him. What about that nephew of yours you were telling me about? I could give him a few lines to work on — suspicions so vague that I don't care to put them on paper. If he could come, I am having a house-party over Christmas, and he might come ostensibly as a guest. Let him turn up on the 22nd, a day before the others. — Yours sincerely,

Fergus O'Brien

"Ah, I see. So that's where I come in," said Nigel ruminatively. "Well, I should like to go down there very much, if you think I come up to the required standard of intelligence and amiability. O'Brien sounds a nice sensible fellow, too. I'd always imagined he was one of the neurotic daredevil type. But you've met him. Tell me about him."

Sir John sucked noisily on his pipe. "I'd rather you formed your own impressions. Of course, he's a bit of a nervous wreck — that last crash of his, you know. Looks damned ill; but you can see the spirit shining through all right still. He has never consciously courted publicity, I should say. But, like all really great Irishmen — take Mick Collins, for instance — he's a bit of a playboy; I mean, it is their nature to do things in the most romantic and colourful way possible; they just can't help it. I should say he had the long memory of the Irish, too —"

Sir John paused, and wrinkled his brow reflectively.

"Is he real Irish?" asked Nigel. "One of the Brian Boru Clan? or just West British?"

"Nobody really knows, I don't think. His origin is shrouded in mystery, as they say. Turned up suddenly in the R.F.C. early in the war, and never looked back. There must be a good deal to him. Genuine integrity, I mean. Popular heroes, particularly in the air, are two a penny nowadays: they flame up and then are forgotten tomorrow. But he's different. Even allowing for the playboy, romantic element in all his adventures, he couldn't have kept his grip on the popular imagination unless he was something out of the ordinary run of

11

'heroes'. It must be some greatness of integrity that keeps the fires of hero worship burning still for him."

"Well, as you say, you'd rather I formed my own impressions," said Nigel provocatively. "But I'd be glad of the outside dope, so to speak, if you've got time. I've rather lost touch with the O'Brien saga."

"I expect you know the salient points all right. He had a bag of sixty-four Germans by the end of the war: used to go out alone and sit up in a cloud all day, waiting for them. The Germans were quite convinced he had a charmed life: used to attack anything of theirs short of a circus. The chaps in his squadron really began to be a bit afraid of him themselves. Day after day he'd go out, and come back with the fuselage looking like a sieve and half the struts nearly shot through. MacAlister in his mess told me it looked as if O'Brien deliberately tried to get killed and just couldn't bring it off; might have sold his soul to the devil, for all anyone knew. And what's more, he did it without drink. Then, after the war, there was his solo flight to Australia in an obsolete machine, flying one day and every other day tying the pieces together after the crack-up. And, of course, there was that incredible exploit of his in Afghanistan, when he took a whole native fort single-handed. And the stunting he did for that film company, chucking his machine all over the place between the peaks of a mountain range. I suppose the culminating feat was his rescue of that explorer woman, Georgia Cavendish. Went looking for her all over some godless part of Africa, landed in impossible country, picked her up out of it and brought her home.

That seems to have sobered even him a bit. The crash at the end of it may have had some effect, too. Anyway, it was only a few months after that he decided to give up flying and bury himself in the country."

"Um," said Nigel, "a colourful career all right."

"But it isn't these spectacular feats — the things every schoolboy has heard about — that have made the legend, so much as the things the public *hasn't* heard of — officially, that is to say, the things that never got into the newspapers, but were passed from mouth to mouth; dark hints, rumours, superstitions almost — some of them fiction, no doubt, and most of them exaggerated, but the greater part founded on fact. All these have swelled up to make a really gigantic mythical figure of him."

"Such as?" asked Nigel.

"Well — one absurd little detail: they say he always fought best in carpet slippers — used to keep a pair in his plane and put 'em on when he got to a thousand feet or so; no idea if there's any truth in it, but those slippers have become as legendary as Nelson's telescope. Then there was his hatred of brass hats — common enough, of course, amongst those who had to do the fighting — but he took active steps about it. Later on in the war, when he had become a flight commander, some B.F. at Wing Headquarters ordered his flight out to do some ground strafing in impossible weather conditions over a nest of machine guns. You know the idea — just to keep 'em busy and justify the brass hat's existence. Well, they were all shot down except O'Brien. After that, they say he spent most of his spare time flying about behind the lines looking for the staff cars. When he saw one, he'd chivvy it all over the countryside, with his wheels a couple of feet above the brass hat's monocle. They say he used to drop homemade stink bombs into the tonneaux, too; fairly frightened 'em out of their wits. But they couldn't exactly prove who it was; and anyway, O'Brien being the popular idol he was, I doubt if they'd have dared to take action. Authority always has been a red rag to him — he didn't give a damn for orders. Went too far, finally. After the war, when his flight was out East, he was ordered to bomb some native village. He didn't see why the natives should have their village blown to pieces just because some of them hadn't paid their taxes, so he made his flight loose off their bombs in the middle of a desert and then flew low over the village, dropping one-pound boxes of chocolates. The authorities couldn't overlook that — he took full responsibility, of course — so he was politely asked to resign. It was soon afterwards that he did his flight to Australia."

Sir John sat back, looking faintly ashamed of his unwonted verbal exuberance.

"So you've fallen under the spell, too," said Nigel, with a humorous cock of the head.

"What the devil do you mean . . .? Well, I suppose I have. And I'll lay ten to one, young man, that you'll be eating out of his hand by the time you've been at the Dower House for a couple of hours."

"Yes, I dare say I shall." Nigel got up with a sigh and began to prowl with his ungainly, ostrich-like stride

14

round the room. This leather-padded, sporting-print-decorated, cigar-and-good-breeding-redolent "sanctum", into which nothing more violent than a *Morning Post* leading article could ever have entered — how utterly remote it was from the life he had just been hearing about, the world of Fergus O'Brien, of dizzy tumblings amongst the clouds, of meteoric exploit and topsy-turvy values: a world where death was threadbare and familiar as Herbert Marlinworth's study carpet. And yet between Lord Marlinworth and Fergus O'Brien there was no more original difference than the excess or deficiency of some little glands.

Nigel shook himself out of these dreamy moralisings, and turned to his uncle again.

"One or two more points I should like to clear up. You said at tea that there were reasons why the press should have been induced to keep quiet about the exact locality of O'Brien's 'retreat.'

"Yes; besides practical flying, he has interested himself a good deal in theory and construction. He is now at work on the plans of a new plane which, he says, will revolutionise flying. He doesn't want the public poking about just now."

"But surely there is a possibility that other Powers may have got wind of this. I mean, oughtn't he to be having police protection?"

"I think he ought," replied Sir John in a worried way; "but there's his blasted cussedness. Said he'd throw all his drawings in the fire if he got so much as a smell of police surveillance. Says he's quite able to look after himself, which is probably true, and anyway that no one else could make head or tail of his plans until they are much further advanced."

"I was thinking there might conceivably be a connection between these threatening letters and his invention."

"Oh, there might. But there's no use getting preconceived ideas into your head."

"Do you know anything about his private life? He's not married or anything, is he? And he didn't tell you who was coming for this house-party, did he?"

Sir John tugged at his sandy moustache. "No, he didn't say. He's not married, though I should think he must be pretty attractive to women. And, as I told you, nothing is known of him before 1915, when he joined up. It all contributes to the newspaper Mystery Man publicity."

"That's suggestive. The newspapers would have been all out to rake up facts about his boyhood, and he must have had some pretty good reason for keeping them in the dark about it. Those threats might be some of his prewar wild oats come home to roost."

Sir John threw up his hands in horror. "For God's sake, Nigel! At my time of life the system can't stand mixed metaphors."

Nigel grinned. "Now there's only one other point," he pursued. "Money: he must be well off to be able to rent the Dower House. I suppose nothing's known about his source of income?"

"Couldn't say. He's had plenty of opportunities of making capital out of his position as Public Idol No. 1. But he's not made great use of them, as far as I know.

But all these questions you'd far better ask him. If he really thinks there's anything in these threats, he'll have to open up to you a little."

Sir John heaved himself out of his chair. "Well. Must be off. Got to dine with the Home Secretary tonight — fussy old hen, he's suddenly developed Communist-phobia; thinks they're going to put a bomb under his bed. Ought to know they don't allow acts of individual violence. Wouldn't mind if they did blow him up, as a matter of fact. His idea of dinner is boiled mutton and grocer's Graves."

He took Nigel by the arm and piloted him towards the door. "I'll just pop in and tell Herbert and Elizabeth not to go giving you away as Sherlock Minor while you're down there. I'll wire O'Brien you're coming on the twenty-second. There's a train from Paddington at 11.45: get you down there in good time for tea."

"So you've got everything fixed, haven't you, you old schemer?" said Nigel affectionately. "Thanks very much for the job — and the saga."

Pausing outside the drawing-room door, Sir John squeezed his nephew's arm and whispered, "Look after him, won't you? I feel I ought to have insisted more strongly on police protection. Those letters would make things pretty difficult for us if anything should happen. And of course you'll let me know at once if you find out there *is* anything behind them. I should simply override his wishes if we had anything definite to go on. Goodbye, boy."

CHAPTER
TWO

The Airman's Tale

As it happened, Nigel did not travel by the 11.45. On the night of the 21st he was rung up by Lord Marlinworth's butler, who said that his master and mistress had been delayed in town and would not be travelling down to Chatcombe till tomorrow. They would be very pleased to give Mr Strangeways a lift down in their car and would call for him sharp at 9.00a.m. Nigel thought it politic to accept this semi-royal invitation, though four or five hours of Lord Marlinworth's reminiscences in such a confined space would be likely to give him a headache.

On the stroke of nine the next morning the Daimler drew up outside Nigel's door. To his aunt and uncle road travel was still a complicated adventure, not to be undertaken lightly. Although the saloon car was as draughtless and dustless as a hospital ward, Lady Marlinworth habitually carried a thick motoring-veil, several layers of petticoat and a bottle of smelling salts for any journey of more than twenty miles. Her husband, in an enormous check ulster, cloth cap and goggles, looked like a cross between Edward the Seventh and Guy Fawkes — a point the cluster of street urchins which had rapidly formed was not slow to take up. A valet and Lady Marlinworth's personal maid were taking the luggage down by train; but the spacious interior of the car was chock-a-block with enough equipment for a polar expedition. Getting in, Nigel barked his shin on a gigantic hamper, and the way to his seat seemed to be paved with hot-water bottles.

When he was at last settled in, Lord Marlinworth consulted his watch, unfolded an ordnance map, took up the speaking-tube and, with the air of a Wellington ordering the whole line to advance, said, "Cox, you may proceed."

During the journey Lord Marlinworth kept up a ceaseless flow of light conversation. As they passed through the suburbs, he commented unfavourably upon their architecture and drew a parallel between it and the makeshift character of twentieth-century civilisation. At the same time he generously conceded that the people who lived there played no doubt a necessary part in the community and were admirable persons in their way. The country reached, he alternated between calling his companion's attention to "pretty peeps" and "noble vistas" and recounting anecdotes of the leading families in each county through which they passed, his wife seconding him with involved researches into their genealogical trees. Whenever they approached a fork in the road, Lord Marlinworth would study his map and give directions to the chauffeur, to which Cox responded with a grave inclination of the head — as if this was the first and not the fiftieth time he had driven the route. Torpor and a haze of unreality stole over Nigel. His head nodded. He jerked awake. His head nodded again. Then he fell finally and uncompromisingly asleep.

He was awoken for a light lunch at twelve o'clock. As soon as they had started, he fell asleep again, thereby missing a remarkable tale about the Hampshire Enderbys, the last head of which family had apparently, at the age of fifty, retired to the top of a lofty tower on his estate, and was never seen again except on the anniversaries of King Charles the First's death, when he used to emerge and fling down red-hot sovereigns to his tenants. When Nigel awoke, they had left the main road and were sliding along a Somerset lane whose hedges almost brushed the sides of the car. Soon they turned left, through a magnificent stone gate. The drive, formally curving and twisting like a hypnotised snake, led them down the side of a combe and up the far slope; there it forked, straight on for Chatcombe Towers, and to the right for the Dower House. Cox was directed to drop Nigel at the Dower House first. As he alighted, Nigel noticed a bizarre addition had been made to the landscape since his last visit to Chatcombe. Fifty yards or so to his right as he faced the front door at the end of the garden, there had been erected an army hut. As he waited for the door to open he wondered idly how O'Brien had managed to persuade Lord Marlinworth to let him erect so unsightly an object on the estate. It also suddenly occurred to him that he had forgotten to let O'Brien know his change of plan, and therefore was not expected till teatime.

20

The door opened. A very large, very broad, very tough-looking man appeared; he wore a neat blue suit, and his nose was about the shape and size of a small pancake. This worthy gave one glance at Nigel and his suitcase — the car had already driven off — and exclaimed:

"No, we don't want no vacuum cleaners, nor yet am I hinterested in silk stockings, brass polish, or parrot seed."

He began to shut the door, but Nigel stepped forward hastily and said: "Nor am I. My name's Strangeways. I got an offer to drive down from London and hadn't time to let you know."

"Oh, I beg your pardon, Mr Strangeways, sir. Come in. My name's Bellamy. Harthur, they generally calls me. The Colonel's out just now, but he'll be back before tea. I'll show you your room. And then I dessay you'd like to stretch your legs around the gawden a bit." He added, with a wistful look: "Unless you'd care to put on the gloves for a round or two. Limber you up after the drive, it would. But perhaps you ain't a devotee of the Noble Art."

Nigel hastily disclaimed it. Arthur looked crestfallen for a moment; but his face soon broke into a craggy grin. "Ah well," he said, "there's some as is 'andy with their maulies, and others as is 'andy with their serry-bellum."

He tapped the small portion of his nose that stood out from the level of his face. "It's OK, Mr Strangeways, sir. I know wot you're down 'ere for.

21

Don't you worry yourself. Mum's the word, sir. I can keep me trap shut. Hoyster is my middle name."

Nigel followed the oyster upstairs. Soon he was unpacking in a cream-washed bedroom, furnished severely but adequately with unstained oak. There was only one picture on the walls. Nigel peered at it short-sightedly, then walked up to it with a cigarette in one hand and a pair of trousers in the other. It was the head of a girl, by Augustus John. Nigel took rather a time to unpack. He was, as he admitted himself, a born snooper. He never could restrain his curiosity about the accessories of other people's lives. He pulled open every drawer in the chest-of-drawers, not so much to dispose of his own effects as in the hope that the last visitor might have left something incriminating behind. They were quite empty, however. There were Christmas roses in a bowl on the dressing table, he noticed. He opened a box on the table beside his bed: it was full of sugar biscuits. He put three absent-mindedly into his mouth, thinking: "A competent housekeeper behind all this." He prowled over to the mantelpiece and fingered the row of books arranged there: *Arabia Deserta*, Kafka's *The Castle, Decline and Fall, The Sermons of John Donne*, the last Dorothy Sayers, Yeats' *The Tower*. He took down the latter; it was a first edition, with an inscription from the poet to "my friend, Fergus O'Brien". Nigel began to revise his preconceptions about his host; it all fitted in very badly with his notion of the daredevil, harum-scarum pilot.

After a bit he walked out into the garden. The Dower House was a long, two-storeyed, whitewashed building, with an overhanging slate roof. It had been built about one hundred and fifty years before on the site of the original Dower House, which had been burnt down. It looked rather like one of those old-fashioned ample country rectories, whose architects seem to have been obsessed by the reproductive power of the clergy. A veranda ran the whole length of the front of the house, which faced south, and was continued along the east face. As he walked round, Nigel saw the wooden hut again; it stood out, more of an anachronism than ever, its windows filled with the blood-red glow of the huge December sun. He went across the lawn and peered in at one of the hut windows. The interior had been fitted up as a workroom. There was an enormous kitchen table, strewn with books and papers; several rows of bookshelves; an oil stove; a safe; some easy chairs; a pair of carpet slippers on the floor. The whole effect contrasted oddly with the guest room he had just left — the one breathing a quiet, distinguished luxury, the other untidy, ascetic and businesslike. Nigel's curiosity, insatiable as that of the Elephant Child, got the better of him. He pushed at the door. Faintly surprised to find that it opened, he went in. He poked about aimlessly for a little; then his attention was attracted by a door in the wall on his left. The living-room looked so large, it had not occurred to him that this was a partition wall. He went through this door and found himself in a small cubicle. It seemed to contain nothing but a truckle bed, a rush mat and a cupboard. Nigel was about to go out again, when he noticed there was a snapshot on top of the cupboard. He went over to it. It was the photograph of a young woman in riding clothes; it was growing yellow with age but the girl's head stood out clearly, hatless, dark-haired, with an expression of sweet madcap innocence on the lips, but in the eyes a shadow of melancholy; a thin, elfish face, promising beauty and generosity and danger.

It was while he was studying this photograph that Nigel heard a voice behind him. "My study's ornament. Well, I'm so glad you could come." Nigel wheeled round. The voice was light, almost girlish in timbre, yet of an extraordinary resonance. Its owner stood in the doorway, his hand outstretched, a humorous quirk on his lips. Nigel came forward, stuttering with embarrassment:

"I . . . I, really I c-can't tell you how sorry I am. Quite inexcusable, prying about like this. My cursed habit of inquisitiveness. Probably should be found examining the Queen's correspondence if I was invited to Buckingham Palace."

"Ah, never mind, never mind. That's what you're down here for. It's my fault being out when you came. I didn't expect you so early. I hope Arthur showed you your room and everything."

Nigel explained his premature arrival. "Arthur was hospitality itself," he added. "He even offered to give me some sparring practice."

O'Brien laughed. "That's fine. It means he's taken to you. Whom he loveth, he chastiseth — or tries to. It's the only way he can express his emotions. He knocks me down every morning regularly — at least he used to till me health wouldn't stand it any more."

24

O'Brien looked a sick man indeed. As they paced to and fro over the lawn Nigel took stock of him. He had not yet really got over his feeling of guilt at being discovered in the hut, and the mental picture he had formed of what the airman would look like had been shattered so bewilderingly by his real appearance. He had expected something hawk-like, whipcord tough, of more than mortal stature. He saw a smallish man, whose clothes hung loosely on him, as though he had shrunk in the night: an almost dead-white face, with raven hair and a neat black beard that half concealed a terrible scar from temple to jaw; large but delicate hands which somehow fitted his voice. His features were homely — not in the least romantic, in spite of the beard and the pallor. Except for his eyes. O'Brien's eyes were dark blue, almost violet, in colour, and as changeable as the sky on a windy spring day — animated one moment, and the next moment clouded over and withdrawn, quite dull, as though the spirit in them had gone somewhere else.

"Look at him now, will you?" O'Brien pointed excitedly to a robin that was hopping about on the lawn in front of them. "He stops quicker than your eye can stop. He stops so dead that the eye can't brake in time: it overshoots him and stops a foot ahead. Did you ever notice that?"

Nigel hadn't ever noticed it. But he noticed how the airman's intonation became more Irish under excitement. And two lines from the "Ancient Mariner" came unbidden into his head:

25

"He prayeth best who loveth best
All things both great and small."

These were about the Hermit. And the airman had become a sort of hermit. Nigel felt that this man could make him see things as he had never seen them before. He knew suddenly, without any possibility of doubt, that he was walking up and down the lawn with a genius.

At that moment two gunshots exploded from some nearby covert. O'Brien's wrist and hand jerked involuntarily and his head twisted round. He smiled apologetically.

"Can't get out of the habit," he said. "Up in the air that meant some fella was sitting on your tail. Bloody awful sensation. You knew he was there all right, but you couldn't help looking over your shoulder."

"Sounds as if they're shooting in Luckett's Spinney. I know this part of the country well. Used to stay every autumn with my aunt when I was a boy. Do you do any shooting down here?"

O'Brien's eyes clouded over, then twinkled again. "I do not. Why would I? I don't hate the birds. Looks as if someone may be going to do a bit of shooting at me, though, doesn't it? You've read those letters. But I mustn't spoil your appetite for tea. We'll get down to business later. Come on in, now . . ."

Dinner was over. Arthur Bellamy had waited at table, with a deftness and speed surprising in one of his bulk, rather like a performing elephant. He was none of your silent, unobtrusive automatons, though, and enlivened

26

the meal with encomia on the successive dishes and crisp comments on the personal lives of almost every member of the village, from the vicar downwards. Nigel was now sitting with his host, sipping brandy in the lounge hall.

"Jolly good housekeeper you've got," he said, looking round at the immaculate order of the lounge, where everything the lounger could possibly require seemed ready to hand, and remembering the Christmas roses and the biscuit tin in his own bedroom.

"Housekeeper?" said O'Brien. "I don't keep one. What made you think?"

"I seemed to detect the trace of a woman's hand."

"Mine, I should think. I like fussing about with flowers and things. Beneath me beard, I'm an elderly maiden lady. So I couldn't have another one about the place. Too much competition. Arthur does most of the chores."

"But don't you have any staff? Did Arthur cook that admirable dinner?"

O'Brien grinned. "The sleuth getting down to it already! No, I have a cook. Mrs Grant. Your aunt recommended her. She has warts, but otherwise she's a paragon. And there's a gorm of a girl comes up from the village every morning when we've visitors to do the cleaning. Judging from her appearance, she deposits more dirt than she takes away. The gardener's a local, too. You'll have to look elsewhere for suspects."

"You've not had any more letters, I suppose?"

"I have not. The fella's saving himself up for the Feast of Stephen, I expect."

"Just how seriously do you take these letters?"

The cloud came and went in O'Brien's eyes. He entwined his fingers in an oddly girlish gesture. "I don't know, shure. I really don't know. I have had that kind of thing before, often enough. But there's something about the way this fella expresses himself —" He cocked his head quizzically at Nigel. "Y'know, if I was going to kill someone, I've a feeling I'd write to him just that way. The usual dotty threatening letter-writer gets his hate off his chest by the mere writing of the letter. He's a physical coward. And he has no sense of humour. Mark me words, he has *no sense of humour*. Now it's only when you're in dead earnest that you can afford to joke about it. We Cartholics are the only people that jokes about our religion. Y'see the implication?"

"Yes, the same thing occurred to me when I read that last letter." Nigel put down his glass on the floor, and moved over to lean on the mantelpiece. In the circle of lamplight O'Brien's white face and black beard jutted out sharply from the shadows, like the head of a king on a coin. The thought came suddenly to Nigel: "How vulnerable he looks, and yet how calm — as if everything was over — like a poet composing his own epitaph with Death looking over his shoulder." O'Brien's withdrawn expression seemed that of one who has already signed the contract with death, sewn the shroud, ordered the coffin, made all funeral arrangements, and awaits the act of dying as something irrelevant — an unimportant detail in the whole huge scheme. Nigel shook himself out of these fantastic musings and turned to business.

"You told my uncle you had some vague suspicions you didn't care to put down on paper."

There was a long silence. At last O'Brien shifted in his chair and sighed: "I don't know if I should have said that." He spoke slowly, picking his words. "It's not as if they could be any use to you . . . Ah, well . . . Here's one thing. Did you notice that in the third letter he said he wouldn't want to kill me till the festive party was over? Now I had this party arranged a week before I got the letter. I'll tell you why I arranged it in a minute. The point is, I never have been one for house-parties. I likes keepin' meself to meself, as Mrs Grant would say. And how could the unknown ill-wisher know I was going to have one if he hadn't been one of the people I'd invited?"

"Or a friend of one of them."

"Yes. It narrows it down, y'see. Now I can't believe it could be one of my guests. They're all friends of mine. But I'm not trusting anyone, just now. I don't hanker after dying before me time." A steely glint appeared in his eyes, making him look momentarily much more like the ruthless airman of legend than the spinsterish recluse. "So I says to meself, after the second letter came, 'Fergus, you're a rich man, and you've made a will, and them that's mentioned in the will know they are.' So, after that joker sent his second letter along, I decided to collect the principal legatees here for Christmas, where I could keep me eye on them — I never did care for having the fella with the gun sittin' on your tail where ye can't see him. The will is locked up in me safe."

"You mean, all the guests coming tomorrow are your heirs!"

"I do not. One or two of them are. And I can't tell you which, can I now, Strangeways? It wouldn't be fair to them. They're probably as innocent as a baby's bottom. Still, there are circumstances in which even your best friend might murder ye for £50,000."

O'Brien's eyes twinkled provocatively at Nigel as he delivered himself of this outrageous dictum.

"You want me just to keep my eyes open, then," said Nigel, "to be a kind of watchdog in sheep's clothing. It's rather difficult when I don't know whom I've got to watch."

The airman's homely, ravaged features lit up in a smile extraordinarily winning. "It's the devil. I wouldn't ask anyone else to do it. You'll just have to take it on trust that I've got good reasons for not telling you who is going to profit by my death, yet. I've heard enough about you, and I've seen enough of you, to be sure that if you can't succeed under these conditions no one could. You've got psychological knowledge, analytical intelligence, common sense and imagination. Don't attempt to deny it, now! You *have*."

It was Nigel's first taste of blarney — that warm, outrageously personal, almost childishly direct flattery which only Irishmen can get away with. He reacted, in the conventional English way, by staring hard at the floor and hastily changing the subject.

"Have you any other theory of possible motives?"

"There's these plans I'm working on. Y'know, it's been proved lately that the interceptor type of aircraft can never be really successful against a large-scale air attack. Bombing planes can attack now from much higher altitudes — ten thousand feet and upwards. Well, now, however fast your interceptor planes climb, they can't reach those high altitudes before the damage is done. It follows that, in the war of the future your big cities and strategic points will have to be protected by a network of planes constantly in the air at different levels. What does that mean, tell me now?" The little airman leapt up from his chair, strode over to Nigel, and stabbed him repeatedly in the chest with his forefinger. "It means that your defence planes of the future must be capable of remaining in the air over long periods. They must be fast, but at the same time capable of hovering, with vertical screws on the helicopter principle. And they must, above all, have a very low petrol consumption, for there simply wouldn't be enough petrol at the present average rate of consumption for fighting planes to keep an adequate force permanently in the air for more than a fortnight. That's what I'm working on now. An improved type of autogyro, with the lowest possible fuel consumption."

O'Brien flung himself back into his chair and combed his fingers through his beard. "I needn't tell ye, all this must be secret as the grave. But I've got wind, through entirely unofficial channels, that a certain foreign Power is getting nosey about what I'm doing, and is employing an English agent to find out. Me plans aren't yet sufficiently advanced to be of much use to them, even if they could steal 'em. But they might think it worthwhile to have me dead before I could bring the plans to completion."

"Do you keep these plans here?"

"They're in the only burglarproof safe in the world — in me own head. I've a great memory for figures and such like. So I burn most of the drawings and calculations that could tell them anything vital." O'Brien sighed. His face in the lamplight looked weary and tortured. His wide mouth, turned down deeply at both corners, suggested the fixed agony of a Greek tragedy mask. "It's a dirty game, though," he went on. "Bomb or be bombed, gas or be gassed — the law of the jungle dressed up to look respectable in that damned hypocritical word 'security'. Man's character isn't grown-up enough to be trusted with the inventions of his brain. The Church in the Middle Ages wasn't being reactionary when it tried to suppress scientific discovery — no more than a father is when he takes a box of matches out of his baby's hand. Ah, I'm not codding myself. I used to enjoy dogfighting up there. I remember singing once at the top of me voice when I sent one poor devil spinning down in flames." His eyes took on a remoter abstraction. "But I had reason. I had reason. I'm too deep in it all now." He seemed to gather himself together and shrink, throwing a glance of peculiar intensity at Nigel, as though to measure his understanding.

"Too deep?" Nigel asked slowly.

"Well, amn't I? Talking what they call pacifism, and working out plans for bigger and better wars," O'Brien answered bitterly. "I'd like to see every airplane in the world scrapped, and to hell with 'progress'. But I'm too old, too fixed in me habits to ahlter annything but the construction of carburettors. It's your generation that's got to change men's minds and achieve real security — and I wish yez luck with it; yez'll need it. Mine knows all about the horrors of war; but it's too tired to do annything about ut. It wants to die, I dare say — y'know more than I do about Freud's death-will; but I can feel ut in me bones. You're young enough to want to live, and it's your lot that's got to see they have the chance to live, even if it means killing off us old ones in the process."

O'Brien spoke passionately, but Nigel felt that his passionate words concealed something quite different, something personal and more deeply rankling. There was a long silence. Then Nigel said:

"Are there any other possible motives for someone wanting to kill you?"

O'Brien's gaze, which had been abstracted, now suddenly sharpened. Nigel thought of the eyes of a boxer warily covering himself up against an imminent blow.

"Enough and to spare," O'Brien said, "but I can't give you anything definite. I've knocked about and made enemies. I expect me bad deeds'll come home to roost some day. I've killed men, and I've made love to women — and ye can't do that without laying up a store of trouble for y'self. But I couldn't give ye a list of them even if I wanted to."

"The tone of your anonymous letter-writer sounds to me like a personal grudge. You wouldn't write like that to a person if you were going to kill him for his money or to get hold of some plans."

"Wouldn't you? Wouldn't it be the most effective way of disguising your real motive?" said O'Brien.

"Um. There's something in that. Tell me about the other guests."

"I'll tell ye a little. I want ye to study them yourself, without prejudice. There's Georgia Cavendish, the explorer; I picked her up out of a nasty hole in Africa once, and we chummed up. She's a remarkable woman, and she lives up to her reputation, as you'll see. Her brother, Edward Cavendish, something in the city, looks like a churchwarden — the maiden lady's prayer — but I fancy he might have been a bit of a boy in his young days. Then there's a fellow called Knott-Sloman; quite a panjandrum in the war; runs a club now. Philip Starling —"

"What? The don at All Saints'?" interrupted Nigel excitedly.

"That's him. D'ye know um?"

"Do I not? He was one of the instructors of my youth. And about the only one who ever nearly reconciled me to Greek accents. He's a grand little man. That's one I can strike off the list of suspects."

"Most unprofessional," grinned O'Brien. "Well, that's about all. No, it isn't. I was forgetting. Lucilla Thrale, a professional peach. Ye'll have to mind yer step or she'll have ye tied up in knots."

"I'll do my best to keep out of Delilah's way. Now, what precautions are you taking or do you want me to take?"

"Ah, time enough, time enough." O'Brien stretched lazily. "I've got a gun, and I've not lost the habit of using it. And I've a feeling the joker that's after me will keep his word about leaving me to digest me Christmas dinner in peace. Did y'ever hear the story about Lord Cosson and the goat?"

The rest of the evening was spent by O'Brien in relating scandalous anecdotes, most of which referred to persons in high office and sustained more than adequately his reputation for contempt of authority. Later, lying in bed, Nigel heard the front door bang and steps going away towards the hut in the garden. His mind was dazed by the mass of contradictions his host's character presented, though he had the feeling that there was a clue, if only he could grasp it, which would bring them all into a visible pattern. Out of his sleepy musings, three points emerged and took shape. First, that O'Brien took these threats much more seriously than he had suggested to Sir John Strangeways. Second, that the light he had thrown on part of the situation left other parts of it in yet deeper darkness. Third, that even under the circumstances it was rather an odd party. Nigel might or might not have been enlightened could he have looked in through the hut window, and seen the wry smile on O'Brien's lips as he settled into his truckle bed, and heard those passionate lines from an Elizabethan dramatist which the little airman whispered to the impassive stars.

CHAPTER
THREE

A Christmas Tale

Nigel was awakened by a thunderous knocking on the door.

"Oh, God, it's happened!" was the first thought that rushed into his mind. It was followed by a banal but terribly clear image of a sentry sleeping at his post. He wetted his lips and croaked, "Come in!" The face of Arthur Bellamy appeared round the door. It was split by a divine-like grin, which changed rapidly into almost comic solicitude when he saw Nigel's expression. "Gorblime, Mr Strangeways, sir, you don't half look ill. White as a sheet, you are, and no error. The colonel says breakfast at nine; but perhaps you'd rather have it up here?"

"It's all right, Arthur," Nigel answered a bit shakily. "I'm not ill. It was just — just a nightmare."

Arthur tapped his pancake of a nose and said sagely, "Ar. Too much of the colonel's brandy. Plays 'avoc with the lights, it does an' all. When the gastric juices curdle, wot eventuates? Mental disorder, sir. Nightmares. Ar."

Nigel had not time to dispute the scientific accuracy of this dictum, for a resonant baritone voice was singing below the window:

"And back to back by the crimson Slaney —"

Arthur Bellamy flung back his head and began to supply a faux-bourdon in a shrill and dismal falsetto. Nigel, never one to be behindhand in such matters, was soon bellowing out a raucous obbligato. A dog or two from the village over the hill joined in: and Lord Marlinworth in his bedroom at Chatcombe Towers tapped his fingers on the eiderdown with dignified deprecation.

When the rendering was over and Arthur departed, Nigel looked out of the window. Fergus O'Brien was standing in the garden below: there was a stack of holly under his arm, and his head was cocked at a hedge-sparrow which moved towards him mouselike over the grass. Soon two thrushes, a blackbird and a robin were standing around him also, their feathers puffed out against the cold, waiting for the bread he had in his coat pocket. What an idyllic scene, how far removed from nightmares, thought Nigel, till the airman turned and he saw in his other pocket the telltale bulge of a revolver, bringing him back to the dark and dangerous reality in which they were living. O'Brien looked up and saw him at the window.

"Go in now," he exclaimed, "or ye'll catch your death of cold." He was quite alarmed.

Maiden aunt, St Francis, intrepid aviator; tender, reckless, fussy, Rabelaisian, ruthless — the outward contradictions of that extraordinary man made Nigel's head reel. But what of the real, the inner man? How could one ever hope to arrive at that? And he, Nigel

Strangeways, was expected to guard him: they might as well ask one to guard a piece of quicksilver, a dragonfly, or a shadow on a windy day.

They spent most of the morning decorating the house. O'Brien threw himself into this with a kind of finicky abandon, dancing from room to room with holly, mistletoe, and evergreens; rushing up stepladders; standing back from his handiwork with hands raised like the conductor of an orchestra. Nigel followed him more soberly. He was intent on fixing the layout of the house in his memory. It was roughly T-shaped, with the main building as the horizontal stroke, and the servants' quarters forming a short vertical stroke. On the ground floor, in the centre, looking south, was the lounge hall in which they had sat last night. To its right were dining room, and a small study — the latter not often in use, it seemed. The whole of the left-hand side was occupied by a huge drawing room, facing south and east, with french windows leading out on to that side of the garden where the hut had been erected. On the northwest side a billiard room had been built on, blocking in one of the angles of the original T, and on the floor above it the space was occupied by two bathrooms. Upstairs were seven bedrooms. Nigel found they had been allotted as follows: walking down the passage which ran the length of the upper floor, from west to east, he had the rooms of Lucilla Thrale and Georgia Cavendish on his right, with the bathrooms facing them. Then came Edward Cavendish's, Nigel's own room, Starling's and

Knott-Sloman's. "And one unoccupied," he said, as they came to a door at the end of the passage.

"Well, yes and no," replied O'Brien, his eyes twinkling like a schoolboy's at the prospect of a practical joke. He led the way into the room. "This is where I sleep," he said.

"But I thought you slept out in the hut."

"I do so. I got used to the ascetic life during the war, and I find ut difficult to sleep now in normal conditions. But," his voice lowered to a conspiratorial tone, "tonight and tomorrow night I'm going to sleep here. On Christmas night and after I'll pretend to go to bed here, but I'll jump on to the veranda roof and off that into the garden, and I'll lock meself up in me little bunk in the hut. Murderous josser comes in here, stabs the bed, and gets the helluva shock when he sees me ating me porridge next morning." The little airman stood back, rubbing his hands with glee. "That ought to make me nights safe, annyway; and in the daytime —" his lips snapped together in a suddenly relentless line, and he patted his bulging pocket — "I can take care of meself. Unless they put poison in me food. And if they can do that with Arthur Bellamy about, they're welcome to me corpse."

"In fact, there's nothing for me to do but watch and pray."

"That's right, me boy," said O'Brien, gripping Nigel's elbow, "with particular emphasis on the 'watch'."

The door opened silently. A grey-haired, harsh-featured woman stood on the threshold.

"Your orrders for today, Mr O'Brien. What will you be wishing for dinner?"

O'Brien gave elaborate instructions. Nigel looked at the woman, her bony hands folded tight over her apron, her lips thin as vinegar. When she had gone, he said:

"So that's Mrs Grant. Wonder how long she'd been outside that door. I feel somehow she disapproves of you."

"Ah, go on. She's a bit of an ould stick, but there's no harm in her. I do believe you're getting nervous, Nigel," he added teasingly . . .

At midday they knocked off work. Nigel went out of doors, and poked about. He found a yard at the back, with stables and a garage. In the latter reposed a Lagonda sports-tourer. The former contained only junk and an old man who was gazing at the handle of a spade with the glassy rigidity of a mystic contemplating eternity. Nigel rightly deduced that this was the gardener. Jeremiah Pegrum was his name, Nigel discovered. He had worked in the Dower House garden and blown the church organ, man and boy, fifty year come Easter. Nigel felt it was too late in life for Jeremiah Pegrum to be taking to murder, and turned to go. He was detained, however, by a hand on his sleeve. The gardener's rheumy eyes took on a semblance of animation, and his next remark made Nigel start. "Yu look aafter Mr O'Brien, zur! 'Tes a dangerous time for him, this Christmastide. Zoon as he came down yur I sez to my missus, 'Mother,' I says, 'new gennulman at Dower House bain't long for this world. 'Znow coming, zur. 'Tes a martal bad time for the old uns and the zick

40

when east wind blows down tu Chatcombe. Powerful ill he looks, zur, and a fine gennulman as ever I knowed. But this wind'll carpse 'im, zure as spinach — if he don't bust hisself up first in that car of 'is."

Nigel wandered through the kitchen garden, round to the east side of the house. The wind was certainly killing. He sheltered for a moment under the lee of the hut. Peering in through the window of the cubicle, his eyes registered that something was missing there. But before his attention could concentrate on it, it was diverted by the arrival of a taxi at the front door. Out of it there bounced a small, rather fat man, immaculately clad: an unmistakable figure, even to Nigel's short sight.

"And if you don't get some new springs in your so-called conveyance, I shall report you to the Minister of Transport," the little man was saying with some heat. Nigel hailed him.

"Hallo, Philip!"

Philip Starling, fellow of All Saints and the foremost authority in England on Homeric civilisation and literature, exclaimed, "Good God, if it isn't Nigel!", came stumping over the grass, shook Nigel by the shoulders, and rattled off, "What the devil are you doing here, old boy? Oh, I forgot. You've a noble kinsman in residence somewhere here, haven't you? Mealy-Mouth? Marshmallow? Marl-pit? Marlinspike? What's his name? No, don't tell me! I've got it — Marlinworth. I've not collected him yet. You must introduce me."

Nigel firmly stemmed the flow. "No, as a matter of fact I'm staying with O'Brien. But what, may I ask, brings *you* down here?"

"Celebrity snobbery, old boy. I've collected pretty well all the aristocracy, so now I'm taking up celebrities — and a lousy dull crew they are for the most part. However, I have hopes of the aviator. A good egg, I should judge, though I've only met him once, at a dinner at Christ Church, and as I happened to be tight at the time — you know the sort of grocer's port they dish out there — my judgement may be at fault."

"And on the strength of meeting you once at a dinner, he asks you down to this very select party?"

"I expect it was my personal charm. Believe me, I've got my ticket; not gate-crashing this time. You sound very suspicious. Do you represent the secret police down here? Guarding the silver or something?"

"Some*one*," Nigel was tempted to reply, but managed to refrain. Starling's air of exaggerated candour was appallingly infectious, and had led three generations of undergraduates into the most wholesale exposure of their private lives. Nigel, however, had become inured to it.

"Well, yes and no," he said: "but for heaven's sake, Philip, don't let on to any of the other guests that I'm a detective. It's quite vital."

"Very well, old boy, very well. The clam will be a babbler compared to me. You know if I hadn't become a don, I should have taken up your profession. I revel in the seamy side of life. But one sees so much of it in the Senior Common-room that there is no need to associate with professional criminals. Yers. Have you heard how the Master of St James was discovered stealing the papers old Wiggens had set for Honour Mods?"

They passed into the house, Philip Starling rattling off his latest scandals, Nigel listening with his personal blend of serious concentration and noncommittal politeness. At lunch the famous airman and the famous scholar occupied themselves chiefly with a discussion of the comparative merits of Greta Garbo and Elisabeth Bergner. They were both brilliant conversationalists, O'Brien with the untutored vivacity of genius, Starling with his almost incredible trained virtuosity. Nigel, listening, reflected that he was probably hearing the last splendour of an art whose delicate tones could not live long against the ubiquitous bawling of the loudspeaker. He muttered to himself:

"Who killed Cock Robin?"
"I," said John Reith,
"Will contribute to a wreath.
I killed Cock Robin."

After lunch O'Brien shot away in his Lagonda and a cloud of dust to fetch Lucilla Thrale and Knott-Sloman from the station. The latter, when they arrived, proved to be a hard-bitten man with china-blue eyes and the impatient mouth of a confirmed raconteur. Lucilla Thrale certainly lived up to O'Brien's description of "professional peach"; she stepped from the car with the air of Cleopatra disembarking from her "burnished throne": even the bleak Somerset wind grew lovesick with her perfume. She was tall for a woman, blonde as a Nazi's dream, full-figured. "O, rare for Antony," murmured Nigel, as she undulated towards the front door.

Philip Starling overheard him. "Nonsense," he said. "Pick 'em up like that two a penny at Brighton any weekend. Won't wear well. No features."

"You must admit she has a presence, a magnificent carriage, Philip."

"Gah! Walks like a jaguar with the gripes," replied the little don with unexpected venom: "you have such old-fashioned tastes, Nigel."

They strolled into the lounge. Knott-Sloman was in the middle of a long and facetious account of some contretemps that had occurred on the journey down. Philip Starling ignored him completely, and to Nigel's intense astonishment walked up to Lucilla, slapped her on the shoulder, and said, "Well, old girl, keeping in the pink?"

Lucilla Thrale stood up to the onslaught well, Nigel thought. She tweaked Starling's cheek, drawling, "Well, if it isn't Philip! And how are all those sweet undergraduates of yours getting on?"

"Much better now that you're no longer in residence, Lucy."

O'Brien, who had been watching the scene with an impish expression, now intervened to make introductions all round. Nigel found himself raked by a long, slow look from Lucilla, which seemed to be calculating accurately the length of his purse and any other qualifications he might possess. Then she half-turned, her green eyes dragging provocatively away from him, and said to Knott-Sloman, "I don't think Fergus is looking at all well, do you? I shall have to take you in hand, Fergus." She took O'Brien's arm with a kind of imperious tenderness. Knott-Sloman was looking displeased. He had not liked Starling's breaking into his anecdote, nor the perfunctory nod with which the little don acknowledged their introduction. Nigel was conscious of an immediate antipathy between the two — the antipathy, perhaps, between the conversationalist, who lives by give-and-take, and the man who must have monologue or nothing.

"Starling?" Knott-Sloman was saying, "haven't I seen your name somewhere ?"

"I doubt it," replied the don, "you don't read the *Classical Review,* do you?"

The latest arrivals were taken to their rooms. Nigel and Starling remained in the lounge.

"I'd no idea you knew that girl," said Nigel.

"La Thrale? Oh, I get about. She used to live in Oxford."

Philip Starling was oddly uncommunicative, Nigel thought, with such an opening for scandalous fantasy in front of him. He had at least expected to be told that Lucilla was the natural daughter of the Vice-Chancellor.

Just before teatime, a distant clanking and rattling were heard. Nigel looked out of the window and saw an extraordinary spectacle. An ancient two-seater was approaching up the drive, with bits of luggage tied on to every available part of the bodywork. A lady was driving it, a green parrot perched on her shoulder, and a huge bloodhound sitting up beside her. As much of the seat as was unoccupied by the bloodhound accommodated a middle-aged man in weekendish tweeds, looking justifiably rather sheepish. The car clattered to a standstill, more out of sheer inanition, it seemed, than through any application of brakes. The lady leapt out and at once set vigorously to work untying the knots which kept the luggage in place. Arthur Bellamy trundled out to help her.

"Well, Arthur, you old ruffian," the lady exclaimed, "not hung yet?"

Arthur grinned delightedly. "Don't seem like it, Miss Cavendish. You're looking a fair treat. And so is Ajax here. And is this your brother? Pleased to meet you, Mr Cavendish."

Georgia Cavendish rushed into the house, and practically flung herself into the arms of O'Brien, her dark, monkey-like face chattering with excitement. She certainly does live up to her reputation, thought Nigel, looking on and grinning involuntarily himself.

Christmas Day. 7.30p.m. For two days Nigel had been watching, with the whole concentrated force of his attention. The superb Lucilla, the colourful Georgia Cavendish, and her pompous, decent, elderly brother; Knott-Sloman, with his professional bonhomie; Philip Starling and Fergus O'Brien — all had passed and repassed under his trained scrutiny: and precious little he had to show for it. His mood alternated between

46

incredulity and an apprehension that was increasing as the Feast of Stephen drew nearer. There were personal undercurrents of feeling among the guests: that was obvious. But the one sign that Nigel was looking for he could not find: it was almost impossible, he believed, to have planned murder against a person and to behave normally towards him in the interim. Yet, as far as he could observe, not one of the guests was less his normal self in O'Brien's presence than out of it. Either someone had the most remarkable emotional control, or the threat came from outside this circle — or the whole thing was a hoax.

Lord and Lady Marlinworth had accepted an invitation to dine at the Dower House this night, and Nigel came downstairs early to be ready for them. As he reached the drawing-room door, he heard a low-toned conversation within. There was no mistaking that resonant voice, its tones indifferent, humouring, a little impatient.

". . . No, not tonight."

"But, Fergus, darling, I want you so. It's quite safe. Why can't I —?"

"You can't because I say you can't. Now be a good girl and do what I tell ye; and don't ask questions, because you're wasting your breath."

"Oh, you're cruel, cruel —" the voice of Lucilla, almost unrecognisably altered from her usual cool drawl, broke; and Nigel had time only to retreat half a dozen paces from the door before she swept out and past him, quite oblivious of his presence. Well, for once you're getting as good as you give, thought Nigel: no wonder O'Brien doesn't want you coming to his bedroom when he means to be out in the hut . . .

The Christmas dinner was half over. At the head of the table O'Brien, his black beard jutting out from his dead-pale face, looked like an Assyrian king; he was at the top of his form, blarneying away at Lady Marlinworth till the old lady was in a positive twitter of delight.

"Fie, Mr. O'Brien, I declare you are the most outrageous flatterer."

"Not a bit of it. Lady Marlinworth looks as if she were at her first ball, doesn't she now, Georgia?"

Georgia Cavendish, in emerald-green velvet, her cockatoo perched on her shoulder, wrinkled up her monkey-face at him and grinned elfishly. At the other end of the table Lord Marlinworth was plying Lucilla Thrale with Edwardian attentions. The girl showed no outward sign of the emotional storm Nigel had overheard. Magnificent in her low-cut white dress, she replied to Lord Marlinworth's sallies with cool provocativeness: but Nigel could see her gaze wandering away to O'Brien and hardening for an instant when it rested on Georgia Cavendish. Georgia's brother was talking high finance with Philip Starling: it was the first time Nigel had heard him on what was presumably his own subject, and there was no doubt he had an acute and able mind. Nigel noticed that, while Philip was talking, Edward Cavendish's eyes kept straying towards Lucilla; considering her nonpareil appearance tonight, there was nothing odd in that: but his expression was revealing by its very guardedness —

he looked at her with the deliberate reticence of a poker player inspecting his hand. Nigel noticed, too, that Lucilla was aware of these glances and studiously avoided returning them. Knott-Sloman was vying with Lord Marlinworth for her attentions. His pale blue, restless, rather stupid eyes kept returning to her mouth and shoulders with a boorish sort of aggressiveness. He held her attention by brute force, as it were, raising his voice to subdue Lord Marlinworth's thin tenor, and piling anecdote on anecdote. He had a coarse charm of his own, undoubtedly, as well as the crude "personality" of the egotist.

All round Nigel the conversation played, rising and falling and blowing to this side and that like fountains on a gusty day. But gradually, in the centre of it all, Nigel grew conscious of a deep nervous excitement. He had the fancy that it was not the cumulative excitement of a successful party, but radiated from one person. He shook his head irritably: what could it be but his own apprehension of O'Brien's approaching zero hour? O'Brien himself looked almost fey. He rose suddenly, glass in hand, shot an incalculable glance at Nigel, and cried:

"A toast! To absent friends — and to present enemies!"

There was a brief, uncomfortable silence. Georgia Cavendish bit her lip: her brother looked vaguely worried: Lord Marlinworth tapped on the table: Lucilla and Knott-Sloman glanced at each other: Philip Starling was smirking with amusement at the general embarrassment. Lady Marlinworth broke the spell.

"What a droll toast, Mr. O'Brien! An old Irish one, I suppose. Such a whimsical people!" The old lady tittered and sipped at her wine; the rest followed suit. Just as they were laying down their glasses, the lights went out. Nigel's heart dropped like a stone. Now it was coming. It was here at last. The next moment he was cursing himself for a hysterical old woman. Arthur Bellamy entered with a flaming Christmas pudding. He set it down before O'Brien, remarking in a perfectly audible whisper, "Took a box of matches to light the blasted stuff, colonel. That there Mrs Grant been swigging it on the Q.T. you betcha life, and filling up the bottle with water." He retired and switched on the lights. O'Brien looked at Lady Marlinworth apologetically, but she was far beyond being shocked.

"What a delightfully outspoken man your butler is! Quite a character! No, not a drop more. I vow you will have me tipsy. Well, just half a glass, then," she giggled. "You know," she proceeded, staring fixedly at him, and tapping his arm archly with her fan, "your face reminds me of someone — someone I met a long time ago. Herbert!" she rapped out, "who does Mr O'Brien remind me of?"

Herbert Marlinworth started, and fingered his silky gray moustache. "I'm sure I don't know, my dear. Possibly one of your — ah — unlucky suitors. I don't think we have had the pleasure of meeting any of the Irish O'Briens. What part of the country do you —?"

"Our seat," replied O'Brien with the utmost gravity, "reposes on the site of the palace of the great king, Brian Boru."

50

Knott-Sloman began to guffaw but, receiving an icy look from O'Brien, turned it into a cough. Georgia Cavendish, her stubby nose wrinkled up in distaste, said to O'Brien:

"I suppose your family has a banshee as well as a castle. You've never told me about it."

"Banshee? That's a kind of fairy or something, isn't it? Can't see a fairy getting much change out of old Slip-Slop," said Knott-Sloman. A curious nickname for O'Brien, Nigel thought, and judging by their puzzled expressions, none of the others knew it. O'Brien cut in quickly:

"A banshee is a spirit that howls about the place when one of the family is going to die. So if anny of yez hears an ululation tonight ye'll know I'm for ut."

"And we'll all come rushing down the stairs and find it's only Ajax having a nightmare," exclaimed Georgia with the barest perceptible tremor in her voice. Lucilla Thrale shivered delicately.

"Brr," she said, "this is getting a morbid party. Death is too fearfully middle-class and Victorian, don't you think? I call it a poor do altogether."

"Dear lady," said Lord Marlinworth, leaping in with Edwardian gallantry, "you need have no fear. Death has only to look at your face once and he will be like the rest of us — a captive at your feet." He sketched a courtly gesture, and continued to the company at large. "The death-warning is not confined to the Emerald Isle. I well recollect a similar phenomenon attaching to the family of my old friend, Viscount Hawsewater. The bell of a ruined chantry on the estate was reputed to toll at night when the death of the head of the family was at hand. One night poor Hawsewater, who was enjoying perfect health at the time, heard it: unfortunately he was tone-deaf and mistook it for the fire-bell: he rushed out of the house, omitting to put on any — if the ladies will pardon me — nether garments. It was bitterly cold that night. He caught a chill, contracted pneumonia, and was dead in two days. Poor fellow. A melancholy end. But it shows one must not dismiss too lightly these supernatural warnings. There are more things in heaven and earth, Horatio, I think. I think so."

At this point Lady Marlinworth thought it best to beckon the ladies into the drawing room. The men gathered nearer to their host.

"Coffee for you, Lord Marlinworth? Coffee, Nigel?" he said, passing the cups along. "Pass the port round. Just reach out if you want nuts — afraid I haven't got any of your speciality, Knott-Sloman: Farquhar's are late with their consignment. You must show us your parlour trick. I bet you're the only person here who can crack a walnut with his teeth." Knott-Sloman duly showed off, and the rest ignominiously failed. O'Brien went on: "I see you are a student of Shakespeare, Lord Marlinworth. Did you ever read any of the post-Elizabethan dramatists? Grand stuff. Shakespeare slew his thousands, but Webster slew his tens of thousands. I must say I like the stage littered with corpses at the final curtain. And what poetry! 'Doth the silkworm expend her yellow labors'." O'Brien began to recite the passage, his eyes looking away into illimitable distance, his voice soft and thrilling. Before he had finished he broke off suddenly, as though ashamed at being betrayed into such emotion by mere words. Lord Marlinworth tapped the table deprecatingly.

"Very striking, no doubt. But not Shakespeare, not Shakespeare. I may be old-fashioned, but I fancy the Bard stands alone."

Before long they joined the ladies. Nigel afterwards retained the vaguest memory of the absurd paper games they played, the blood-curdling ghost stories that were told, the general horseplay, for he felt sleepier and sleepier — as well he might after such a dinner. One thing he remembered clearly — the resonant voice and infectious laughter of Fergus O'Brien, contrasting so strangely with the fey look in his eyes, the look of one seeing things beyond the world's edge. When Lord and Lady Marlinworth took their leave at 11 p.m. and some of the men adjourned to the billiard room, Nigel went up to bed. He wanted to rest. Hoax or no hoax, he meant to be near the hut tonight. O'Brien might be able to look after himself, but four hands were better than two. The hut . . . zero hour . . . "Look after him, won't you?" . . . four hands better than . . . zero hour . . .

CHAPTER
FOUR

A Dead Man's Tale

Nigel, coming awake by slow degrees, was conscious first of light and then of silence. The light seemed to be striking down at him from the ceiling, which was surely odd on a winter's morning. The silence was not, now that he listened to it more attentively, exactly silence; but a damping-down of all the country sounds, of dog-bark, harness-jingle, wagon-rumble, cockcrow, and footfall, as though some gigantic soft pedal had been pressed down over the countryside. Nigel wondered vaguely if these phenomena were the after-effect of drugs. Then he pointed out to himself, rather laboriously, that he did not take drugs. Then his mind started working properly, and he exclaimed, "Snow!" He went to look out of the window. Yes, there had been a fall in the night: not enough to overload roofs and branches, but blanketing earth and all its sounds. Nigel's heart contracted suddenly. O'Brien! The hut! He ran along to the room in which O'Brien had pretended to be sleeping, and looked out towards the hut. A single trail of footsteps, half obliterated by the snow, led to it from the veranda. There was a thin layer of smooth snow on the veranda roof. "Thank God,

54

that's all right," Nigel muttered. "No one but O'Brien has been out there. Nothing has happened after all." Returning to his room, he looked at his wrist watch. Eight-forty. He had slept late. So had O'Brien, it seemed: he was usually out feeding the birds by this time. Well, after a dinner like that, what could you expect? But a little flaw of apprehension crawled over Nigel's heart again. He would have been told if — Arthur Bellamy would have told him. But Arthur had not been out to the hut; or, if he had been out, he had not come back. And why hadn't he called Nigel?

Nigel hurried on his clothes. A nightmare sensation was gnawing at him — the sensation he had felt as a boy, dreaming that he was late for school. He ran downstairs. Edward Cavendish was stamping up and down the front veranda in an overcoat.

"Getting up an appetite for breakfast," he said. "Everyone seems very sleepy this morning. I wasn't called at all — though I suppose one couldn't expect that in this house." His tones were a little pettish.

"I'm just going out to the hut to see if our host is awake," said Nigel. "Coming?"

Nigel's uneasiness must have communicated itself to Cavendish, for the latter preceded him with alacrity round the corner of the house. The trail of footsteps stretched out before them from opposite the french windows to the hut door, a distance of about fifty yards. Nigel hurried out, unconsciously keeping well away from this trail, Cavendish a little ahead of him. He knocked on the door of the hut. There was no answer. Nigel looked in at the window, and what he saw made him leap for the door, thrust it open and stumble inside. The enormous kitchen table was still there, strewn with books and papers; the oil stove and the easy chairs were as he had seen them last. One of the carpet slippers was there on the floor, too; but the other was on the foot of O'Brien, who lay in a heap beside the desk.

Nigel knelt down and touched one of his hands. It was dead cold. It did not need the dried trickle of blood from his heart, the scorching of black lapel and white shirt-front to tell Nigel that Fergus O'Brien was dead. A revolver lay beside the stiffened fingers of his right hand. His eyes were blank, but his black beard jutted out indomitably even in this hour of defeat, and some whimsy of death had set his lips into a smile — the half-impish, half-sardonic smile with which he had looked down the dinner-table only twelve hours before. Nigel never forgot that look. It seemed to forgive him for his own failure, to invite him to be amused at the way death had outwitted them both. But Nigel was very far from being amused. In a few days he had come to feel for O'Brien an affection and deep respect he had never felt for anyone but his uncle before. He had failed; and the completeness of that failure was the measure of his determination to win through to the truth in the end.

"Keep still, and don't touch anything!" he snapped at his companion. Cavendish was not in a state to touch anything. He was standing against the wall, mopping his brow with a handkerchief, breathing heavily, and staring at the body and the revolver as though he

56

expected the one to leap up and the other to explode at any moment. He made some incoherent sounds, then controlled his voice and said:

"What on earth? Why did he —?"

"We shall find out. Close that door — we don't want everyone looking in. No! Keep your hands off it! Use your elbow."

Nigel made a hasty survey of the room and the adjoining cubicle. The bed had not been slept in. Nothing seemed out of place anywhere. The windows were shut and locked. The key was on the inside of the door. Nigel felt the oil stove; it was cold as O'Brien's hand. The hut was icy, too. He looked round in a puzzled way, as though missing something.

"I wonder where his —"

"There's Bellamy," interrupted Cavendish, standing at the window. "Shall I call him?"

Nigel nodded absent-mindedly. Cavendish shouted "Bellamy!" at the top of his voice; but the sound seemed deadened and, though he shouted again, it had no effect. Nigel opened the door, using a handkerchief to turn the handle. Arthur Bellamy was standing on the veranda, blinking into the sun and rubbing his eyes with his huge fists.

"Arthur!" he called. "Come over here, and keep off that single trail of footprints. Didn't you hear us shouting for you?"

"Can't hear much from in there when the door's shut," said Arthur, lumbering over the snow like a bear. "The Colonel had it sound-proofed like. Says 'e can't work with the shindy the cocks and 'ens and whatnot make round about 'ere."

"That's why no one was awakened by the shot," thought Nigel.

"'Ere, wot is all this, Mr Strangeways, sir?" said Arthur, now approaching the door and suddenly realising that there was something unusual in the situation. "Ain't the Colonel in there? I was coming to call him. I overslept, you might say, and —"

Nigel's expression silenced him. "Yes, the Colonel is in here. But he won't be working here any more," Nigel said gently, and let Arthur Bellamy come in.

The big man staggered, as though he had collided with a wall. "So they got him!" he gasped finally in a high, hoarse voice.

"Who 'got him'?" asked Cavendish, bewildered. No one paid any attention to him. Arthur, who had been bending over O'Brien, straightened himself, as it were, with a giant effort — like Atlas with the sagging sky on his shoulders. Tears were pouring down his face, but his voice was firm as he said, "When I gets my hands on the — wot did this, I'll beat his — carcase into a — paste, I'll —"

"Hold it, Arthur. Some of the others will be coming out in a minute." He drew the big man aside, and whispered to him quickly. "We know this isn't a suicide, but it's going to be damned difficult to prove. There'll be no harm the rest thinking we think it's suicide, for a bit. Pull yourself together now and act up."

Arthur acted up. "Strite, guv'nor? You're sure it's sooicide? Ar, the gun there and that scorching on his coat. I reckon you must be right."

Cavendish, looking through the door, said, "Some of the others are on the veranda. They must have heard our voices. You'd better tell them to keep off those footprints. Oh, God, there's Lucilla. She mustn't see this."

Nigel went to the door and hailed the guests. "Stay where you are a minute. Yes, all of you. Arthur, just walk round the hut and see if there's any trail up to the back. We'd better make sure, before they all start tramping about."

Arthur moved away. "But look here, Strangeways," Cavendish protested, "you can't let those women come in here and see —" He shuddered.

"I can and I propose to," said Nigel brusquely. He did not intend to lose this golden opportunity for studying reactions. Arthur returned and informed him that there were no footprints at the back of the hut. Nigel spoke to the guests huddled on the veranda.

"You can come out now, but keep well away from that single track of footmarks. O'Brien has met with an accident."

There was a gasp, and Georgia Cavendish came running out ahead of the rest. They were all dressed, except for Knott-Sloman, who was wearing an overcoat over his pyjamas, and Lucilla Thrale, who had on a magnificent grey mink coat over what looked suspiciously like nothing else at all. With her silver-gold

59

hair and white throat and frozen expression she was a veritable Snow Queen.

Nigel put his back to the far wall of the hut, and said, "You can come in. But stand still and don't touch anything."

They filed in and stood fidgeting in a row, like a company of amateur actors with bad stage fright. For a second they did not know where to look. Then Georgia pointed a trembling finger, bit her lip hard, said in a small solemn voice, "Fergus. Oh, Fergus!" and fell deathly silent. Knott-Sloman's face grew taut and his pale blue eyes seemed to turn to stone. "Good God! Dead! Is he dead? Who — did he do it himself?" Philip Starling pursed up his lips and gave a long whistle.

"He *is* dead," said Nigel, "and everything points to suicide."

Lucilla Thrale's frozen expression suddenly broke up like a landslide. Her scarlet mouth dropped open; and with a violence that appalled everyone she screamed out: "Fergus? Fergus! You can't! It's not true! Fergus!" Then she reeled and fell back into Knott-Sloman's arms. The little group split up. Nigel glanced at Georgia. She was gazing at her brother now with an indecipherable look. Suddenly aware of Nigel's scrutiny, she dropped her eyes and walked out, bending and just touching O'Brien's hair on the way.

"Look here, Strangeways," Knott-Sloman exclaimed angrily. "What the devil do you mean by letting these ladies come in and — it's outrageous."

"You can all go out now," said Nigel impassively. "Stay in the house, please. You will be needed for the formality of questioning. I am just going to ring the police."

Knott-Sloman's face grew purple, and knotted veins stood out. "Who the hell are you to give orders here?" he roared. "I've stood just about enough of your buck." He broke off. Nigel was looking at him, a very different proposition from the mild, bespectacled, amiable creature of the day before. His tow-coloured hair stood on end berserk fashion, his boyish expression had been left behind with the jokes and crackers of last night, his eyes looked dangerous as the muzzles of machine guns. Knott-Sloman capitulated, and retired to the house grumbling. The others followed. Lucille Thrale, who was getting full emotional value out of the occasion and behaving like a tragedy queen, was being supported into the house by Georgia and Philip Starling. Nigel told Arthur to stay on guard in the hut and to see if he could find anything missing there or out of place. He himself went into the house and phoned up Taviston. He was put through to Superintendent Bleakley, who promised to come at once with a police doctor and other accessories. Taviston was a good fifteen miles distant, and Nigel spent the intervening time putting through a trunk call to his uncle in London. Sir John Strangeways' reception of the news was typical of the man.

"Shot . . .? Suicide to all appearances . . .? You don't think so . . .? Well, go to it . . . I'll send Tommy Blount down if they call in the Yard . . . No, don't blame yourself, boy; I know you did your best. He didn't give us a chance . . . Going to be a rumpus about this, though. I'll have to see what we can do about nobbling the Press . . . So long. Let me know if you want anything . . . Oh, right. Who? Cyril Knott-Sloman, Lucilla Thrale, Edward and Georgia Cavendish, Philip Starling. Right, I'll have 'em looked up . . . So long. Be good to yourself."

Ten minutes later the police car arrived. Superintendent Bleakley was a man of middle height. His straight back and waxed moustache suggested military service; a brick-red face, the faint Somerset burr in his voice, and something unwieldy in his gait, pointed to the blood of many yeomen ancestors in his veins. The martinet quality of his training and the deep inherited *laissez-faire* of the countryman were always at odds within him. He was followed out of the car by a sergeant, a constable and the doctor. Nigel met them.

"My name is Strangeways. My uncle's Assistant Commissioner. I've done a certain amount of work as a private inquiry agent, and I was staying down here with O'Brien in that capacity. I'll give you details later. We found O'Brien at nine forty-five in that hut over there: he had been shot. Nothing has been touched. There was this single trail of footprints leading to the hut. No others."

"What's all this, then?" asked Bleakley, pointing to the tracks that had been made by the other guests. "Seems to have been a proper stampede."

"There are several other visitors. They *would* come out here. I kept them off the important prints," said Nigel mendaciously.

They entered the hut. Bleakley looked at Arthur suspiciously, Arthur at Bleakley belligerently. The body was photographed from several angles. Then the doctor got to work on it. He was a taciturn man, but agreeably unprofessional both in his clothes and his manner. After a bit, straightening up on his knees, he said:

"Looks like a clear case of suicide. See the powder burning here? Shot fired into the heart from a few inches range. Here's the bullet. You'll find it checks up with that revolver, Bleakley, or I shall be very surprised. Only point against suicide is that he isn't holding the revolver. Suicides generally grip on the weapon they've used — cadaveric spasms, it's called. Still, it's not invariable. There are no other injuries except these bruises on the right wrist. He would be killed instantaneously." The doctor looked at his wristwatch. "M'm. I should say death took place between ten last night and three this morning. The post-mortem may narrow it down. The ambulance will be along here directly, I suppose."

"These bruises, doctor, how do you account for them?" said Nigel, bending over the body and looking at the two faint purple marks on the underside of the wrist.

"Hit himself against the edge of this table falling, I should think."

Bleakley was staring in a ruminative way at O'Brien's feet. "Surely he didn't walk out here in carpet slippers," he said, and began rummaging around the hut. In a minute he discovered, behind one of the armchairs by the left-hand wall, a pair of patent-leather evening

63

shoes. "These belong to the deceased?" he enquired sharply of Arthur Bellamy.

"The Colonel's shoes those are," said Arthur dully, looking inside them.

"The Colonel's? What Colonel?"

"He means O'Brien," said Nigel.

"Well, we'd best see if they fit those footprints outside before the sun melts 'em away altogether."

Bleakley took the shoes up gingerly, using his handkerchief. Nigel put his fingers on the soles. They were quite dry. They went outside. The shoes fitted accurately into the footprints. It was true that the snow falling after the prints had been made had obliterated any peculiar features of the tread, except that the indentation of the toes seemed deeper than that of the heels; but to the superintendent the identification seemed decisive.

"That clinches it," he said.

"Just a minute, before you make up your mind," said Nigel, drawing out of his pocketbook the threatening letters and O'Brien's covering note. "Read those."

Bleakley took out, rather surprisingly, a pair of pince-nez, rustled the papers formidably and began to read. When he had finished, officialdom and human interest struggled for a moment in his expression. "Why weren't we informed about this? Well, that'll keep. This is a mighty queer set-out, sir. Did Mr O'Brien take these threats seriously?"

"I think he did."

"He did? Well I never. You know, sir, this'd be a thundering big case, Mr O'Brien bein' who he was, if

— But no, it's impossible; you can't get round the evidence of them footprints. Still, just to make sure. Doctor Stephens, will you look out particularly carefully for any evidence at the post-mortem that might point to — something else than suicide." The doctor smiled sardonically and shrugged his shoulders. "Oh, there's the ambulance. You can take his prints now, George, and then they can take him away. See you later, Doctor. Thanks. Now, George" — he turned to the sergeant again — "go over the hut for fingerprints — the gun, the shoes and that safe especially: not that it's going to be much help if all those people have been in here since," he added, the martinet coming uppermost.

"I told them to touch nothing," said Nigel. "I was watching them hard, and I'm pretty sure they didn't."

"Well, that's something. Now you, what's your name?" He spun round abruptly to Arthur, who had been standing in the background.

"Arthur Bellamy, late aircraftman, discharged 1930, heavyweight champion of the R.A.F.," the big man reeled off. Bleakley's parade-ground rasp had made him involuntarily stand to attention.

"What is your position here?"

"I was the Colonel's personal servant, sir."

"What do you know about all this?"

"Wot do I know about all this? I know the Colonel was expecting trouble. I was going to watch this 'ut all last night, though he *did* tell me 'e'd 'ave my blood if I came anywhere near it, only I got so blasted sleepy I couldn't keep my eyes open. So sleepy I forgot to bolt

65

the front door. Next thing I knew it was nearly nine o'clock this morning. That's all I know, except that when I lays my hands on the — who did it, I'll twist his guts round his — earhole."

"So you don't think the Col — Mr O'Brien committed suicide?"

"Suicide my — ," replied Arthur coarsely. " 'E'd no more do it than — than 'e'd 'ave killed one of them little birds 'e used to feed with bread crumbs every morning." Arthur's voice shook at the remembrance.

"Very well. Is this Mr O'Brien's revolver?"

"Yus. No doubt about that."

"Now who would be likely to come into this hut?"

"The Colonel was very particular not to let anyone in. He always locked it when there was company about. I came in to clean it most days, but no one else but 'im and Mr Strangeways will have been in here."

"Then any other fingerprints we found would be a bit suspicious. We've got Mr O'Brien's, and I'll take yours now, Bellamy, and yours, Mr Strangeways, if you've no objection. Not that I think there's anything in it. Still, we might as well do the thing properly."

They submitted to the process. Then Bleakley said, "You get on with it now, George, and see if you can find a broken cufflink anywhere; the one on O'Brien's right wrist was snapped in half — did it when he fell, I expect. You come with me, Bolter. I'll want you to take down depositions."

The superintendent jumped higher in Nigel's estimation. He might be only a country dumpling, but he noticed things.

"Now first we've got to try to find out when the snowfall began here," Bleakley was saying as they went over to the house. "It started about midnight with us. Do you know, by any chance, sir?"

"Afraid I did the same as Arthur — fell asleep on the job," said Nigel bitterly.

Bleakley noticed the bitterness in his voice, and changed the subject tactfully. "A good lad, that George. His dad and mine worked on a farm down to Watchet. Now, sir, can you give me a line on the other people staying here, before I interview them?"

Nigel gave a succinct account of his fellow guests, omitting all conjectures and nuances. To keep out of earshot, he led Bleakley round by the kitchen garden and the stable yard, and by the time they had reached the back door he had finished his descriptions. He was so absorbed by them, in fact, that he did not notice the face that regarded him and Bleakley with a forbidding expression from the kitchen window. As they entered a harsh voice said, "I'll thank ye to wipe your feet and noat come sullying ma clean passage." Mrs Grant stood in the kitchen door, her fingers folded tightly over her apron. Nigel began to giggle uncontrollably; the anticlimax was too much for his strained nerves. Mrs Grant fixed him with a dour regard. "This is noat the time for unseemly murrth, with a mon lying deid oot yonder."

"And who told you your master was dead?" asked the superintendent smoothly.

The slightest flicker appeared in Mrs Grant's granite-grey eyes. "Ah hairrd that woman screeching," she said.

"What woman?"

"Miss Thrale. It was an ill day when she set foot in this house, the painted hoor. I have always been in respaictable families before."

"Come, come, this is no way to talk with your master just dead," said Bleakley, genuinely shocked.

"He broaght it on himself, consorrting with that hussy. It is the Lorrd's judgement. The sinner shall perish before Him."

"Well," said Nigel, recovering himself, "we can discuss the theological aspect of the case later. What we're concerned with at the moment is facts. Can you tell us, Mrs Grant, what time it began to snow last night?"

"I dinna ken. I went to bed shairp at eleven and bolted the back door. It wasna snowing then."

"You saw, or heard no unauthorised persons about the place yesterday night, I take it?" asked Bleakley.

"That slut, Nellie, went home to the village when she'd washed up. After that, I hairrd nothing but Mr O'Brien's friends rampaging and blaspheeming in the drawing room," said Mrs Grant severely. "And now I'll thank ye to let me get on with my wurrk. I havna time for chattering with beesy-bodies."

They retired, Bleakley frankly mopping his brow. The guests were in the dining room. Georgia was trying to persuade Lucilla, who was now clothed, though scarcely in her right mind, to drink some coffee. The rest were making spasmodic efforts to eat breakfast. Their heads all turned nervously when the door opened. The superintendent seemed rather nervous himself. He was not used to high life, his professional activities having been mainly confined so far to poachers, petty thieves, drunks and errant motorists. He twisted his moustache and said:

"I will not trouble you for long, ladies and gentlemen. There seems no doubt that Mr O'Brien committed suicide. But I just want to get a few details settled up, so that there will be no trouble at the inquest. Now first, can any lady or gentleman tell me what time it began to snow here last night?"

There was a stir, a relaxation, as though everyone had been expecting some more sinister question. Starling and Knott-Sloman glanced at each other. Then the latter said:

"Cavendish and I went to play billiards between eleven and half-past, I suppose it was. Starling came to look on. About five minutes after midnight — I remember because I heard the hall clock striking — Starling said, 'Hallo, it's beginning to snow.' He was standing at the window. Weren't you, Starling?"

"That seems quite satisfactory," said the superintendent. "Was it falling heavily, Mr Starling?"

"A few flakes at first. It got heavier quite quickly, though."

"Did anyone happen to notice when it stopped?"

There was rather a long pause. Georgia, Nigel noticed, was looking uncertainly at her brother. Then she seemed to make up her mind about something, and said:

"About quarter to two — I can't tell you exactly, because my travelling clock has gone funny — I went into my brother's room and asked for some sleeping draught. He'd packed it in his luggage. He was awake and got up to get it, and I noticed then that the flakes were coming down much thinner. It probably stopped soon after that."

"Thank you, Miss Cavendish. You were just going to bed then, Mr Cavendish?"

"Oh, no. I went up soon after twelve. I couldn't get to sleep, though."

"That is quite clear, I think. Now just one more question. The coroner will want to know when Mr O'Brien was last seen and whether he showed any signs of — of what he was going to do."

After some discussion, the following points emerged. O'Brien had been with Lucilla and Georgia in the drawing room for a quarter of an hour after the Marlinworths had left. Then, about eleven-fifteen, the ladies had gone up to bed. O'Brien had looked in at the billiard players after this. He had stayed there for twenty minutes or so, and then said he was sleepy and going upstairs to bed.

"So Mr O'Brien was last seen somewhere round about eleven forty-five," Bleakley summed up.

As to the other question, there was more difference of opinion. Cavendish and Knott-Sloman had noticed nothing about O'Brien, but that he seemed in exceptionally good form. Philip Starling thought he had

70

looked "rather weird and worked-up". Georgia agreed that he had been at the top of his form, but insisted that he had looked more than usually white and ill, and that she had felt some great strain under his gaiety. Lucilla, being asked her opinion, threatened to go off into another fit of hysterics, and cried out: "Why do you torture me? Can't you see that I — I — loved him?" And then, as though shocked into sanity by the admission, she said, with unnatural calmness: "The hut? What was he doing in the hut?"

Nigel interposed quickly: "Well, I think that's all we want, isn't it, Bleakley?"

The superintendent took the cue, and after informing them that they might be required not to leave Chatcombe for a day or two, went out with Nigel and Bolter to the hut again. There they found the sergeant very pleased with himself. He had found the bit of broken cufflink lurking behind one of the legs of the big table. He had also discovered four distinct sets of fingerprints. One on the handle of the revolver, on the safe, and in other parts of the room, presumably O'Brien's. There were no prints on the shoes. Bleakley had no doubt that two of the other sets would prove, on expert examination, to be Nigel's and Bellamy's. Whose was the fourth? Those prints on the shiny window-sill and the cigarette box on the bookcase? Nigel's heart leaped up. Here was the X, the unknown whose existence he had yet to prove. Then, as suddenly, it sank again. Edward Cavendish had come into the hut with him; he had been standing by the bookcase and later had moved over to the window. Almost certainly they would be his. He suggested this to the superintendent. They went back to the house, detached Cavendish from his sister and Lucilla, and asked him to let them have his prints, for comparison with those on the window-sill and cigarette box. He made no demur, though he seemed nervous and flustered at the suggestion. Back in the hut again, Bleakley shook his head sadly at Nigel.

"No, sir," he said, "it's no manner of good. They say dead men tell no tales, but it isn't true here. The story is clear enough for a babby to see. I don't like to think of a fine gentleman like Mr O'Brien taking his own life, but you can't go against the evidence."

"The evidence," said Nigel slowly. "I believe I could make this dead man tell a very different tale, just on the evidence we've got so far."

CHAPTER
FIVE

A Twisted Tale

The superintendent twirled his moustache indeci-
sively. There was something compelling about this
young Mr Strangeways' quiet confidence. His army
training had given him a possibly misplaced belief in
the superior wisdom of what he would never have
thought of calling "the officer class". And what a
case this would be if — Bleakley decided to listen. It
was perhaps the wisest decision he ever made in his
life. He sent George off post-haste to Taviston with
his prints, and Bolter into the house to fetch some
breakfast for Nigel.

Gesturing, now with an impaled sausage, now with a
marmalade spoon, Nigel took up his parable. "I'm
going to take as my hypothesis that O'Brien was
murdered, and see how the evidence fits in with that.
You can be the advocate for *felo-de-se*. Pull me up
whenever I seem to misinterpret or contradict the facts.
Between us we ought to thrash out the situation pretty
thoroughly. Now first, the psychological evidence."

Bleakley twirled his moustache importantly. He was
gratified that Mr Strangeways took for granted his
knowledge of the meaning of these scientific terms.

"Anyone who knew O'Brien well would tell you that he was the last person to put an end to himself. Even my short acquaintance with him convinced me of that. He was a remarkable character — an eccentric one, you might say; but not unbalanced. He had the physical courage to shoot himself, I'll admit; but he had equally the moral courage to refrain from shooting himself. I don't believe he would have any qualms about taking life — we know that in the air he was quite ruthless, and I can imagine him even murdering a man in cold blood if he had sufficient incentive — for revenge, for instance. He must have had a terrific will-to-live for him to have come through all he did, and you are asking me to believe that a man with such survival power could just go quietly into a corner and shoot himself."

"It wasn't so quietly, sir. Several of them said he seemed all worked up like and excitable last night."

Nigel's eyes glinted behind his spectacles and he waved a sausage forcefully in the air.

"Ah, that's just it. If O'Brien had been going to shoot himself, one would have expected him to be distrait, reserved, the stiff upper lip with an *occasional* outburst of semi-hysterical hilarity. But he wasn't anything of the sort. He was uniformly gay. It was high spirits, not hysteria. The excitement beneath the surface, plus that fey look about him, are just what one would have expected from a man of almost reckless courage before going into battle. Which is exactly what he *was* doing. X's ultimatum expired at midnight. Unfortunately

74

O'Brien must have underestimated his adversary's power this time."

Bleakley scratched his knee. He did not like to admit that Nigel's last reasonings had taken him right out of his depth. Then, with a desperate effort to get back to solid ground, he said:

"That may be so, sir. But don't you remember? The writer of those letters said something about how Mr O'Brien mustn't balk him of his revenge by committing suicide. Now, that might've been just what Mr O'Brien did, see."

"That's a bright idea of yours, Bleakley. It would have tickled O'Brien's sense of humour to forestall the fire-breathing Mr X like that. But I don't believe it. And, don't you see, X probably put that bit about suicide in deliberately; he had laid his plans to commit murder and make it look like suicide; and this was just another detail to impress the idea of suicide on our innocent minds."

"Very ingenious, Mr Strangeways," said the superintendent obstinately; "but it's all up in the air, in a manner of speaking. It's not evidence, sir."

Nigel jumped up, walked over to the safe, set his coffee cup on it, and brandished the spoon at Bleakley.

"Very well, then, try to keep this one out of your wicket. If O'Brien intended to commit suicide, why, why, why did he ask me down here to help him repel the would-be murderer? If he wanted to be dead as much as all that, why go to such trouble to prevent someone doing the job for him?"

Bleakley was evidently impressed by this argument. "That's a very pretty point, sir. I suppose, though, he might have intended to kill himself, yet not wanted the person who made those threats to escape unpunished."

"Unlikely, I think. And all that paraphernalia of carrying a revolver and pretending to be sleeping in the house — Oh, I hadn't told you." Nigel explained O'Brien's ruse. "Now why in the name of Bach, Beethoven and Brahms should he have bothered himself with such precautions against death if death was what he wanted?"

"I don't know about — er — about the gentlemen you mentioned," said Bleakley cautiously, "but it certainly don't seem sense. Nor," he added, "don't it seem sense for a man who was on the lookout for a murderer and not intending to be murdered to let someone walk up to him and put a gun right up against his waistcoat — and his own gun, too. Nor yet don't it seem sense," his moustache bristled belligerently, "for a murderer to walk away from the hut through an inch of snow and leave no tracks. Why, sir, it's soopernatural — that's what it is, soopernatural."

"It must have been someone he could never have thought of suspecting," said Nigel slowly; "and yet it's queer. The very reason he had this particular party down was that he suspected some or all of its members."

"What's that, sir?" The superintendent started upright in his chair.

"Stupid of me. I keep on talking as though you knew all I know about it." Nigel mentioned the hints which

O'Brien had let fall about his will and the aeroplane plans. "So you see, there is quite enough motive to be getting on with. And there may have been another motive that O'Brien didn't reckon on at all. You remember what Mrs Grant said about Lucilla Thrale. Well, I happen to know for certain that she was O'Brien's mistress — Lucilla, I mean, not Mrs Grant." Bleakley gave one explosive guffaw, then assumed his most ferociously official expression. "Lucilla tried to persuade O'Brien to let her come to his room last night: not unnaturally, he staved her off: "soft hands cling to the booted spur", or however it goes. Now supposing O'Brien had cut out somebody else with the fair Lucilla. The somebody else would not be pleased. He might even carry his displeasure as far as murder. It has been done before. And there is a strong smell of personal hatred about those threatening letters."

"Ar, Sex," said the superintendent profoundly. "Churchee lar fem. Why, only last week my old woman was in a fair taking, and just because —" He was spared further revelations by a not altogether convincing attack of coughing and the appearance of Arthur Bellamy. Arthur whispered hoarsely into Nigel's ear, then departed, eyeing Bleakley with the expression of a man who is not quite sure whether the object before him is a slow-worm or an adder.

Nigel looked down his nose, and said dreamily, "I wonder. Disappearance of a young woman in riding kit. Where has she gone, and why?"

"What's this, sir? A young lady disappeared? Out of the house, do you mean? What is the party's name?"

"I don't know her name. And she has not disappeared out of the house exactly. She was in this hut till yesterday — No!" he exclaimed with a sudden violence that made Bleakley clutch the arms of his chair, "now I remember. I will explain all. I asked Arthur before you came to look round the hut and see if anything was missing. He has just told me that the photograph of a girl that used to be on the cupboard inside the cubicle there is gone."

"Probably Mr O'Brien burnt it before he shot himself. Suicides often —"

"Ah, but I've just remembered that on the day the other guests arrived I happened to look in at the window and got the impression that something was missing. I'd noticed the photograph there the afternoon before. I forgot about it, because just then Philip Starling turned up. But I know now. It was this photograph that had disappeared. Now why should O'Brien remove it?"

"It was not a photo of either of the ladies staying here?"

Nigel shook his head.

"Well, I reckon it's naught to do with this business." The superintendent got up cumbrously and stretched himself. Perhaps he felt that he had been twisted too easily round Nigel's finger, too easily persuaded of something that was against all reason and all criminal textbooks. At any rate, he put on his official manner and said, "I'll bear in mind your suggestions, Mr Strangeways; but I don't think I have sufficient grounds for —"

Nigel advanced on him with his ostrich strides, took him by the shoulders, and pressed him down into the chair again in a friendly but firm manner.

"No, you don't," he said, grinning. "I've not nearly finished yet. So far has been merely theorising, bombarding the clouds to try to bring down rain. Now we'll come down to earth ourselves and deal with the material evidence. You'd better have some coffee, or smoke a pipe, or bring out the hypodermic syringe, because I'm going to spread myself over this with some abandon."

Bleakley's official shell could not stand the strain of this good-humoured informality. He emerged from it, not without relief, grinned amiably, and started chewing a piece of toast. "Now," said Nigel, looking — with his thick glasses, his rumpled hair and clothing, his air of precise abstraction, and his demonstrative forefinger — rather like a university lecturer on Aristotle. "Now, I don't pretend to have got any explanation of the footprints — or rather, the absence of them. We'll leave them aside for the moment. Let us consider O'Brien's movements last night. About eleven forty-five he told them in the billiard room that he was going up to bed. His plan was to jump from that window on to the veranda roof — it's only a few feet — and from the roof on to the ground, go over to the hut, lock himself in presumably with revolver. But from the evidence of the snow he couldn't have gone out till somewhere round about one-thirty. Why did he stay in his bedroom till then? Everyone else had gone up an hour ago or more. Why should he wait in the obvious danger spot an hour and a half after the Feast of Stephen had begun? And another curious question: Why didn't he go out by the window as he said he was going to do?"

"How do you know he didn't?"

"Because I looked out of that very window this morning, before I went downstairs. The snow on the veranda roof showed no trace of anyone's having passed that way. It was quite smooth. What does that suggest?"

"Either that he went out that way before the snow began to fall heavily —"

"In which case, he didn't make the footprints over the lawn," interrupted Nigel excitedly.

"— Or else that he went down the stairs, out of the front door, and so on, not long before the snowfall ceased."

"Exactly. Now, if O'Brien wanted to be killed, why should he not have waited in his bedroom, the obvious place for the killer to come to? If he didn't, why alter his plans and invite death by going out of his door, walking along the passage and down through the lounge, with the killer for all he knew wide awake and listening for such a move. He would be simply giving himself away."

"Yes, sir," said Bleakley, scratching his head, "put like that, it do sound as though he must have gone out before the snow began."

"Then who made the tracks?" asked Nigel unemphatically.

"Why, that's obvious — the person who killed h — Dash it, sir, you've been and hypnotized me like into saying what I never —" Nigel's eyes were shining with the mild benevolence of the schoolmaster who has trapped a favorite pupil.

"But what about the shoes, Mr Strangeways, sir?" went on the Superintendent, seeing a way out. "How did they get hold of Mr O 'Brien's shoes? You answer me that, sir."

"We don't know for certain they were his shoes. All we know is that his shoes tallied with the footprints. It might mean simply that he and X wear the same size."

Bleakley whipped out his notebook and made a note. Here obviously was a line of action. But, even as he wrote, his pen slowed to a standstill.

"I reckon I'm getting fair mazed," he exclaimed irritably. "I was forgetting that these blamed footsteps were going to the hut, not coming from it. It's no good, sir."

"I know. We haven't got over that yet. The only clue the footsteps give us is that whoever made them was running. The impress of the toe was deeper than that of the heel, as you noticed. *A priori*, this might apply equally well to O'Brien or a murderer. Neither would want to be seen going out to the hut, so they'd try to get there as quickly as possible. Anyway, I've got another idea about those shoes: I'll tell you it when we arrive at that point." Nigel resumed his professional manner and went on: "Assume O'Brien has arrived at the hut, some time about midnight. Assume, if you like, that he intended to kill himself. He locked the windows, but not the door — for it was not locked when we found him dead. Contradiction number one:

Why lock windows and not door? He takes off his shoes and puts on carpet slippers. Would a person like him — or anyone — change their shoes before committing suicide?"

"Might be just force of habit."

"It might; but it's a point worth noticing. My uncle told me, too, that there was a legend about O'Brien's always putting on carpet slippers when he went into action in the air. Sounds as if he felt he was going into action again — against an unknown enemy."

"I call that pretty far-fetched," protested Bleakley.

"But possibly worth the carriage," murmured Nigel, quoting Dr Johnson; "and interesting in relation to the fingerprints on the revolver."

The superintendent's brick-red face looked blank as a wall.

"Supposing O'Brien intended to commit suicide. He would either have been quite determined about it, in which case he would simply have pulled out the revolver and shot himself without bothering to change his shoes; or he might have wavered at the last moment, in which case he would surely have fingered the gun nervously and there would have been prints on the muzzle. But he *did* change his shoes, and there *were* no prints except on the handle."

"That's downright clever, sir, that is. But it's not conclusive, not by any manner of means."

"'Little drops of water, Little grains of sand' — you know. Here's another. How many suicides have you heard of who have shot themselves in the heart?

Through the temples they do it; or else put the muzzle into their mouth."

"Ah. I'd wondered about that," admitted Bleakley.

"To proceed. Your theory is, I presume, that he shot himself, and struck his wrist against the edge of the table as he fell, bruising himself and breaking the cufflink. I have two objections to that. A blow of this type would make a single bruise, not two; and the little chain of a cufflink is surely not so weak that the impact of an arm falling limply on a table edge would break it. Now imagine this pipe is a revolver. I am pointing it at you and you seize my wrist with your right hand to deflect the muzzle away from yourself. You would probably try to push it away with your left hand, too. Come on, man, fight! You see. Your thumb and fingers would leave two bruises on the inside of my wrist, just where they were on O'Brien's, and my cufflink might quite conceivably be snapped by a strain."

Bleakley tugged furiously at his moustache. "By God, sir, I believe you've got it. The murderer comes in. O'Brien at once, or maybe after a bit of talk, suspects him and draws his gun. The murderer somehow or other distracts his attention, seizes his wrist, forces the gun round and — that accounts for his getting it at such close range and in the heart. Then the murderer tidies up all signs of a struggle, rubs any fingermarks off the muzzle, makes it look like a suicide, and —" he groaned. "There we are up against it again. *Flies* back to the house, I suppose."

Nigel evaded this point. "To return to the shoes. Just where did you find them?"

"They were on the floor over there, half hidden by that armchair."

"When you say half-hidden, you don't mean three-quarters, seven-eighths or altogether?"

"I certainly don't, sir. I could see the heels without moving the chair at all," said Bleakley with some heat.

"Well, this morning, after I'd made sure O'Brien was dead, it occurred to me to wonder where were the shoes in which he had come to the hut. I looked all round; hadn't time to open cupboards and things, but I looked by that chair, and I could swear there weren't any shoes there then."

The superintendent's expression changed to the shocked anguish of one who, munching placidly a mouthful of pheasant, suddenly bites on a piece of shot; then to the wild surmise of one pursuing the shot tortuously with his tongue through the masticated mass.

"Gor!" he said finally. "Why, that means —"

"Taken in conjunction with the fact that (a) there were no prints on the shoes, (b) that their soles were quite dry although the stove had gone out long before, the point is — as old Uncle Sherlock would say — highly suggestive," Nigel interrupted. "However, it's not a point that would carry any weight by itself in the courts. It might not even be enough to persuade your chief constable that this is a case for further investigation. However, there's one thing more." Nigel was speaking half to himself now. "I shall look a prize zany if it doesn't come off." He twitched his shoulders, as though shaking off indecision. "Are you by any

84

chance a nob at opening safes, Bleakley? It would save time and put me out of agony."

The superintendent walked over to the safe and inspected it for a minute. "I reckon I could manage this one. It's only a matter of time and patience, if you've got the knack like. A friend of mine, Harris, at the Yard, taught me how. What's on your mind, sir?"

"O'Brien told me that he kept his will in there. If we find that safe empty, we shall have almost certain proof he was murdered; and it will begin to clear up the question of motive, too."

For nearly half an hour Bleakley worked over the safe. His touch was surprisingly delicate, and his head was cocked like a violinist's while he tunes his instrument. Nigel prowled restlessly about, lighting cigarette after cigarette, pulling out books and putting them back in the wrong places. At last there came a final click, an oath from Bleakley. The safe door swung open. The safe was empty as Mother Hubbard's cupboard.

CHAPTER
SIX

The Don's Tale

Bleakley was now convinced, and sprang into a furious activity with which his companion could not and would not compete. Nigel had an extraordinary capacity for absorption in the task in hand; it was one of his strongest points as a detective. While he had been exerting all his powers to achieve his preliminary aim — the persuasion of Bleakley against the suicide theory — his mind had been immersed in the facts to the exclusion of any emotional significance. It was simply a matter of arranging them in a convincing pattern, or rationally working out a problem to which he already knew intuitively the only possible answer. Death levels all, and for Nigel's purpose up till now all the facts had had to be equal in value, equally devoid of emotional content. A mathematician working out a problem cannot afford to let his mind wander to the Hebrew significance of the number 7 or to modern superstition about the number 13. So to Nigel nothing had been relevant but the cut-and-dried logic of facts. O'Brien had been simply a dead body, of neither more nor less value than the snow on a veranda roof or the prints on the handle of a revolver. But now, as though it had been a dog obediently playing dead, O'Brien's body jumped up again before his eyes and took on life. From now on, O'Brien was to be the centre of everything: it was his living personality alone that could lead them to the hand which had killed it. Nigel walked out of the hut, leaving the Superintendent to his proper activities. They had agreed that the members of the house-party should for as long as possible be undisillusioned as to the manner of O'Brien's death. One of them, of course, had never had any illusions about it; but there was no harm in his believing that the police were still pottering about at the end of the garden path up which he had led them. Nigel strode about in the park, allowing the concentration of his mind to diffuse and play upon the personality of O'Brien.

While Nigel was trampling the fast-melting snow, the superintendent was weaving a web of complicated activity. First, Bolter was sent to keep an unobtrusive eye on the house; from his point of vantage he noticed Knott-Sloman steer a battered two-seater up the drive and away in the direction of the village, and Georgia Cavendish and her brother setting out for a walk in the park. Bleakley telephoned to the chief constable, giving him a résumé of the case and arranging for an interview with him that afternoon. He then got in touch with headquarters and ordered reinforcements. His next move was back to the hut, which he now examined with elaborate thoroughness. For this task he enlisted Bellamy's services. They discovered that they had both served for a time in the same station in India; and, uniting in some very flowery invective against a certain

87

quartermaster there, they soon thawed the previous frigidity between them. Bleakley's main object was to find further proof of a struggle's having taken place in the hut. He asked Bellamy to look for anything out of place.

"That reminds me," said Arthur, "them shoes you found behind the chair. Didn't ought to have been there. The Colonel always put 'em in the cupboard next door. Very meticularrus the Colonel was in 'is 'abits."

Bleakley registered silent exultation. Another point scored by his — by his and Mr Strangeways' theory. He pointed to the table and said:

"Mr O'Brien doesn't seem to have been so tidy with his papers."

"Ar. He let himself rip there. I tried to tidy it up one day and — gawd! — he didn't 'arf give me his tongue; a treat it was, a real eddication to listen to. 'You leave this — table alone, you — son of a —' 'e, sez. 'There's method in my madness,' 'e sez — I can 'ear 'im saying it now — 'and if you lay yer — paws on it you'll 'ave confusion thrice confounded,' 'e sez. Wot they call a hepigram, that is."

"So you wouldn't know if there was anything wrong there now?"

Arthur Bellamy stood for a moment over the table, fingering his battle-ram of a jaw.

"'Ere," he said, "'ere, wot's this? The Colonel used to sling all his letters down in a heap over there: that box marked 'Letters' he used for keeping papers in — calculations and such like. Now all the letters 'ave got into the box and the papers 'ave got piled over 'ere."

Arthur made no further discoveries, but the superintendent was quite satisfied and shortly after dismissed him. As Arthur was going out he turned and whispered hoarsely:

"When you and Mr Strangeways gets 'old of the barstard who did this, just give me five minutes alone with 'im, chum — just five minutes — you know, unofficial like. You can tell the judge 'e ran into a lorry trying to escape. Be a sport, matey."

Arthur winked, giving himself temporarily the appearance of a rhinoceros about to run amok, and departed. Bleakley worked hard for another half-hour, but the stream of clues seemed to have dried up, and there was no trace of a will to be found or of any drawings or formulae. By this time his reinforcements had arrived. He sent one man to make tactful enquiries in the village: whether any inhabitant had been in the park last night or any stranger been noticed about the place lately. He didn't expect any results from this, but elimination plays a larger part in police work than deduction. A second man he stationed to guard the hut. A third relieved Bolter, who now went into the house with the superintendent.

Nigel Strangeways, engrossed in the prospects and retrospects over which his inward eye was ranging, suddenly awoke to find himself almost walking slap into his uncle's house. Chatcombe Towers was thoroughly English, not only in its architecture, but in the wanton illogicality of its name. Generations of Marlinworths, aided and abetted in their whimsies by an obsequious succession of architects, had combined to evolve an all-in, catch-as-catch-can, and devil-take-the-hindmost riot of brick and stone. Balustrades, cupolas, buttresses, battlements, ornament Gothic and rococo stunned the bewildered eye. The only architectural feature which the building did not possess was, needless to say, a tower. Yet the house had a sort of eccentric dignity and wit and charm like that of some old aristocratic rip resting on her wild oats, Nigel had to admit.

He rang the bell and was admitted into a hall which would have been enormous but for the acute feeling of claustrophobia imparted by a whole herd of stags' heads that seemed to be breathing in concert down one's neck. The supercilious expression on their faces was repeated in that of the butler: indeed, fitted out with moth-eaten hair and a good pair of horns, his head could have been mounted on the wall and no one any the wiser. Ponsonby, having expressed his gratification at Mr Strangeways' presence amongst them again and given the weather a pontifical but qualified blessing, proceeded suavely as a crankshaft in oil towards the morning-room door. As some geologist, lost, starving and distraught amongst the Himalayan ranges, might rush at the side of a mountain and assault it with his little hammer, so Nigel suddenly felt an insane desire to strike a spark of humanity out of the butler. He clutched his elbow and hissed melodramatically: "Terrible doings at the Dower House, Ponsonby! Mr O'Brien has been found shot. He is dead. We suspect the worst." A flaw, no larger than the chipping of a geologist's hammer on the Himalayan ranges, appeared on the butler's face.

"Indeed sir! Very painful, I am sure. No doubt you will wish to apprise his lordship of the fatality."

Nigel gave it up, and, finding his uncle in the morning room, apprised him of the fatality. Lord Marlinworth's eyes protruded and he gobbled a little. "God bless my soul!" he finally ejaculated. "Dead, you say? Shot? Poor fellow, poor fellow. A tragic end. And to think that only last night he was sitting, *inter laetos laetissimus,* at the head of the festal board. Violence, they say, begets violence. A life violent, colourful, adventurous — to such a life any other manner of death had been anticlimax. Elizabeth will be much distressed: she took a great fancy to the young man. 'The last of the Elizabethans,' I called him — a pretty *lusus verborum,* I flatter myself. And exceedingly well connected, too, I gather: one of the Irish O'Briens, you know —"

Lord Marlinworth, after a shaky start, was now well into his stride and settled down to obituary. At lunch the news was broken to Lady Marlinworth. Once over the first shock, she behaved with a calmness and practicality surprising in one of such brittle, Dresden-china appearance. "I must go over at once and see that nice Cavendish gel. If she feels able to see anyone. Though I fear she will be quite prostrate".

Nigel smiled inwardly at the idea of the tough little explorer being "prostrate."

"Why should *she* be particularly upset?" he asked.

Lady Marlinworth shook a delicate, jewelled forefinger at him.

"Oh, you men, you men! You never notice anything. I may be an old woman, but I can at least see when a gel is head over heels in love. Such a charming gel, too. Not a beauty, perhaps, and a little eccentric in her ways. Bringing a parrot down to dinner is not quite — Still, *autres temps, autres moeurs*; and one must allow some latitude to a young person who spends her life wandering about amongst savages. In my young days it would not have been encouraged at all. Where was I? Oh, yes, the gel was in love with poor Mr O'Brien. A very suitable match it would have been, too. It was really most naughty and inconsiderate of him to go and get killed like that. The poor gel will be quite heartbroken."

"Elizabeth always has been a — hum — inveterate matchmaker. Haven't you, my dear?"

"I say, Aunt," said Nigel, "how do you mean 'go and get killed like that'? The doctor has no doubt it was suicide."

"The man's a fool, then," said the old lady spiritedly. "I've never heard such wicked nonsense. It was an accident. Mr O'Brien would no more kill himself than Herbert would."

Herbert started, then smoothed his moustache with some complacence. Lady Marlinworth went on:

"I shall call on Miss Cavendish this afternoon. Is there anything else you would like me to do, Nigel?"

"Yes, yes, there jolly well is. You said at dinner last night you had seen O'Brien before, or someone like him. Now I want you to try and remember where. Please. It's really important."

"Very well, Nigel, I'll try. But I won't have you stirring up mud about him; I simply won't have it. Promise me, now."

Nigel promised. After all, the mud was already stirred up so thoroughly that the lady who sits at the bottom of the well was totally invisible.

While Nigel had been listening to his uncle's funeral oration, the superintendent had begun another inquiry among the guests. He found Philip Starling and Lucilla Thrale in the lounge. Lucilla had miraculously conjured up from somewhere a dress that conveyed the suggestion of widow's weeds and at the same time was an invitation to all comers. Starling, sitting on the opposite side of the fireplace, had to admit there was a touch of genius in the way Lucilla had taken every vestige of make-up off her face. She really did look rather impressive and Andromache-like. Not every vestige, though, perhaps; the little don wondered maliciously whether those two dark smudges under her eyes were not the result of artifice rather than of grief. The superintendent said:

"Do either of you happen to know anything about a will made by the deceased? I have been unable to find one in the hut, though I am informed that he kept all his private papers there."

Lucilla rose to a statuesque position, one rounded arm flung across her eyes.

"Why do you torment me? What do I care about wills? They cannot give Fergus back to me," she said in low, broken, thrilling tones.

"Don't be an ass, Lucy," said Starling acidly; "it's the superintendent who wants to find the will, not you. Anyway, why shouldn't you want it found? It won't give Fergus back to you, as you so dramatically put it, but it will quite likely give you a nice handful of his boodle."

"You contemptible little mannikin!" she flashed back at him. "There *are* things in the world more valuable than money, though you may not be capable of understanding them."

Starling flushed angrily. "Oh, for God's sake stop play-acting, my good girl. You never were a success on the stage, and you're a bit old now for a comeback."

Bleakley hastily interposed. Lucilla looked like committing physical assault. "Now, now," he said soothingly, "we're all a little overwrought. I take it you know nothing of a will, Mr Starling?"

"You take it correctly," the little don snorted, and stumped off upstairs. Bleakley next met Edward and Georgia Cavendish coming in from their walk. To them he put the same question. Edward denied all knowledge of the whereabouts of the document. Georgia was silent for a moment, and then said:

"I don't know where he kept it, but he did tell me once that he was leaving me some of his money."

"Why not ask his solicitor?" said her brother.

"We shall get into touch with him in due course, sir."

Cavendish looked at him in a puzzled way. Bleakley went on hastily:

"Do you know of any relatives of the deceased with whom we should get into touch?"

"Afraid I don't. He never told any of us about his relations, I don't think, except that his father and mother had been dead for some time. Oh, I believe he once said something about some cousins who lived in Gloucestershire."

A few minutes later Knott-Sloman arrived back. The superintendent met him in the yard. "Just been out for a spin in the Cavendishes' car," he volunteered. "Blow away the cobwebs and all that. Stopped for a drink in the village. I can recommend the Beehive."

"I just wanted to ask if you knew anything about O'Brien's will. We can't find it," said Bleakley.

"No, I don't know. What's the idea?"

"Well, sir, you being a friend of the deceased, I thought you might have perhaps witnessed it."

"See here, what are you getting at?" said Knott-Sloman, his eyes cold and guarded. "Are you suggesting I am trying to suppress something? Because — let me tell you —"

"Oh, no, sir. Of course not; it's simply a routine inquiry."

But Knott-Sloman went off looking both offended and thoughtful; and Bleakley kicked himself for the tactical error. That question about the witnesses to the will might set minds working and tongues talking — might suggest to someone, once it got about, that the police were not so satisfied with the suicide theory as they pretended to be.

On his return after lunch, Nigel dragged Philip Starling away from a peculiarly savage article he had begun to write exposing the imbecilities committed by a recent editor of the *Pythian Odes,* and brought him to his own room.

"Look here, Philip, I've got to have the dirt on all these chaps, and you can probably give me some of it. In return I'll give you an exclusive story — which'll damned well have to remain exclusive for the present. But first I'll have to ask you a question. What's all this between you and Lucilla?"

Starling's cynical, arrogant, yet oddly appealing face grew tense. His eyes turned away. Then he said lightly:

"I like thumping great blondes. Lucilla does not like small men."

He spoke in identically the same tones as he used in relating his most fantastic scandals; but Nigel knew that he was being serious now.

"I see," he said. "I'm sorry. Not that I think you're missing much."

"Lord, no. She's a bitch, all right. And one of the world's most barefaced self-deceivers. Look at the way she's acting up now. The field marshal's widow walking in the funeral cortege. Couldn't get O'Brien to sign her marriage lines on earth, so her marriage has got to be made in heaven. Gah! She makes me sick."

"O'Brien likely to have left her some money?"

"Might have. She was pretty thick with him. And at the very top of the gold-digging profession. You and Bleakley seem curiously interested in his will. What's the hurry?"

"O'Brien was murdered," said Nigel negligently, lighting a cigarette.

Philip Starling gave a long-drawn whistle.

"Well, you should know," he said at last.

"And if you pass the news on there'll be another murder," smiled Nigel. "Now tell me more about La Thrale."

"She turned up at Oxford a few years ago, acting in the Thespians Repertory Company. And what a ham-actress, too. However, she compensated for her failure on the boards by her success in the bed. Drove the proctors silly. They had to intrigue to get her out of the place finally. Her face was launching too many overdrafts among the undergraduates."

"And then?"

"She went up to London. No visible means of support, but a series of guardian angels. Cavendish was the last of the angelic succession. She turned him down for O'Brien. Always did have an incredible nose for the sinking ship, the little rat. Cavendish has been getting into rather a sticky position financially this year, you know. I'm not sure she didn't really fall for O'Brien. First time she'd had to do the chasing, and she had to like it. He'd got her properly taped, and she was beginning to realise he didn't give any more for her than she'd given for her previous playmates. Lucilla in the role of cast-off glove would have been an interesting spectacle — and she wouldn't take it lying down, either —"

"Stop, stop, stop!" cried Nigel, clapping his hands to his ears in mock desperation. "I can't stand more than one motive at a time, and you've already given me three. Edward Cavendish might have killed O'Brien because (a) he'd taken away his girl, or (b) he wanted to expedite his legacy, or both; Lucilla might have killed him on the hell-has-no-fury-like-a-woman-scorned cue. It only needs you to tell me that Georgia is O'Brien's cast-off mistress and Knott-Sloman an agent of the OGPU and we shall have a perfect case against everyone in the household. Oh, I'd forgotten Mrs Grant. Her motive could be religious mania."

"What about me? It's rather humiliating to be left out like this. I've always fancied myself as a potential murderer. The trained mind applying itself to the practical problems of life, you know." Starling's face wore its most irresponsible and babyish expression, but his eyes were sharp; he looked like an overgrown infant prodigy.

"I should head the list of suspects with your name, Philip, only that I can't conceive any possible motive for you."

"No. If I had felt the need to bump off anyone in this outfit, my dear Nigel, it would have been Knott-Sloman. A really squalid fellow. Was a brass-hat in the war and runs a roadhouse in the peace, and if you can tell me a more nauseating combination of activities I'll eat my hat. Add to that the fact that he is an anecdote-addict and eats nuts between meals, and Dante would have had to think out a special circle of hell for him. Woof!"

"Where's his roadhouse?"

"Near London. Kingston bypass or somewhere. Very posh and popular. He's just the sort of fellow to make a success of a thing like that. Smacks the women on the bottom and wears all his medals on his dinner-jacket, no doubt."

"I wonder how O'Brien came to take up with him."

"You may well ask, old boy. Blackmail, probably. Sloman and Lucy are suspected by the cognoscenti of working in partnership over something or other, and blackmail would be just about his mark."

"Ah," said Nigel ironically, "I was waiting for something like that. Now you've only to give me a nice, succulent motive for Georgia, and I shall be quite happy."

"No, no. I yield to no one in my love of scandal for scandal's sake. But Georgia is a good stick. Everything that a woman should be — attractively ugly, eccentric without being a frump, witty, a good cook, sensible and sensual, faithful, and a perfect seat — I am told — on anything from an armadillo to a camel."

"She's everything, in fact, except a thumping great blonde," said Nigel maliciously.

"Everything, as you say, except a thumping great blonde. Not that I wouldn't have made an exception to my rule, and applied for the job; only she was booked. O'Brien, you know. Yes. He was very fond of her, and she was right in the deep end over him — wouldn't look at anyone else. Can't think why they didn't get spliced."

"That's what you meant when you said she was faithful?"

"And to her brother, too. He must be ten years older, but she looks after him like an only son. The only time I've seen her fussy was at some party or other when he threw a faint. You'd think the end of the world had come, the way she behaved. Oh, yes, she dotes on Edward. God knows why. He's quite a decent old trot, but definitely in the Beta class."

"I thought he seemed to have brains."

"He has, of a sort — the financier's type of brain. Enough to make a fortune, but not enough to leave well alone when it's made. Georgia is going to have her hands pretty full with him in the near future. Fellow's on the edge of a nervous breakdown already. He's been going about all this morning with a long face and twitching hands. Gives you the pip to look at him. Heaven knows Oxford is a neurotic enough place to work in, but it must be lotus-land compared with the Stock Exchange."

"How are the other inmates reacting?"

"Well, Lucilla's standing about in a series of funeral urn poses: positively reeks of tragedy — a widow bird sat mourning for her love, 'widow' being the courtesy title and 'bird' the courtesan one. I really believe the girl is a bit upset about something; she never did have the talent to put up such a good act. Knott-Sloman, thank God, has been out of the house most of the time, and comparatively silent when he was in it — the atmosphere is not a favourable one for the bottom-slapping *raconteur*. Poor Georgia has been wandering about most of the time looking like the ghost of an organ grinder's monkey. It's really more than I can bear to look at her — makes me want to weep buckets. In spite of it, she's the sheet-anchor of the party: a ministering angel to Edward, and a trained nurse for

Lucilla — and that must be a pretty grinding job, considering the way Lucy groans and bays and sniffles all the time about her broken heart and her dead hero, as though Georgia's heart wasn't ten times as big and fifty times more broken."

The little don was quite flushed with his generous denunciation.

"Yes," said Nigel, "the real broken heart does not advertise itself."

"Is not puffed up."

"Neither vaunteth itself unseemly," replied Nigel antiphonally. "However," he continued, "there is a time to play quotation-games and a time to refrain from playing quotation-games. Will you please, Philip, instead of searching the Scriptures, apply the trained mind to another practical problem? To wit, how does a chap go fifty yards over snow an inch deep without leaving tracks?"

"Faith, old boy, faith. Levitation. Fellow's a yogi. Or possibly used stilts."

"Stilts?" said Nigel with sudden excitement. "But no, that won't do. They would leave marks, too, and Bleakley has been all over the ground; he'd have noticed them. I wonder, now, what sort of impressions snowshoes make. Visible, anyway, I should think. It must be something ludicrously simple."

"If you were to give me the context, I should have less difficulty in determining the correct reading," said Starling donnishly. "I thought there were a perfectly good set of footprints."

"Going the wrong way, unfortunately. Unless the murderer found himself all of a sudden through the looking-glass and had to walk away from the house to get to it."

Philip Starling's face took on its most infuriating infant-innocence expression. "And that, in a sense, is just what he did. Your Greek compositions, Nigel, admirable as they often were, suffered from over-elaboration. Straining after style, you were apt to make elementary mistakes. Blind spots, you called them —"

"Oh, heaven," Nigel interrupted, "I never thought I should have to undergo another tutorial."

Starling continued imperturbably. "Now if you'd not spent all your time at your private school inking your fingernails, and at Oxford drinking coffee in some low dive, you would have come across the adventures of Hercules. The little affair of the Cacus and the oxen, for instance."

Nigel buried his face in his hands and groaned bitterly. "I shall have to take to rabbit breeding," he moaned.

"Cacus," the don went on mercilessly, "as every schoolboy knows, stole some oxen. Hercules, the Bulldog Drummond of the period, went to recover them. Cacus, showing remarkable intelligence for one of such abnormally overgrown physique, dragged the oxen backwards by their tails into a cave. Impression made on Hercules' mind — which incidentally was about on a par with Drummond's for low cunning, obtuseness, greed, humourlessness, cruelty and bestial arrogance — was that the oxen had gone in the opposite direction."

"All right, all right," groaned Nigel. "Don't rub it in. I've made the world's most childish howler. But, by Jove, this alters the complexion of everything. X walked backwards into the house; that's why the toemarks were deeper than the heel. But there were no other tracks. Therefore he went out before there was enough snow to take an impression — between twelve-five and twelve-thirty, say. He's going to get a nasty jar when he finds we know that."

They talked for nearly an hour more, until the winter evening was darkening into night and the image of buttered toast loomed large in the mind. Starling had begun to say:

"By the way, Nigel, I suppose you noticed at dinner how O'Brien —"

When he was interrupted by a commotion downstairs. A woman's voice gave a stifled shriek; feet could be heard running fast somewhere; a long silence; then someone was calling out, "Mr Strangeways! Mr Strangeways!" and footsteps were pounding up the stairs. Whatever O'Brien had said or done at dinner was not to be recounted just now. Nigel opened his door. Bolter was outside, mopping his brow, his red face working with excitement.

"The super wants you, zur," he said. "Mrs Grant found un in the pantry — she went to get the victuals for tea — his skull be nearly zplit oapen. A ghaastlee zight 'e be, zur."

"Good lord, the super laid out now; not dead, is he?"

103

"You mistake my meaning, zur. Bain't the super. 'Tis that man of Mr O'Brien's — what's his name? — ar, Bellamy. Bellamy it be, zur. In a pool of blood."

CHAPTER
SEVEN

Telltale

Arthur Bellamy's rendezvous with the murderer had taken place sooner than he had expected. Not that he could have known much about it. He had been struck down from behind, in the passage that led from the main part of the house towards the kitchen and scullery. It was a dark passage, so that, even if the blow had been struck some hours earlier, he might very well not have seen his assailant. There was blood on the stone floor just on the far side of the swing-door that divided the servants' quarters from the rest of the house; from there, smears and spots of blood pointed a clear trail along the passage to the pantry door: no attempt had been made to clean them up: they and the pool of blood on the pantry floor were still wet. Superintendent Bleakley had little difficulty in reconstructing the deed. The assailant had either followed Bellamy into the kitchen passage or been in hiding behind the swing-door which opened into it; probably the latter. He had struck him with some weapon which was yet to be found. He had then taken hold of his victim, presumably by the heels — for to take him by the shoulders would have been impossible without getting blood on to one's clothes — dragged him along into the pantry, let the body slump on to the floor, closed the door, and — Bleakley added — congratulated himself or herself on a neat little job. The superintendent knew the body had been dragged, not carried, by the clear trail it had left on the rather dusty floor of the passage.

Unfortunately, that seemed likely to be the sum of his knowledge for the present. The person who might have been expected to know something about it, Mrs Grant, had been taking her usual afternoon nap in her bedroom: and, as she made it quite clear, she always slept the sleep of the righteous. Nigel doubted, in fact, whether she would have curtailed her legitimate period of sleep even for the Judgement-Day trumpets: she seemed more concerned with the mess that had been made in her pantry than with the fate of Arthur Bellamy. This still hung in the balance, and would hang for an indefinite time. He was still breathing when they found him. The local doctor, hastily summoned, declared that there might be a chance of saving his life. The superintendent, for obvious reasons, wanted him conveyed to the safety of a hospital; but the doctor refused to be responsible for the results of moving him so far in his present condition. After some argument, Bleakley gave in. Bellamy was taken up into his own bedroom: a policeman was stationed at the door, with orders not to admit anyone except the doctor or the superintendent, under any circumstances whatsoever, and a trained nurse sent for.

While some of his men were searching the kitchen quarters, the outbuildings and the grounds for the weapon, Bleakley herded the guests into the dining room, preparatory to beginning his inquiry. He first asked whether any of them objected to their private rooms being searched. He would be able to obtain a search warrant, of course; but time, in a case like this, might prove important; and as none of them could possibly have anything to conceal, etc., etc. The superintendent was a different man from the homely, puzzled individual who had talked with Nigel in the hut only a few hours before. Thought removed from the sphere of action meant little to him; but now, with all the familiar detail of action about him, he showed himself to possess a mind lucid and orderly, and the personal dignity of one who is working single-mindedly towards a definite goal. Nigel had had a few words with him before the inquiry started. "Well, this looks like clearing things up a bit," he said.

"That's right, sir. I thought I'd made a fool of myself this morning, letting out that I was interested in that will. But it's brought our man out into the open, and a darned sight sooner than I should have imagined. Only hope it's not done for Bellamy."

"You mean, it suggests that Arthur Bellamy was one of the two witnesses to the will."

"Exactly, sir. And if he was, he'll know who the other witness was and possibly the provisions of the will, too. The murderer took the will, knowing that its contents would prove motive against him."

"Getting it out of the safe how?" Nigel interrupted.

"Must have known the combination, sir; means it was one of Mr O'Brien's intimate friends, and that fits in with everything we've got so far."

"H'm. It would not be impossible to pick holes in that. Still, go on."

"Well, assuming the murderer does not want the contents of this will" — at the word "this" Nigel nodded vigorously with sudden comprehension — "divulged yet, or ever maybe, it would be natural for him to try and finish off Bellamy. His knowing that Bellamy was one of the witnesses suggests that he was the other."

"But does not necessarily imply it. We must remember, too, that a witness to a will cannot benefit by it. Therefore, if this murder was done in order to obtain money under the will, the murderer cannot have been a witness."

"Well, sir, if the murderer was not one of the witnesses but knows who the other was — and there'd be no use his killing Bellamy if he didn't — then that other witness is going to be for it in the near future, if we don't look out."

"By Jove, yes, you'll have to keep your eyes open. Though it's not impossible that this second witness might be in league with the murderer."

"You don't often find conspiracy to murder, sir. Very few people would trust anyone else with a secret like that."

"Macbeth and his wife. Thompson and Bywaters. It's not uncommon in cases when sexual passion is involved. And there's a hell of a lot of sexual passion lying about in this party."

Bleakley was pondering the sinister significance of this idea as he went into the dining room to confront his guests. No sign of it, however, appeared on his brick-red, deceptively bucolic face. No one raised any objection to a search of their bedrooms. Bleakley accordingly sent up the sergeant, who had returned from Taviston, to carry out this task; and retired with Nigel and Bolter to the little study, leaving a constable at the dining-room door to send in the guests one by one and also to pick up any illuminating bits of conversation that might be dropped there. Philip Starling was disposed of first. Mrs Grant had already deposed that Bellamy had been in and about the kitchen premises till about two-thirty, when she knocked off work for her afternoon sleep. Starling had been talking with Nigel upstairs from two-twenty till the alarm was given, and he was therefore out of it. He repeated his assertion that he knew nothing of any will: nor did he know who were O'Brien's solicitors.

Lucilla Thrale was sent for next. She swept in and took the chair offered her at the end of the table like a queen. Bolter emitted an audible gasp of admiration, and Nigel felt that even the superintendent could scarce forbear to cheer. Lucilla met this more or less silent applause with that almost imperceptible lift of the head, that faint arrogant awareness of lip and eyebrow which are the beautiful woman's acknowledgement of admiration. Bleakley fingered his stiletto-like moustache and settled his tie. He first asked the formal questions as to her age, address, etc. Then, with a rasping cough, he set to work.

"Now, Miss Thrale, I'm sure you will not mind answering a few other questions. Bolter there" (Bolter puffed out his already very adequate chest) "will take down what you say, and later you will be given a copy of the deposition and asked to sign it, if you find it correct."

Lucilla inclined her head graciously.

"First of all, Miss Thrale, do you wish to amplify the statement you made this morning about Mr O'Brien's will?"

"Amplify it? How can I?" she said in her cool, husky, slightly insolent voice. "Fergus — Mr O'Brien — never spoke to me about a will."

"Put it this way, do you think you are likely to benefit by it?"

"I dare say," she replied indifferently.

Slightly nettled, the superintendent leant forward and said:

"What was your relationship with the deceased?"

Lucilla flushed: then threw back her magnificent head, and, looking through Bleakley rather than at him, replied:

"I was his mistress."

A half-strangled sound, suspiciously like "Cor!" proceeded from Bolter.

"Hrrm, hrrumph. Just so. Well now, to revert to the occurrences of last night, ma'am. You heard no suspicious sounds after you had gone to bed?"

"I went to sleep at once. What suspicious sounds would there be?"

Nigel, crushing out his cigarette, said mildly to the superintendent, "I don't think Miss Thrale realises that O'Brien was murdered."

Lucilla's hand flew to her mouth. She gasped. Her pale face grew paler still and seemed to shrink.

"Murdered? Oh, God! Fergus — who?"

"We don't know yet. Perhaps you can tell us if he had any enemies."

"Enemies?" Lucilla's eyelids dropped: their long lashes swept down; her previous repose of attitude seemed to have tightened to a nervous immobility. "Such a man will always have enemies. I cannot tell you more."

Bleakley was silent for a moment. Then he said briskly, "Now if you will just tell us, as a matter of form, your movements this afternoon."

"I was in the lounge till about three o'clock. Then I went up to my room to rest. I did not come down again till I heard the noise downstairs. It is terrible, terrible! No one is safe in this house! Who will it be next?"

"Don't you worry yourself, ma'am. We have the matter well in hand. Anyone with you in the lounge?"

"Miss Cavendish sat with me for a bit after lunch. She went out before I did — about a quarter of an hour before. I don't know where she went," Lucilla said coldly, "and I think Mr. Knott-Sloman looked in once. Yes, it was ten to three. He came to compare his watch with the clock."

"Now, just one more question, Miss Thrale, and I hope you will understand that it is merely a formal matter of cross-checking all movements. Have you any means of corroborating that you were in your room from" (he glanced at his notes) "three o'clock till you heard the alarm?"

"No, I have not," she said quickly and decisively — a little too quickly, as if she had anticipated the question and decided on the answer beforehand. "I do not have witnesses of all my movements."

"The loss is ours," murmured Nigel with impudent gallantry. Lucilla gave him a freezing look, and swept out. Knott-Sloman was summoned next. He entered jauntily, smoking a cigar, and wearing the expression half-hearty, half-ingratiating with which he welcomed visitors to his roadhouse.

"Well, well, well," he said, rubbing his hands. "So this is the inquisition. Not so alarming as I always imagined this sort of thing to be. What we always found out at the Front — the worst part of a show was waiting for it to begin."

He declared himself to be Cyril Knott-Sloman, age fifty-one ("But a man's no older than he feels, what?"), bachelor, proprietor of the Fizz-and-Frolic Club, near Kingston. He knew nothing of O'Brien's testamentary dispositions. He did not fancy his chances as an heir ("Put my money on Lucilla for the inheritance stakes; a fast mover, that filly."). When asked whether he had heard anything during the night, he looked hard at Bleakley, then said:

112

"Aha, I thought so. You gave yourself away this morning, superintendent. So you don't think O'Brien did it himself. Well, I don't either. He was not the fellow to take the easy way out. Poor old Slip-Slop. It's hard to believe that he's gone west. One of the best, he was. I wish I could help you, but I slept like a log all night long."

"Can you tell us any possible motive there might have been for killing O'Brien? Was he the sort of man to make enemies?"

"Well, anyone who's got a packet of money like that is a bit liable to dirty work, what? Damn it, I shouldn't have said that — sounds as if I was trying to get one in at Lucilla — ridiculous, of course, the girl couldn't kill a wasp. Forget it. Apart from that I can't imagine anyone wanting to do him in. Everyone liked him; you couldn't help it. Though I thought he'd got a bit queer in his ways since I met him last."

"Where was that?"

"Out in France. Hadn't seen him since 'eighteen. Turned up suddenly one night last summer at my club with Lucilla."

"Very well, sir; now if you'll just inform us of your movements from lunchtime today."

Knott-Sloman's eyes narrowed. "Darned difficult to remember everything, y'know. I'll try, though. Let me see. Cavendish and I played billiards after lunch; that would be from about two o'clock till a little after three."

"You two were in the billiard room the whole of that period, I take it?"

"Rather. Had to keep an eye on each other to see there was no monkeying with the score," said Knott-Sloman facetiously.

"Miss Thrale was mistaken, then, when she said you came into the lounge about ten to three?"

After the slightest hesitation Knott-Sloman replied, showing his teeth in an apologetic and dentifrice-advertisement smile. "Of course. Damned silly of me. Just shows how difficult it is to remember everything. I went into the lounge for a minute to compare my watch with the clock there. I had some letters to write and didn't want to miss the afternoon post. Found it was later than I thought, so Cavendish and I just finished off that game, and then I came in here, wrote my letters and walked down to the village with them. Didn't get back till after you'd discovered poor old Bellamy. How is he? Going to turn the corner, I hope."

The superintendent said that there was some slight hope of Bellamy's recovery. He asked next whether there had been anyone else in the study while Knott-Sloman was writing his letters.

"Yes, Miss Cavendish was there. She was busy quill-driving too."

Bleakley was about to dismiss this witness when Nigel, who had been sitting hunched-up in his chair, gazing noncommittally down his nose, roused himself and said:

"You say you knew O'Brien in the war. Were you in the R.A.F.?"

Knott-Sloman gave him an insolent stare. "So Saul also is among the sleuths. Well, wonders never cease. If you want to know, I was a pilot till 'sixteen: then I got a job on the staff. I came across O'Brien because I held a command in his sector from the summer of 'seventeen. Quite satisfied now?"

"Can you tell me the name and address of anyone living who was in O'Brien's flight or squadron or whatever it is?" Nigel answered imperturbably.

"Let me see." Knott-Sloman appeared to be taken rather aback. "Anstruther, Greaves, Fear, McIlray — they all went west, though. Ah, I've got the man for you. Jimmy Hope. He was living somewhere down this way when I heard of him last: a chicken farm just outside Bridgewest — Staynton; that was the name of the place."

"Thanks. You interested in aeroplane engines?"

Knott-Sloman surveyed him insolently. "Not particularly. Are you?" He turned to Bleakley. "Perhaps when your assistant has finished with the round games he will permit me to go."

Bleakley looked inquiringly at Nigel, who said in his most infuriating manner, "O.K. We'll get down to a bout of consequences tomorrow, if the gentleman cares to play."

Knott-Sloman scowled at him and departed. Bleakley raised his eyebrows at Nigel and was about to say something, when a constable entered hurriedly. A poker had been found in the incinerator. It naturally enough bore no signs by now of having been used for the attack on Bellamy: but Mrs Grant swore that she had used it at lunchtime to poke the kitchen range, and she conceded grudgingly that even the slut Nellie would not be such a fool as to put it in the incinerator. Nellie was not on the spot to confirm this, as she always went home for a few hours after washing up the lunch things, but Bleakley arranged that she should be sent to him as soon as she returned.

"That incinerator's in the scullery," he said. "Whoever it was had to go into the kitchen for the poker, and go right through the kitchen again to hide it in the incinerator. Lucky for him Mrs Grant takes her nap upstairs in her bedroom. She must be a sound sleeper, and no error, to sleep through all that."

"If, indeed, she was asleep at all," said Nigel in tones of bloodcurdling suggestiveness.

The superintendent looked startled, then contemplative, then amused. "No, sir," he said, "you can't pull my leg like that. Mrs Grant may be an old — but she don't go about shooting people and battering them with pokers, I'll lay my pension on it. Well, we'd better get on with it. Miss Cavendish next."

Philip Starling's description of Georgia had been very accurate, Nigel thought, watching her as Bleakley put his preliminary questions. Her eyes, that the night before had been so happy and vivacious, now were cups of sorrow — dazed, forlorn, hopeless as a ghost's; she moved as though her whole body were bruised; yet in its steely control and the restraint of hand and feature there was something indomitable.

"Yes," she was saying, "Fergus did say he was going to leave me his money, or some of it. I've got all I need, really; but we used to joke about how I would have enough to explore Atlantis when he was dead. He was very ill, you know, and didn't expect —"

Her voice shook very slightly and she had to stop. There's only one country you want to explore now, thought Nigel, and that's the country O'Brien has gone to.

Georgia knew nothing more about the will. When told that O'Brien had been murdered she was silent for a moment and then said, "Yes," with a shuddering intensity, as though submitting to a blow she had for a long time seen coming. Then she beat her small brown hand on the table and exclaimed:

"No! Who would ever kill him? He had no enemies. Only cowards and bullies get murdered. He was very ill. The doctors said he could not live for long. Why can't you leave him in peace now?"

Bleakley tilted back his chair and looked at her intently. "I'm sorry, miss, but there doesn't seem any chance of it being suicide. Why, you're the only one of his friends who hasn't said that he was the last person to kill himself."

After this outburst, Georgia Cavendish withdrew into herself again, answering Bleakley's questions in an absent-minded way. She corroborated Lucilla's statement that she had been with her in the lounge from lunchtime till about two forty-five. She had then gone into the study to write a letter: Knott-Sloman had come in a little after three o'clock — she could not be sure of exact times. He was still there when she finished her letter and went up to her room. She had stayed in her room till she heard the commotion below. She had no witness to this. Lucilla had been just behind her as she ran downstairs. When Bleakley had finished, Nigel said:

"I'm afraid this is a very impertinent question, Miss Cavendish; but will you tell us just how things stood between you and O'Brien?"

Georgia looked at him hard; then, as though he had passed some test, she gave him a friendly smile and said:

"We loved each other. We really did ever since that first time we met in Africa — at least, I did. But we didn't seem to realise it till just lately. As soon as I — I knew, I wanted us to get married: I like carrying things to extremes," she added with a ghost of her old impish smile. "But Fergus said the doctors had told him he was a dying man, and he didn't want to saddle me with a corpse. I thought that was all rot, of course, but he stood firm. Said Nature had not intended me for a sick nurse. So we just — we were lovers."

"I see," Nigel smiled at her gravely. "Now please don't be offended — I believe what you have told us — but it does rather conflict with Miss Thrale's testimony and, er, general behaviour, and so forth."

"This is damned difficult," said Georgia, clasping her hands and pressing them into her lap. "You see, it's like this. She was — she had been Fergus's mistress. She *is* a pretty grand piece of work, after all. But when Fergus and I — well, woke up to each other, he didn't want her any more. Damned odd, but there it is. He really had her down here to sort of break it to her — always the gentleman, you know, and all that. Apparently she didn't quite grasp what he was driving at — I mean, this official mourner stuff she's putting on now — no, that's catty of me — she *did* love him — why shouldn't she? Oh, hell!"

Georgia relapsed into confusion and Bleakley tactfully dismissed her, asking her to send her brother along next. As soon as the door was shut he cast an eloquent glance at Nigel.

"That puts Miss Thrale in a nasty position, don't it, sir?"

"We don't yet know for certain that O'Brien had officially paid her off," Nigel replied; but Georgia's evidence had undoubtedly given a definite direction to the case.

Edward Cavendish entered, wearing the same bewildered and harassed appearance that he seemed to have worn since he and Nigel found the body in the hut. He sat down heavily in the chair that was offered him, looking a good deal more than his fifty-three years. The superintendent questioned him as to his address and occupation, then asked whether he could not, as an old friend of O'Brien, give them some inkling of the motive for the murder.

"You're misinformed about that, Superintendent," he said. "I'm not an old friend of O'Brien's. Only got to know him this year. My sister introduced us."

"Well, sir, let us say 'friend', then. You had got to know him pretty well, I take it."

"No. He used to ask my advice occasionally on investments; he had considerable capital; but we were dissimilar types and had quite different interests."

"A friend for the sake of advantage, as Aristotle puts it," murmured Nigel, gazing beneath almost closed lids at Cavendish's big, round, well-shaved, pale face; the eyes behind rimless glasses — eyes in which the professional reticence of the big-business man could not conceal some deep perturbation; the lines of anxiety on the forehead and the thinning, pomaded hair. His mouth suggested sensuality and even ruthlessness; yet there was something curiously babyish about his expression as a whole, something that no doubt appealed to the mothering instinct in his sister.

Bleakley was now asking him about his movements since lunch.

"I was playing billiards with Knott-Sloman till about three o'clock. Then I went out for a walk in the park."

"Meet anyone on your walk, sir?"

"No, I can't say I did. Very poor alibi," he added with a ghastly attempt at a smile. "I got back between four and a quarter past, and a constable told me Bellamy had just been discovered."

"Was Mr Knott-Sloman with you all the time in the billiard room?"

"Yes. No — I remember; he went out to find the time — about ten minutes before we stopped playing, it was."

"Just went into the lounge and came back again, did he, sir?"

"Well, I wouldn't quite say that. He must have been out five minutes at least."

The superintendent could scarcely suppress a start of surprise, and Bolter's pencil remained poised in mid-air.

"You're sure of that, are you, sir?" asked Bleakley, as unemphatically as possible.

"Yes. Why not?" Cavendish looked at him in a puzzled way. Then his whole expression changed. He seemed to be nerving himself for some crucial utterance. He moistened his lips and said:

"Look here, Superintendent, are you sure about this murder business? I mean, couldn't it have been suicide? Damn it all, I can't believe that anyone here —"

"I'm sorry, sir. There can be no question about it on the evidence we have got so far."

Cavendish looked again at Bleakley and Nigel, as though weighing something in his mind. His fists clenched and unclenched.

"The evidence," he muttered: "but supposing I —"

Whatever disclosure was coming did not arrive, for at that moment the sergeant entered, looking portentous as a Greek tragedy messenger, and laid a piece of paper before the super.

"Found it in Mr O'Brien's bedroom," he whispered to Bleakley, "folded up and used as a window wedge."

Bleakley gave one look at the paper: his eyes bulged and his waxed moustaches seemed to quiver like wires. He pointed to the paper and said to Cavendish:

"Recognise this handwriting, sir?"

"Yes. Er — it's Miss Thrale's; but —"

"Bring Miss Thrale in, George."

While the sergeant was fetching Lucilla, Nigel leant across the table and looked at the paper. On it was written, in a large, slap-dash kind of handwriting:

I must see you tonight. Can't we forget what has happened since — Meet me in the hut after the others have gone to bed. Please, darling, please. Lucilla.

Lucilla Thrale entered regally, pausing for a moment in the doorway as though waiting for the applause to die down. But this time there was no applause. Bleakley stood up, held the note in front of her, and rapped out:

"Did you write this, Miss Thrale?"

Her hand flew to her throat. A deep flush rose in her face.

"No!" she cried. "No! no! no!"

"But Mr Cavendish testifies this is your handwriting."

She turned on Cavendish, bending forward, her fingers hooked like claws. Her voice, cold and harsh at first, rose to a shrill distraught screaming.

"So *you* testify, do you? You would like to give me away, wouldn't you. You were jealous because I left you for a better man. Jealous! You white-faced, double-crossing skunk, pretending to be respectable, and all the time — You hated Fergus. It was you who killed him! I know you did it! I —"

"Now then, Miss Thrale, that's enough of that. Did you write this note?"

"Yes, yes, YES! I wrote it. I loved him. But I didn't go to the hut — I didn't, I tell you. He wouldn't let me —"

She looked round at the cold, incredulous faces.

"It's a frame-up," she screamed at Cavendish. "You're trying to put this on me!" She turned to Bleakley, pointing wildly at Cavendish. "Can't you hear? He's planted it on me. He put it in my room this afternoon! I saw him."

"The note was not found in your room, Miss Thrale. If your other statements are as false as this one, you're going to find yourself in a very awkward situation."

"Just a minute, Bleakley," interrupted Nigel. "Cavendish, were you in Miss Thrale's room this afternoon? You said nothing about it in your statement."

Cavendish's cheeks were flaming, as though Lucilla had been boxing his ears. Dignity and anger seemed to be struggling for supremacy in his countenance. The image of a churchwarden accused of stealing from the collection bag rose unbidden into Nigel's mind. Outraged dignity and righteous anger were in the man's voice when he spoke.

"Very well, then. As Miss Thrale has chosen to make these ridiculous accusations, she cannot expect me to be tender to *her* reputation. I *was* in her room this afternoon, and I'll tell you why."

"No, Edward! Please! I was upset — made to say what I did. You know I didn't mean it." Lucilla's voice was broken and pleading, but Cavendish did not even look at her.

"When Knott-Sloman came into the billiard room again this afternoon he said Lucilla — Miss Thrale — wanted to see me in her room. We finished our game and I went up. Miss Thrale made me a proposition.

123

Either I should pay her £10,000 or she would let the police know that she had been my mistress. She had letters of mine. She said that if our relationship was disclosed it would do me great damage publicly: she also said that the police would soon be looking for motives, because O'Brien had been murdered, and the fact that O'Brien had taken her away from me — as she put it — would seem to them a very sufficient motive for my having killed him. I told her that I was not accustomed to being intimidated by blackmailers. She then swore she would also tell the police that I had killed O'Brien in order to benefit by his will and get myself out of those difficulties, as well as from motives of revenge. I replied that, if O'Brien *had* been murdered, the police would investigate the position of every one of this party, and the state of my finances would be discovered soon enough. I had naturally intended to keep quiet about all this. This is why I said I was out for a walk this afternoon, when actually I was in Miss Thrale's room most of the time. I did go out for a little after that, by the way. But now Miss Thrale has chosen to make these accusations in public, I see no point in further dissimulation. I have no wish to retaliate; but, as things have gone so far already, Superintendent, I suggest that you ask Knott-Sloman how much of this £10,000 blackmail money was to be his share."

CHAPTER
EIGHT

A Tale of Woe

As Nigel drove with Bleakley towards Taviston that evening the sun that had melted the last night's snow was drawing up mists like thick woollen combinations about the lower parts of the hills. Or so he unromantically described it to himself. The road switchbacked up and down and round these hills, so that now they would be travelling through clear air and looking down on a kind of lake of steam, now they plunged downwards into a patch of it and could see nothing much beyond their own radiator cap. The constable who was driving dashed with speculative abandon into these patches and, emerging on the far side still on the road, muttered to himself audible congratulations. Bleakley was to drive back with Nigel later that night, as he felt it imperative to be on the spot just at present. If they managed to get through the fog, which would be much worse after dinner. But no fog, Nigel was thinking — not even the dense and universal steam that first covered the earth as it hung cooling in space — could hope to compete with the utter caliginous inspissated fog in his own mind.

The series of revelations they had just been hearing, like magnesium flashes in a dark room, had only served to blind the eye. Each fresh clue seemed to lead in a different direction and then to break off in the hand before it had got them anywhere. For the fifth time Nigel forced himself calmly to review the web of contradictions. Lucilla Thrale had denied Cavendish's accusations: she admitted that he had been in her room after lunch, but swore they were just having a friendly conversation. A curious place for light chat, Nigel had reflected, but you couldn't be certain. Lucilla emphatically denied having been in the hut last night, her denials finally reaching such a pitch of hysteria that Bleakley had to turn her over to Georgia Cavendish and salve his official conscience by detailing a man to see she made no attempt at escape. Knott-Sloman, faced with Cavendish's charge of complicity in the blackmail, had first blustered and threatened several kinds of action, from physical assault to legal redress; then he had cooled down and magnanimously declared that he would forget it all, as poor old Edward was really knocked-up and not responsible. Poor old Edward, however, persisted in his statement, though he could give no satisfactory reason for connecting Knott-Sloman with Lucilla over the alleged blackmail. Knott-Sloman and he also continued to contradict each other as to the length of time the former had been out of the billiard room.

This brought Nigel's sorely belaboured mind back again to the problem of Bellamy's assailant. Every one of the household except Philip Starling had had the opportunity. Lucilla could have done it between two forty-five, when Georgia had left her in the lounge, and the time when Cavendish came up to her room; with the exception of that minute (or was it five minutes?) when Knott-Sloman was in the lounge: or he and she might have done it together then, Knott-Sloman wielding the blunt instrument and Lucilla keeping cave. Georgia had no witnesses to her movements from about three o'clock till the body was discovered. Her brother could have slipped out of the billiard room after Knott-Sloman, though this was unlikely, as he could not have known how long Knott-Sloman was going to be; but Cavendish also could have done the deed after he had left Lucilla's room. Knott-Sloman himself, apart from a possible complicity with Lucilla, might have attacked Bellamy after Georgia left the study and before he went to post his letters. It seemed on the whole more likely that a man had made the assault. The position of the wound suggested someone fairly tall behind the poker, but did not imply it. Nor was it impossible that a woman should have had the strength to drag him by the heels into the pantry. Almost anyone might have done it, including Mrs Grant.

So much for opportunity. Knowledge of the ground? O'Brien had only rented the Dower House a few months ago, and none of the present party had visited there before. Except for Mrs Grant, therefore, they all started from scratch. On the whole, a woman would be more likely to have learnt the layout of the kitchen premises and Mrs Grant's habits, and to know where poker and incinerator were to be found. But, as the job had presumably been premeditated, there was nothing to prevent a man finding out the details beforehand. Then there was the question of timing the assault. Nigel imagined that the assailant must have watched for Bellamy to come through the swing-door from the kitchen premises, hurried into the kitchen, seized the poker, and hidden himself behind the swing-door in time to catch Bellamy on his return. The only thing there seemed no doubt about was that the poker had been the weapon. Nellie had been interviewed by Bleakley when she came back from the village, and had sworn first indignantly and then tearfully that she never put pokers inside incinerators and Mrs Grant was that strict she'd have her skin off if she touched her poker, the old cat. To Nigel it appeared that Mrs Grant ought logically to be chief suspect, though why she should have done it he couldn't imagine. Calvinist Cook Cracks ex-Serviceman on Crumpet. Grand. One expected a Calvinist to disapprove of everyone else on principle, but scarcely to carry this disapproval to the length of poker-work.

That brought him back again to the question of motive. On the whole it was sensible to suppose that Bellamy had been attacked because he knew something about the will which someone wanted hushed up. It was significant that the attack had taken place soon after the superintendent had begun to show an embarrassing curiosity about the will. If Bellamy had been a danger to the murderer for some other reason, one would have expected the murderer to have settled him on the same night as he killed O'Brien, not to have waited for fifteen hours or so, giving him plenty of time to make any disclosures and attacking him in the much more hazardous daylight. But this was not really conclusive. Bellamy might have found out something that morning which made him a menace to the murderer; something about aeroplane plans, for instance, or about the erotic tangle which was rendering their search for a motive so complicated. Again, was it not conceivably possible that the attack on Bellamy had no connection at all with O'Brien's murder? At the thought that there might be two trails to follow Nigel groaned aloud.

"It's a teaser, sir, isn't it?" said Bleakley. "Still, we've not been on the job twelve hours yet. There's plenty of time."

"You know," said Nigel, "I'm more and more convinced that we shan't get to the bottom of it all until we've found out a great deal more about O'Brien. It's he, and not the murderer, who is the real mystery man. I think I shall concentrate on that myself. We know nothing about his parents, for instance, or what he was doing before the war, or where he got his money from."

"We'll find it, sir, we'll find it. Slow but sure. I shall send out inquiries as soon as I get to headquarters; and particularly as to who his solicitor is, if he used one at all. What's bothering me most, Mr Strangeways, is that we haven't really got a good case for murder at all. You and I knows it was. But Treasury counsel must have something more to go on than theories and gossip. Them footprints in the snow, for instance. What jury's going to believe that they were made by someone walking backwards? They'll say we've been reading too many blood-and-thunders. Without we get proof that O'Brien was in the hut when the snow began to fall, we simply haven't a case to take to court at all."

Arrived at headquarters, the superintendent busied himself with a number of reports that had recently come in. First, the post-mortem had only confirmed the doctor's original conclusion: death had been caused by a bullet entering the heart, and the police expert confirmed that it had been fired from the revolver which had been found in the hut. The post-mortem had also confirmed that O'Brien was suffering from a disease which must have killed him within a couple of years. The doctor was not prepared to narrow down the period within which O'Brien had been killed, though he did not mind venturing unofficially the opinion that death had probably taken place between midnight and 2a.m. On the other hand, he admitted that his first explanation of the bruises on the wrist was not satisfactory, and agreed that they might very well have been caused by a struggle for the revolver. The fingerprints on its butt tallied with those of O'Brien; and the other sets found in the hut had been demonstrated to belong respectively to Bellamy, Nigel and Cavendish.

The man who had been sent to make inquiries in the village reported that a tramp had turned up at the rectory on Christmas night; he had been given some dinner but had not, oddly enough, asked for anywhere to sleep. He had been seen walking out of the village about 11p.m. in the direction of Taviston, which would bring him past the gates of Chatcombe Park. The rector had declared that the tramp did not seem quite right in his head; after putting down a good deal of the rector's port, he had talked vaguely about knowing where he could lay his hands on something worth a great deal of money. Bleakley pricked up his ears at this point, and made arrangements for the man to be brought in for questioning as soon as he could be found. None of the villagers, as far as this constable could learn, had been near the park last night. He had discovered, however, at the post office that a gentleman answering to the description of Knott-Sloman had come in hurriedly that afternoon and bought stamps. The postmistress, who in an English village performs the same news-spreading function as the tom-tom in the jungle, had noticed something bulky in his overcoat pocket; and later, when she was sorting the post, came upon a large, fat envelope, addressed in an unfamiliar hand. With that intelligence, initiative and public spirit which have recently raised the postal service so high in popular favour, she had even noticed the destination of this package. It was addressed to Cyril Knott-Sloman, Esq., the Fizz-and-Frolic Club, Nr. Kingston, and marked "Not to be sent on".

The same thought struck Bleakley and Nigel simultaneously. Bleakley reached for the phone and made a trunk call through to New Scotland Yard. He asked that this envelope should be examined before being delivered to its address tomorrow morning, and should be held if found to contain anything resembling plans or formulae.

"He knew we would be making a thorough search as soon as we suspected murder, Mr Strangeways, so he'd naturally want to get rid of them as soon as he could."

"We can take that a step further. Knott-Sloman went into the village to post that package before it had been suggested that we even suspected murder. Why, unless he knew that murder had been committed and a search might begin any moment, should he be in such a hurry to get rid of it? And how could he know it was murder, unless —?"

"By gum, sir, that's good reasoning, that is. But wasn't it taking a big risk sending them by post?"

"We don't know what is in the envelope. It may be an embroidered bed-jacket for his Aunt Amelia's canary. But you must remember he had no reason to suppose, when he sent off the package, that we knew anything about O'Brien's invention or a possible attempt on it; therefore we would not be likely to examine anything he sent off by post."

"But if he was the murderer, it must have been him as sent those threatening letters. He must've allowed that O'Brien might show them to the police, and the police would be bound to ask him what reasons anyone might have for wanting to get rid of him; the fact O'Brien was working on those plans would come out then."

"I don't believe that, if he was after the plans, he wrote those letters. It would have been crazy to put O'Brien on his guard, even in such an indirect way. And I don't believe either that if his object was to steal the plans, he would premeditate murder. There *is* a possibility, though, that O'Brien caught him stealing them, held him up with his revolver, somehow let Knott-Sloman get too near him, and was shot in the ensuing struggle."

"Yes, that might have been the way of it," said Bleakley. "Well, I'm due at the chief constable's in five minutes. If you'd care to come along . . .?"

The chief constable greeted them with geniality and a cloud of cigar-smoke. He was a large, untidy, dog-and-gun-looking man, with country squire written all over him: his heavy white moustache was stained with nicotine and his fingers might have been cleaner; but there was a kind of easy, paternal competence about him which was reassuring. He was very popular with all ranks of the force under his control, for he never fussed the superior officers or browbeat the rank-and-file. He soon had his visitors settled with cigars in their mouths and drinks at their elbows.

"It's very good of you and the superintendent to let me in on this," said Nigel.

"Not a bit of it, Strangeways; you were in it already; on the ground floor, as they say. We wouldn't have got as far as we have without you. Though I don't mind telling you I rang up the Assistant Commissioner — just to make certain you were your uncle's nephew, and *compos mentis* and free from foot-and-mouth, and so on, what?" Major Stanley laughed heartily and took a prodigious gulp at his whisky-and-soda. "Well now, Bleakley, if you'll tell me just where we stand, like a good fellow."

The superintendent twirled his moustache ("I wonder does he keep it in a plaster mold at night," speculated Nigel dreamily) and launched forth into a detailed statement of the case. He concerned himself mainly with ascertained facts, only bringing in theories when they were necessary for the explanation of some action of his own. It was easy to see, though, from his treatment of the facts, which way his suspicions tended.

"H'm," said Major Stanley, when the superintendent had finished, "expect you wish you'd stuck to crossword puzzles, eh, Bleakley? Still, I think you've done very well. Can't see any further lines we ought to open up just at present. Things'll sort themselves out by degrees. As I see it, Miss Thrale and what's-'is-name — Knott-Sloman — are the most likely suspects, with Edward Cavendish keepin' well in the picture. Trouble is, we haven't got sufficient proof yet that O'Brien was murdered at all. Bleakley told me over the phone your case against suicide, Strangeways, and damn' clever it was, too. Mind you, I think you're right; but it's too clever for the average jury to swallow. They can't follow anything but a stinkin' aniseed sort of trail. Comes of givin' a vote to every hayseed and short-weight grocer in the — However; hrrumph, where was I? Ah, yes. Apart from the fact that murder has not been sufficiently proved, I don't think we can take any action yet. That note Miss Thrale wrote is pretty damning at first sight — a queer set of crooks you seem to have up at the Dower House, Strangeways — but counsel for the defence is goin' to say: 'Would a woman who proposed to murder a fellow write a note like that, which would give her away completely unless it was destroyed, when she could just as well have made the assignation by word of mouth?'"

"About the note: there seem to me two possibilities," Nigel struck in, smoothing his sandy hair. "Either he received it before dinner, and the conversation I heard between her and O'Brien was his answer to it — you remember, he said 'Not tonight' — in which case he folded it up absent-mindedly and stuck it in his window frame. I can't quite believe that: anyone might have found it, and O'Brien was not the sort of chap to let a woman expose herself in that way. Or else he put it in his pocket; the murderer discovered it there and half-hid it later, hoping that — if murder was suspected — it would be found and throw suspicion on to Lucilla. Guh! What a mouthful. It's made my mouth dry as ginger. Sorry to interrupt you, Stanley."

"Not a bit of it. I think that second theory of yours is very sound, Strangeways; even if it turns out wrong, it would obviously be premature to take any action against Miss Thrale at present, don't you agree, Bleakley?"

"I do, sir."

"Then we've got a goodish case against Edward Cavendish as far as motive goes, but not a shred of evidence. What size shoes does he take, by the way?" the chief constable added lazily, his face almost invisible in cigar smoke.

"Same as Mr O'Brien. Knott-Sloman takes a size smaller; Starling a size and a half; and the ladies, of course, smaller still," replied Bleakley, not without complacence. "Mr O'Brien had large feet and hands for his height."

"Aha," said Major Stanley jovially, "can't catch you nappin'. So any of 'em might have worn his shoes and made those footprints. Still, I should concentrate on them: try to find out who could have put 'em back in the hut next morning, and so on. Feller looks a bit conspicuous totin' a pair of shoes about. Of course, the prints may not have been made in O'Brien's shoes. If they weren't, Cavendish must be our man. Then this Knott-Sloman: sounds a nasty piece of work; might have been caught by O'Brien pinchin' his plans, or if there's anything in what Cavendish said about blackmail — he and Miss Thrale might have been tryin' it on with O'Brien; O'Brien determines to finish him off or give him a bad fright, threatens him with the revolver, but Knott-Sloman pounces on him and the thing goes off. However, I don't want to put ideas into your head. What I'm just wonderin' is — have another drink, Bleakley — seein' that most of the people in the case are not locals, whether we oughtn't to call in the Yard. I'm not questioning your ability, but I think it's a pretty big mouthful for us to chew, and the papers are goin' to make a hell of a shindy about it — it's their last chance to cash in on the O'Brien legend. What do you feel about it, Bleakley?"

The superintendent seemed relieved rather than offended by the suggestion, and it was arranged that Major Stanley should ring up the Assistant Commissioner at once. Bleakley and Nigel now took their leave. Bleakley wished to call in at his home to collect a few

136

things for the night. While he was doing this, Nigel was engaged in conversation by Mrs Bleakley, a lady whose figure resembled nothing so much as a succession of built-up areas. She produced an equally massive teapot and a flow of sombre statistics about road casualties occasioned by fog. When the superintendent came down in mufti with his bag, she said in her rich, chesty voice:

"Bleakley, you're a fool to go out on a night like this. I've just been telling Mr Er about that chara that went over the edge at Follisham Corner — only last month, it was, and a fog just like this. Tempting Providence is what I call it, and me just buying two lengths of flannel at the sales to make you up some new nightdresses. You'll back me up, Mr Er, won't you?"

"That's all right, mother. Don't be a fidge-fadge. I know the road like the back of my hand," interposed Bleakley. He gave his spouse a resounding kiss, and led the way out to the car. The constable who had driven them in had been left at the station; for Bleakley proposed to drive back himself. The fog was certainly much thicker, though after leaving the town they found sections of the road where visibility was comparatively good. Nigel sat back in a kind of trance, watching the trees and hedges that seemed to pounce at them out of nothingness, like spirits out of a magician's incantations. The beams of the headlamps thrust feebly up into the fog, wavered and fell back, like fountains of light playing at half-pressure. Every now and then a yellow tinge crept into the greyness ahead, and Bleakley drew in to the side to let another car pass. After a while they left the main road and began to climb. The air was clearer here and they could make better speed, though Bleakley still seemed to take the corners more by second sight than by calculation. Nigel was no driver, and therefore able to close his eyes, oblivious of the hazards they might be passing through. He felt tired as death, but he was not to get any sleep for the present. A muffled oath from the superintendent and the dead check of brakes brought him wide awake. In the deflected haze of the headlights a body could be seen lying half on the bank and half on the road.

"Oh, lord," muttered Nigel, "not *another* corpse: this really is going a bit too far."

His prayer, as it happened, was granted. As Bleakley jumped out and bent over it, the body raised itself piecemeal from the ground and was resolved into a tramp. He staggered a little, blinked, and exclaimed huskily but in the most gentlemanly of accents:

"Great Scott! The Aurora Borealis!"

He then rubbed his eyes, and, perceiving the source of the illumination, said:

"I beg your pardon, gentlemen, I fancied myself for a moment back again behind my huskies in the frozen North. Allow me to introduce myself: Albert Blenkinsop is the name. You see me rather at a disadvantage, I fear. *Non sum qualis eram,* as the bard has it."

He swept off his bowler hat with a courtliness not at all diminished by the fact that the rim came away in his hand while the crown remained in position.

138

Bleakley was staring at him as if he was the winning ticket in the Irish sweepstakes. Nigel quickly seized Bleakley's arm and whispered:

"Leave this to me!" He turned to the tramp and said, "Can we give you a lift anywhere? I don't know if we are going your way."

"Any way you are going will suit me admirably, old man," replied Albert Blenkinsop, his gesture a consummate blend of politeness and magnanimity. Nigel followed the indescribably tattered figure and its bundle into the back of the car. Albert Blenkinsop leant back, produced a cigar stub from some cache in his rags and lit it. Then sighing with satisfaction he waved his arm airily and began to talk.

"As I was saying, I have seen better days. I am one of Fate's laughing stocks. Time and again life has given me to sip of her brimming abundance, only to dash the cup from my lips. Bitter words, you will say, but amply justified. You see me now in somewhat reduced circumstances. You would be surprised to hear, perhaps, that I am a rich man. Yes, I could take you this minute to a bank in Moscow where a hundred thousand rubles of mine are locked up. I happened to be over there when the Revolution broke out. I was able to assist a certain grand duke, who must be nameless, to escape; the hundred thousand rubles was a token of his gratitude — very lavish the old aristocracy was, though barbarous according to our standards of civilisation. Unfortunately the Bolsheviks got wind of the part I had played in the affair, and but for the fact that I was warned by a charming little lady — one of the corps-de-ballet there and quite infatuated with me — I should not have got away with my life. As it was, I left the country with nothing but a few rubles, a faked passport, and a signed photograph of the Czar which I managed to conceal in the sole of my boot. I would not burden you with an old man's reminiscences. Such episodes are commonplace in my life. It is just an example of the way I have been from beginning to end a plaything of Fate."

The tramp sighed and relapsed into reverie.

"A heartbreaking business for you," said Nigel gravely. Albert Blenkinsop turned abruptly upon him and tapped him on his top overcoat button.

"You might well think so. But what *is* money?"

"Well," Nigel answered cautiously, "money is not everything." He had evidently given the right answer. Albert Blenkinsop leant back again and gestured expansively.

"That is profoundly true," he said. "As soon as I saw you tonight I said to myself: 'I don't know who this young man is, and I don't care. He may be an old Etonian: he may be the Trunk Murderer. That is not Albert Blenkinsop's concern. But what I *do* know is that he is sympathetic. An old head on young shoulders,' I said to myself, and I am a judge of faces. Yes, time and again in my checquered life I have asked myself that identical question, 'What *is* money, after all?' And I have always answered, as you so well put it just now, 'Money is not everything.' And shall I tell you what *is* the most important thing in life?"

"Yes, I should be most interested."

"Romance. Life without romance is like Hamlet without the Prince of Denmark. I will tell you a little experience of my own to illustrate this truth. Five years ago I was in the theatrical world. A young girl came to me for an audition. She had not been in my room two minutes when I said to myself, 'That girl will go far.' I spent every penny I had in building her career — a divine creature — the theatre was in her blood. We fell in love, I need hardly say: a few months of paradise, and then she passed out of my ken. The other day I happened to be walking down Shaftesbury Avenue: there was her name, in electric letters six foot long. I sent in my card, just for old acquaintance' sake. The reply came back, 'Miss X regrets she has never heard of Mr Blenkinsop.' Ingratitude, you may call it. The young are harsh in their judgements. To me the whole thing is different. For me those electric letters in Shaftesbury Avenue spelt one word only — Romance."

The superintendent was chafing more and more visibly, so Nigel thought he had better drag Albert Blenkinsop back to the present.

"And what are your plans now?"

Blenkinsop leant forward impressively.

"Well, I don't mind telling you that I could lay my hands on a very tidy sum of money, if only —"

Bleakley made a gargling sound that seemed likely to prelude some official pronouncement. The tramp, however, with several significant nods and winks in his direction, remarked to Nigel in a stage whisper:

"Sorry, old man, but is your friend quite trustworthy?"

"Oh, yes, rather. Though I couldn't vouch for him when he is in drink."

"Well, it's like this. A friend of mine, a man very high up in the scientific world — for obvious reasons I cannot disclose his name at this stage — has discovered" (Blenkinsop's voice fell to a thrilling whisper) "iron ore in Berkshire. I thought that would surprise you. It surprised me. Of course the thing's a goldmine, my dear fellow, a veritable gold-mine. He wishes me to come in with him and exploit it. In fact, I am on my way there now. Unfortunately, funds are rather low with me. I need capital. In short, if you happen to have £100 to spare, it would be a genuine gilt-edged investment."

Bleakley's back looked utterly deflated. Nigel said:

"Afraid I haven't. If ten shillings would be any use?"

Albert Blenkinsop was not in the least discomposed. He accepted the note with a nice blend of gratitude and independence.

"I suppose you didn't have much of a Christmas," Nigel said.

"I can't complain. I had dinner with the rector of an old-world little hamlet near here — a charming fellow, though not altogether sound on the Manichaean heresy, I thought. An old friend of mine, Lord Marlinworth, has a place just outside the village."

"Yes, he's my uncle. We're staying at the Dower House."

"Indeed? Well, well. What a small place the world is. I had thought of dropping in on his lordship last night, but when I had walked some way into the park I heard midnight strike, and it seemed a bit late for a social call."

"What a pity you weren't near the Dower House: isn't it, Bleakley? My friend and I had a wager on," Nigel explained; "it all hinges on whether someone was in a hut in the garden before twelve-thirty or not. Now if he *was*, and you supplied the evidence, I should feel bound to give you a percentage of my winnings."

Bleakley winced at this flagrant leading of a witness.

"As it happens," said Blenkinsop, "I can be of assistance to you over that point, I believe. I did find myself near a sort of hut last night: not long after midnight. It was just beginning to snow, I remember, and I thought 'any port in a storm'. Unfortunately there was someone in there already."

"Really," said Nigel with elaborate negligence. "I wonder was that our man."

"A fair-sized, thinnish fellow. A military man, I should say, by the cut of his jib. Blue eyes and a hard-bitten face. Seemed to be looking for something. A treasure hunt in progress, I dare say. Yes, it must have been. Because a few minutes later he slipped out, and just after that another fellow went in — a small fellow with a white face and a black beard. I thought it was time for me to move on then. My presence might have been misunderstood. Luckily I found a barn not far from the park gates. We old campaigners are used to living hard, but I have had enough experience in the Arctic Circle to know the dangers of going to sleep in snow."

"This first fellow, did he go back to the house?"

"That I couldn't say. I was looking in at a window at the back of the hut. He went off to the right and was swallowed in the darkness."

"Well, I win my bet, and here's your rake-off." Nigel handed over another note, and then consigned Albert Blenkinsop to the less tender mercies of Bleakley, who by this time, judging from the colour of the back of his neck, had reached boiling-point and would explode incontinent unless provided with a safety valve.

CHAPTER
NINE

A Tale Curtailed

Nigel Strangeways went to bed that night staggering with exhaustion. The day's stress and activity, culminating in their drive through the fog and the fantastic episode of Albert Blenkinsop, had produced in him that deadened state of the senses where everything seems to be happening to one through a kind of local anaesthetic. As though he was a holy man towards the end of a long fast, people and things appeared to him infinitely more remote and less important than at normal times. The electric light that blazed in the hall as they entered seemed to be inside his own head. He saw Georgia and Lucilla, Philip Starling, Cavendish and Knott-Sloman as through the thick glass of an aquarium, moving about with the unnatural slowness of fishes. The one advantage of this, he reflected as he tumbled wearily into bed, is that it dehumanises one. If I hadn't had all this work to do, I should have been moping about, remembering what a grand fellow O'Brien was and tormenting myself for my abject failure to help him. Like poor Georgia. How she must have been suffering! Still, she's tough. The sort whose wounds heal cleanly. Or isn't that wrong? Isn't it the superficial people, like Lucilla Thrale, who recover quickest and most completely, simply because they can never receive more than superficial wounds? The murderer must be feeling pretty blue, too. So certain he had rigged up a really watertight suicide, and then to find that it was leaking in every joint before a few hours were up. Driven already to the desperate expedient of attempting a second murder to cover up the first. Yes, he must be feeling bad. And perhaps someone else here may be as great a danger to him as Bellamy. Perhaps he is sitting up in bed now, revolving a dozen schemes in his head, planning mischief, knowing that somebody else must die if he is to live.

The thought made Nigel sit up in bed and reach for a cigarette. His head felt extraordinarily light and clear now. Sleep could wait for a bit: there was still work to be done before he earned it. The murderer. Bleakley and the bloke from Scotland Yard will attend to material facts far more effectively than I can, he thought. My angle must be the personal one. Very well, let's be thoroughly unorthodox and start with the question, which of these people here is most capable of this kind of murder? The evidence goes to show that there was a struggle. It follows that this murder was unpremeditated: no one who had planned to kill O'Brien would let him get near enough the gun to grab it. Anyway, it was *his* gun. That suggests X coming in for some purpose other than murder, O'Brien holding him up with his revolver, either because X was doing something he shouldn't have been, or because O'Brien suspected him of being the writer of the threatening letters, and being overpowered by X in a struggle. The first of these would fit Knott-Sloman; it would imply that he hadn't found what the tramp said he was looking for and had gone back, thinking O'Brien was asleep. Or alternatively Knott-Sloman might have been trying on a bit of blackmail with O'Brien. Damn' fool to pick on a man like O'Brien for that. Neither alternative seems very alluring. Lucilla? She might have gone to make a last appeal to O'Brien not to throw her over: she gets the final bird and sees red, picks up his gun or pulls it out of his pocket, etc., etc. This fits in with the note she wrote to him. A much more attractive theory. Only snag, would she have the strength to worst O'Brien in a struggle and make those bruises? What about Cavendish? He might have gone to the hut (a) to have it out with O'Brien about Lucilla, or (b) to ask for money to tide him over the crisis. A very odd time to choose for such a discussion. On the other hand, if O'Brien refused to hand over Lucilla or some cash, Cavendish might have been driven on the spur of the moment to do something desperate. On second thoughts, it must have been the cash, for the evidence goes to show that O'Brien wanted to get rid of Lucilla. Quite a sound theory, and backed up by the present state of jitters that Cavendish seems to be in.

Who else? Philip and Georgia. Philip is out, because he couldn't possibly have done the attack on Bellamy. And Georgia could have no conceivable motive. She loved O'Brien. But wait a minute. She was desperately fond of her brother, too. Is there any situation under which she might kill one man she loved out of love for the other? Yes, if she knew she or Edward inherited by the will, she might just possibly have killed O'Brien to save her brother from financial ruin. Sounds damned melodramatic. Surely O'Brien would have given her the money if she had asked for it? Anyhow, it suggests premeditated murder, which this obviously wasn't.

But wasn't it? What's the evidence for an unpremeditated one? The disarrangement of the papers on O'Brien's table, the broken cufflinks and the bruises. Those are the only things that pointed to a struggle. Oh, yes, and the fact that O'Brien's gun was used. Can I get round them? The papers might have been disarranged by Knott-Sloman before O'Brien came into the hut or by the murderer seeking to remove some evidence afterwards. The cufflink *might* have been snapped when O'Brien fell, or it might conceivably have got broken in some quite irrelevant way. The bruises? Surely that is insuperable. O'Brien wasn't fighting earlier in the day. Oh, lord! *He was*, though. After dinner there was a lot of fooling about and horseplay. He and Knott-Sloman were trying that test of strength with a knife. Sloman did have hold of his wrist for a bit then. I must have been stupefied not to remember it before. But still, you can't get round the gun. Nobody who planned to shoot him could have planned to do it with his own gun, surely to goodness. But hold on! If X planned the murder, he presumably planned the suicide, too. Ergo, he must have arranged somehow to get hold of O'Brien's gun. How could he do that when O'Brien was on his guard? Only if he was a person O'Brien trusted implicitly and held above all suspicion. In other words —

Nigel shrank at the result of this equation. X = Georgia Cavendish. He most decidedly didn't want it to be Georgia. Still, there were those anonymous letters. Surely it's too much of a coincidence that X should threaten to kill O'Brien on the Feast of Stephen, and then he should get killed more or less by accident on the same day by a hypothetical Y. It *might* have happened. Y *might* have done X's work for him. But it's a pretty indigestible lump to swallow. Let's suppose, then, that the murder was premeditated and committed by the author of the threatening letters. Which of my gallery of suspects fits the frame best? Cavendish. Has the brains to plan it, but surely not the nerve to carry it out. Moreover, there's something reckless and flamboyant about those letters which simply won't square with the personality of a staid, outwardly respectable — even though in fact somewhat disreputable — city man. Knott-Sloman has the nerve to have carried it out — he's hard-boiled enough. On the other hand, it's doubtful whether he's got the intelligence to have planned it, and the grim humour of the letters is very different from his brand of facetiousness. Nor can one see any reason why he should want O'Brien dead: very much to the contrary, if he hoped to blackmail him. The melodramatic touch in the letters would fit Lucilla quite well; she is capable of the *crime passionel*, but surely has neither the nerve nor the brains for a premeditated one. Georgia? She has the guts, she has the intelligence; what's more, she is capable of the flamboyant yet cold-blooded humour of those letters. The crime fits her at every point. Except motive. An appalling chill crept over Nigel. Supposing she really hated O'Brien; suppose, like Clytemnestra, she had made up to him only in order to put him — and everyone else — off their guard. Melodramatic; but O'Brien had lived in a world of melodrama. Nigel was compelled to admit that here again Georgia stood out as the most likely suspect.

He had cleared a patch of the jungle, anyway. Like a beast that has turned round and round in tall grasses to trample its lair, his mind curled up and went to sleep in the little clearing it had made. When he woke it was high daylight and his clock said half-past eleven. He went downstairs in his dressing gown and ate some cold sausages. Lady Marlinworth had sent over one of her maids to take Arthur Bellamy's place, so the household was running fairly smoothly again. As he was eating, Bleakley popped his head in to say that Arthur was still unconscious, but hanging on to life, and that Albert Blenkinsop had sworn to Knott-Sloman as the first of the two men he had seen entering the hut. Bleakley proposed to take no further action till the arrival of Detective-Inspector Blount from Scotland Yard, who was expected by midday. Nigel went upstairs again and put down on paper the arguments he had worked out before going to sleep last night. They still looked damnably convincing. He felt uneasy. Georgia; her gallant bearing and mischievous monkey smile; her parrot and her bloodhound; the eccentricities which she wore as naturally as the eight-fifteen business man

150

wears his bowler and umbrella and folded newspaper. How had Philip described her expression? "The ghost of an organ-grinder's monkey." Surely a murderess couldn't act that utter forlornness of sorrow. She wouldn't look like that if she had hated O'Brien. "Ah, yes," whispered the relentless voice, "but supposing she really did love him: supposing she had to choose between his life — the life of a dying man — and her brother's ruin? Might she not have done it then? And wouldn't that account for her death-in-life look — the look of one who cannot cross Lethe, stretching out her arms to the farther bank?"

Nigel shook himself impatiently. He was getting morbid. What he needed was a bit of company. He found his fellow guests sitting about glumly in the lounge. As he entered their eyes all turned to him with a hoping-against-hope expression. They might have been the survivors of a shipwreck, stranded on an island out of the trade routes, and he the one who has come down from the lookout place on the hill. There was a moment of constrained silence, and then Edward Cavendish said, "Well, any news?"

Nigel shook his head. Cavendish certainly looked in a bad way: there were dark circles under his eyes, and their expression of agonised bewilderment seemed to have sharpened since yesterday. He looked strangely like a small schoolboy who has lost his books and hasn't done his prep and has a painful appointment with the headmaster before lunch.

"Have to get your news from the papers," grumbled Knott-Sloman, who was sitting near the fire and cracking walnuts with his teeth. "The police don't know any more about it than you or I."

"It's really an infernal nuisance," Cavendish went on in worried, petulant tones. "I ought to get back to the city tomorrow, but we've been told we've got to stay here for the inquest, and God knows how long they'll keep us after that."

"Don't worry, Edward. A few days can't make much difference one way or the other." Georgia's voice was tender, motherly, yet assured and matter-of-fact.

"It's scandalous," exclaimed Knott-Sloman. "No one admired and respected O'Brien more than I did. At the same time —"

"— You want to get back to your fizz and your frolic," interrupted Philip Starling sourly, not looking up from the *Times* leading article. Knott-Sloman looked daggers in his direction, but they were blunted on the impervious back of the *Times*. Lucilla, in an odalisque pose on the sofa, drawled:

"The whole thing's a crashing bore, of course. But the police are so stupid, they won't find the murderer till all of us are murdered in our beds. It's what they call the process of elimination."

"All but *one* of us, Lucy," said Starling politely.

"I consider that a damned tactless and uncalled-for remark," said Knott-Sloman. "As good as accusing one of us of being a murderer. No doubt you feel quite safe yourself, after the way you've succeeded in sucking up to the police: though I could tell them a thing or two which might alter their attitude to you."

152

Philip Starling laid down his *Times* in a leisurely way and, fixing Knott-Sloman with his most hubristic and irritating stare, said:

"That's just what's wrong with you retired army men. Not content with practically losing us our Empire through sheer inefficiency, you settle down in Cheltenham or some low nightclub and spend the rest of your lives in malicious gossip. Gossip, gossip, gossip — like a lot of old women. Tchah!"

Knott-Sloman rose in his wrath. "My God! You damned little squirt. What the devil d'you mean by talking like that? It's — it's an insult to the Service. You, you" — he collected himself for a crowning piece of invective — "you rotten little highbrow."

"Yes. Yes. Just what I thought. A moral coward," said Starling briskly, walking right up to Knott-Sloman. "Daren't attack me except in public. Very typical. Squalid fellow." He suddenly darted forward his hand, whisked Knott-Sloman's tie out of his waistcoat, and stumped from the room before his flabbergasted adversary could recover his breath. Lucilla suddenly burst out into a peal of laughter.

"Oh, dear!" she bubbled. "Oh, Law-love-a-duck! What a riot! Poor Cyril, you *were* outclassed, weren't you? Now do tuck your tie in and stop looking like Second Murderer."

Knott-Sloman went out, tucking in his tie, but still looking very definitely like Second Murderer. Nigel noticed that Lucilla had dropped her distinguished-widow pose, for tactical reasons, perhaps, and resumed the girl-about-town manner. He remained for a few minutes talking to Georgia Cavendish. Lucilla seemed quite willing to console herself with Edward. Then a message came for him that Bleakley would like to see him in the morning room. The superintendent, who looked very cock-a-hoop, introduced him to Detective-Inspector Blount. Blount was a man of middle height, with a bland, youngish face, but almost entirely bald. He had a dry and precise, yet courteous manner, horn-rimmed glasses and rather impersonal eyes. He would have been mistaken anywhere for a bank manager. Bleakley could scarcely restrain himself till the preliminary politenesses were over.

"Got some good news for us, the inspector has, Mr Strangeways."

"I'm glad. We need it."

Blount handed an envelope to Nigel. "These are the reports you asked the Assistant Commissioner for — as much as we could get in the time. Shall I tell him the other points, sir?" he asked Bleakley.

"You fire ahead."

"First, we examined the package addressed to Cyril Knott-Sloman at the Fizz-and-Frolic Club. It contained a number of letters written by Edward Cavendish to Miss Thrale — letters of a compromising character." Blount looked up over the top of his horn-rims to see how Nigel was taking it. He added, with an inflection of dry humour, "There were no plans or formulae, I'm afraid, sir."

Nigel smiled. "I'm afraid the superintendent has been betraying my romantic processes of thought to you."

154

"However, the package also contained a note from Knott-Sloman to the deceased. This note suggested that, if O'Brien was a gentleman, he would make Miss Thrale some recompense for having trifled with her affections: and if he did not certain steps would have to be taken."

"So that's what he was looking for," murmured Nigel. "Funny he didn't destroy it at once."

"We have also discovered and got into communication with O'Brien's solicitors. They have no knowledge of any will made by the deceased. But they have in their possession a sealed envelope which was entrusted to them last October by O'Brien with strict injunctions that it should not be opened till a year after his decease. It is not improbable that it may contain a will."

"That's queer. He told me he kept it in his safe. Still, we can't expect everything all at once. And you've given us all we can digest for the moment," said Nigel.

The superintendent, who had been looking like a rather overloaded cornucopia, positively bursting with good things, could contain himself no longer.

"Ah, Mr Strangeways, sir, but that isn't all. The inspector has kept the *bonne booch,* as you might say, to the last." He hastily gathered the remnants of his official dignity about him, twirled his moustache, and nodded severely at Blount. "Please continue, Inspector."

"Very well, sir." Blount's mouth betrayed the slightest quirk of amusement. Then he proceeded, in the well-modulated but impersonal tones of a chairman reading the annual report. "After we discovered the contents of the package sent off by Knott-Sloman, the

155

Assistant Commissioner suggested that unofficial investigations should be made at the Fizz-and-Frolic Club. I went down there late last night. Working on a line also suggested by the Assistant Commissioner, and simulating an advanced stage of inebriety, I wandered at large over the premises. In the course of these investigations I found myself" — Blount's eyes twinkled faintly — "in Knott-Sloman's private office. There I discovered a typewriter, with which I managed to write a few lines before I was — er — thrown out. On returning to the Yard I handed over this writing to an expert, who declares that it was made by the same machine on which the threatening letters to O'Brien were written."

"Oh, my hat," said Nigel slowly, his face a comical mixture of surprise and relief. "Well, that seems to sew everything up pretty decisively."

Blount was looking at him, his eyes suddenly keen as steel. "It doesn't fit in with your theories, sir?"

"Couldn't we drop the 'sir'? Always makes me feel like a schoolmaster. No, it doesn't fit in. But my theory will just have to be altered to accommodate it." He thought hard for a minute, then said, in rather a strained voice:

"Look here, will you read this? Dark thoughts of blackest midnight born. I'd like to have 'em off my conscience."

He handed over to Blount the loose pages on which he had put down his reasonings of the previous night. While Blount and Bleakley put their heads together over these, Nigel studied the reports his uncle had sent.

They added little to what the omniscient Philip Starling had told him. They were confirmation that Edward Cavendish had got into low water, but he had already admitted this himself. Knott-Sloman evidently had a bad reputation. His club had come under the notice of the police once or twice, but he had been clever enough to avoid any serious charge. They had also picked up rumours of blackmail in connection with him, but naturally these were only rumours. Nothing significant came to light about Starling, Lucilla or Georgia. Sir John Strangeways had also sent along a detailed dossier on O'Brien. Nigel flipped through this. The most remarkable thing about it was what it didn't tell him. O'Brien seemed not to have been alive at all till he joined up in London in 1915, giving his age as twenty. After he had become famous several papers had invited him to put his name to his life story as written by them, but they had never succeeded in tracing it back beyond 1915 — and what the press couldn't ferret, Nigel reflected, must be concealed in the king of all burrows. Scotland Yard had got into touch with the Special Branch in Dublin; but they knew nothing of O'Brien's early years, and as the name under which he had joined up was probably an assumed one, it didn't seem likely that they would have much success in tracing him.

"Well, Mr Strangeways," Blount said, "this is very interesting. I am not sure whether we should let it modify our attitude to Knott-Sloman — after all, it's mainly theorising." He sketched a neat, apologetic gesture. "As I see it, the facts all point to Knott-Sloman as the murderer, probably in collusion with Miss

157

Thrale. It is as good as proved that he wrote the threatening letters. We know that he was hanging about the hut after midnight when O'Brien came out of the house. Now my theory is this: Sloman writes the threatening letters —"

"Why?" interrupted Nigel. "Surely would-be murderers don't advertise their intentions?"

"Because he planned to fake the murder as a suicide. To do so, he had to use O'Brien's gun. O'Brien wouldn't have been carrying a gun unless he was on his guard against some threat. That's why the threat had to be made."

Bleakley beamed proudly from Blount to Nigel, as though showing off an infant prodigy. "We never thought of that, Mr Strangeways," he said.

"Then Sloman got Miss Thrale to write that note. They wanted O'Brien in the hut, where the murder and fake suicide could be done without interruptions," the inspector continued.

"Why wasn't the note destroyed, then?"

"I suggest that either O'Brien folded it up and stuck it in the window absent-mindedly, or that Sloman found it on his body, kept it till the suicide fake was exposed, and then put it there to throw all the suspicion on Miss Thrale. From what I've heard about him he's quite capable of double-crossing. I imagine he must have been talking with O'Brien for at least a quarter of an hour, possibly manoeuvring to get near the revolver. That would put the actual murder about twelve-thirty. Faking the suicide and generally tidying up might take him ten minutes longer. Then he looks out and finds

158

himself trapped by the snow thickening on the ground. He daren't walk out, in case the snow should stop before it had filled in his footprints. So he sits down and thinks it out, and finally lights on the idea of wearing O'Brien's shoes and walking backwards."

"M'm," said Nigel. "He must have taken a long time to think it out. The snow was thinning at quarter to two, which suggests that the tracks must have been made somewhere about one-thirty; otherwise they would have been far more obliterated. It was nearly an hour before the bright idea struck him. Well, I always thought he was a bit of a numbskull, in spite of having been on the staff in the war. The wonder is that he could have thought up all the rest of the bag of tricks."

"He had to get the shoes back into the hut," the inspector went on. "No doubt that was done when Mr Strangeways was holding his reception there the next morning." Blount's voice was at its driest, but the whimsical sideways glance he gave Nigel over his spectacles took the sting out of his words. "Did you happen to notice whether Knott-Sloman was carrying a spare pair of shoes?"

"I can definitely state that he was not," Nigel replied with equal seriousness; "but he was wearing an overcoat and could easily have got them stowed away somewhere in it."

"Good. That brings us to the attack on the man Bellamy. I have been examining the place where it was made, and I think it would have been difficult for one person to synchronise it successfully. We shall have to make some experiments before we can be definite on the point. But the *easiest* method, if I may so put it, would have been for someone to have kept watch on the passage and the main staircase, after Bellamy had come out from the kitchen passage, while his accomplice hurried into the kitchen, took the poker and hid behind the swing-door. A good place to keep watch would be from the door of the lounge. Knott-Sloman and Miss Thrale were together for five minutes, Cavendish has deposed, in the middle of the game of billiards. That would have been ample time. I gather your chief objection to such a theory, Mr Strangeways, is the lack of motive for a *premeditated* murder by Knott-Sloman. Now you know what penalties are attached to blackmail. Supposing O'Brien had told Sloman that he intended to expose him as a blackmailer. Wouldn't that have given Sloman a sufficient motive to do away with him? He might easily prefer the risk of hanging for a sheep to the certainty of going to prison for a lamb."

"Yes," said Nigel, "you make it all sound most convincing. What action are you going to take?"

"The superintendent agrees that we should wait to see if we can't get more evidence. In any case, the chief constable must be consulted first. But there can be no harm in asking Sloman to explain — er — some of the disputed points of evidence, don't you think, sir."

"That's right," said Bleakley. "I'll fetch him in."

Knott-Sloman entered, his hands in his pockets, a bold stare in his pale-blue eyes. The inspector introduced himself, then said:

160

"There are certain points, sir, in which your evidence conflicts with — er — other evidence we have received. We shall be glad if you can assist us. At the same time, you are not compelled to answer our questions, and you may wish to consult a solicitor first."

Knott-Sloman, who had been fidgeting about, suddenly sat stone-still. It was as though someone had begun sniping from a nearby roof. "Well, let's hear your questions first," he said.

"You gave evidence, I think, that shortly after midnight on the night of the crime, you stopped playing billiards and went straight up to bed?" There was the slightest emphasis on the "straight".

"Yes, of course." Knott-Sloman eyed Blount warily. "No! Damned silly of me! Quite forgot. I went out first for a breath of air."

"In the snow, sir? I don't expect you stayed out long."

"No, just looked out of the door and came in again."

The inspector's voice became smooth, paternal, but faintly censorious, like that of a bank manager speaking to a client about a not very serious overdraft.

"I'm just asking, because we have evidence that you were in the hut about twelve-fifteen."

Knott-Sloman bounced up from his chair and struck the table with his fist. "This is all a damned bluff!" he shouted. "I'll not stand for any more of this insinuation."

"That's as you like, sir," said Blount smoothly. Then his voice turned hard as granite. "But it's by no means insinuation. We have a reliable witness" — Nigel blinked at the word "reliable" — "who testifies to having seen a man in the hut at that time, and has since identified the man as yourself."

Knott-Sloman's bold stare challenged the inspector for a few seconds. Then it crumpled. He made a rather ghastly attempt at a conciliatory laugh.

"Oh, all right, then. You fellows seem to know everything. Yes, I did just look into the hut."

"For what purpose, may I ask, sir?"

"No, you bloody well may not," exclaimed Knott-Sloman, with a brief return to aggressiveness. Blount unexpectedly and adroitly shifted his ground.

"A package, addressed by you to yourself at the Fizz-and-Frolic Club, has come into our possession," he said conversationally. "It contained certain letters written to Miss Thrale by Edward Cavendish. In view of the charges of blackmail made by Cavendish against Miss Thrale and yourself, you may think it advisable to give some explanation of how these letters came into your hands."

Knott-Sloman's eyes flickered from Blount to the superintendent.

"Well, that's a bit of a facer," he said with an apologetic laugh. "I don't like letting a woman down, but . . . It's like this: Lucilla — Miss Thrale — gave me a package yesterday. She said she wanted me to put it in some safe place. Seemed to me rather curious then, but of course I didn't know what was in it. I can see now she wouldn't want letters like that about the place when there was likely to be a search. But it's ridiculous to talk about blackmail. I'm afraid poor old Cavendish's financial worries have made him a bit unbalanced. There's nothing criminal in a woman keeping her old love-letters, is there? Or perhaps the police don't allow us to do even that nowadays."

"I see," replied the inspector in tones of polite but devastating incredulity. "No doubt then you will be able to give us an equally — er — satisfactory explanation why in one of these letters there was also a note written by you to O'Brien suggesting that some pecuniary redress should be made to Miss Thrale."

"What the devil? But I couldn't find it —"

"So *that's* what you were looking for in the hut."

Knott-Sloman's resistance crumbled like a collapsing house. His expression was a shameful mixture of panic and baffled rage.

"So the little bitch double-crossed me! She must have had the note and put it amongst her letters. I suppose she told you to examine them, too. My God, and after I'd written it for her, too."

"You admit, then, that you wrote it?"

"Yes, of course. And if I'd known Lucilla was going to do the dirty on me like this, I'd have cut off my right hand before I — I'd better explain. I was sorry for her. O'Brien had treated her badly, and frankly I thought he ought to pay for it. Perhaps the method was a bit unconventional, but I didn't want him to be dragged into a breach-of-promise case."

"Your motive sounds most laudable, sir, but I think the law might use a harsher word than 'unconventional' for your proceedings."

"Just a minute," Nigel broke in. "Did Miss Thrale actually suggest that you should approach O'Brien on these lines? And when did you give him the note?"

"Yes, she did. I gave it to him after tea on Christmas Day," Knott-Sloman said sullenly.

"Why do it in writing? Why not have talked to him about it?"

Knott-Sloman twisted in his chair. "Well, y'see, I was going to talk to him later, of course. But he was a bit hot-tempered, y'know, and I thought — well — the note would give him time to think things over and cool down."

"You were going to talk to him in the hut that night? Or was Miss Thrale going to? Is that why she wrote *her* note asking him to meet her there?"

"No, damn you, I wasn't!" shouted Knott-Sloman, goaded beyond endurance. "And I neither know nor care what Lucilla was doing."

"If you weren't going to the hut to talk to O'Brien, for what purpose did you go?" Blount pursued.

"Well, if you must know, I wanted to recover that note of mine, in case he hadn't destroyed it. It occurred to me, thinking it over, that the note might be misconstrued if anyone else found it."

"Just so. I take it, then, that you went to the hut, but failed to find the note. How do you account for its being amongst the letters you sent off the next day?"

"God knows. Presumably Lucilla got hold of it somehow."

"Which suggests that she also went to the hut, either before or after you did. Did you know that she had made a written assignation with O'Brien there?"

164

"No."

"When you failed to find the note in the hut, you went straight back to the house? You did not wait till O'Brien came out?"

"I did NOT! Are you trying to plant this murder on me?" Knott-Sloman's voice rose and cracked. He was almost blubbering. Then with a great effort he controlled himself and said, "When I was in the hut, I thought I heard a noise near the house. I went out quickly and hid amongst some bushes to the right of the hut. I saw O'Brien cross the lawn and enter the hut. That's all I saw. I went straight back into the house after that and to bed. Take it or leave it. It's the truth. You won't get any more out of me."

To everyone's surprise Blount took him at his word and told him he could go. The object of this manoeuvre was at once apparent, for Blount asked the superintendent to fetch Lucilla Thrale in before she could have any conversation with the last witness.

"Now, Miss Thrale," the inspector began without preamble, "you say you did not go out to the hut on the night of the murder?"

"Of course I didn't. I was in bed."

"In spite of having made an appointment there with O'Brien?"

"How many more times do I have to repeat it? I didn't go because Fergus had told me he didn't want me to."

"Exactly. You gave a packet of letters yesterday to Mr Knott-Sloman, asking him to put them in a safe place for you. Was it your suggestion that he should address them to his club?" Blount's abrupt change of direction took Lucilla off her balance.

"No. No, I . . . I didn't know what he was going to do with them. Oh, God, you haven't read them?" she gasped, as realisation dawned on her. The rest was something like a rout. Lucilla strenuously but not very convincingly denied that the letters had been kept for the purposes of blackmail and had been disposed of because a general search was feared. She had handed them over to Knott-Sloman after lunch. Faced with the note that Knott-Sloman had written to O'Brien, she denied furiously that he had written it at her suggestion, called him no gentleman and a good deal worse for having said so, and refused to admit any knowledge of how it had come to be amongst the letters from Edward Cavendish. The inspector told her that she had been accused by Knott-Sloman of putting it there, and therefore presumably of having got it somehow from O'Brien. At this her indignation rose to fever pitch, and Blount thought it expedient to let her go.

"She'll only think up a lot of lies about Knott-Sloman in revenge; and we've got quite enough lies already in this case to drive us insane," Blount explained.

"Well, you've certainly driven a good-sized wedge between the pair of them," said Nigel.

"Yes. We'll get something from them soon. They're both thoroughly rattled; that's when the criminal feels compelled to take some action. And *that's* when he begins to make mistakes."

Action indeed followed fast enough, though it was not quite what the inspector had bargained for. At about six-thirty the maid, Lily Watkins, whom Lady Marlinworth had sent to replace Bellamy, entered Knott-Sloman's room with a can of hot water. She was thinking of her young man and humming to herself. But, when she saw what was lying on the floor beyond the bed, her humming abruptly ceased. She dropped the hot-water can, screamed, and rushed out of the door screaming.

CHAPTER
TEN

Told in A —

Nigel and Inspector Blount were sitting in the study. They had been going over some of the salient points of the case, but the conversation had somehow or other turned to cricket and they were now discussing the new lbw rule. Into this academic dispute the cries from overhead dropped like a bomb. They sprang to their feet and tore upstairs, Bolter, who had been on guard at the front door, hard on their heels. On the landing they met Lily Watkins. She was sobbing convulsively and could only point to the door of Knott-Sloman's bedroom. Blount hurriedly ordered Bolter to keep everyone downstairs, and ran into the room. The first thing they noticed was a smell of bitter almonds on the air; the next was the disarray of the bed; the eiderdown and top blanket seemed to have been dragged right over to one side. Then they saw the body. It was lying on its back, one hand convulsively clutching the bedclothes. The jaws were set hard, and there was froth at the corners of the mouth. But it was chiefly the wide, unwinking, atrocious stare of those pale-blue eyes that had sent Lily Watkins screaming from the room. Cyril Knott-Sloman was dead, beyond question or remedy.

168

Blount gave him one swift glance, knelt to feel the heart, and snapped at Nigel: "Cyanide poisoning. We're too late. Ring up a doctor." The local practitioner, as it happened, was out on a case, so Nigel got into touch with the police doctor at Taviston, who promised to come along at once. Nigel also had a few words with Bleakley, who had returned to Taviston that afternoon to clear up arrears of routine work. "So he's gone and done it," Bleakley's voice came over the wire. "Well, that looks like the end of this case, sir. Pity we let him slip through our fingers like that. Still, least said soonest mended. I'll come along with Doctor Wills and bring the photographer."

When Nigel returned to Knott-Sloman's room, he found Blount looking about him in a puzzled way.

"What's wrong?" asked Nigel.

"I'm looking for something he could have drunk the stuff out of."

There were plenty of signs of eating in the room. Knott-Sloman did not apparently confine his vice of nut-eating to public performana. There was a plate of assorted nuts on the table beside his bed, and another plate on the dressing table containing broken shells. There were even a few fragments on the floor. But, except for the glass on the carafe, there seemed to be no possible receptacle for poison. Blount had already taken up this glass, using his handkerchief to grip it, but it had no smell and no visible mark of having been used recently.

"This type of poison is generally taken in solution. One would expect to find a small phial, probably in splinters," he said, and began for the second time to scour the whole room. There was no trace of what he was looking for. Nigel, who had been indulging his propensity for snooping, thrust his head aimlessly into the wardrobe and began going through the pockets of Knott-Sloman's clothes. Out of one he drew a flask. It was about half-full of brandy.

"Could he have put the poison in this?" he asked.

"He could," replied Blount dryly, "but he could not have put it back in that pocket, I doubt. Cyanide poisons, when a lethal dose is taken, act like lightning, as a general rule. They result in almost immediate loss of muscular power."

"Mightn't he have eaten some, then?"

"I believe there have been cases of people eating potassium cyanide. But he wouldn't have carried it about loose in his pocket, and I can't find anything here he might have kept it in. The smell would betray it, if there was such a receptacle."

"Well, dash it all, he did take the stuff. There must be evidence somewhere. Suicides don't bury their phials neatly in the back garden to avoid making litter."

The inspector's eyes gleamed. "Exactly, Mr Strangeways. And that is why I am now going to lock this door and examine the other rooms. I am not as a general rule in favour of murders," he added cryptically, "but your uncle will give me what-for if it's proved that I've let a suspected murderer slip out of my hands. Now I want you to go and keep that crowd downstairs corralled up somewhere. Tell Bolter to send me the sergeant — he's about the place — and then to

170

telephone for a police matron. I've got to have those women searched. The sergeant can do the men. Until then, you've got to keep 'em amused. Find out when Knott-Sloman was last seen, and all that. But don't let out there's any doubt about suicide. If you can find out tactfully where the members of the household were from teatime onwards, it'll be all to the good. But there'll be plenty of time for that later."

The inspector's calm authority and competence were refreshing to Nigel. His mind felt woolly and without initiative. Too much had been happening and far too rapidly in the last couple of days. He went downstairs and sent Bolter off on his errands. The party had been collected in the drawing room. Lucilla, Georgia, Edward Cavendish, Philip. Nigel involuntarily counted them off on his fingers. One, two, three, four. Lily Watkins, the kitchen-maid, Nell, and Mrs Grant were there, too, sitting bolt upright on hard chairs. The whole picture looked curiously like one of a Victorian household assembled for morning prayer. Mrs Grant, at any rate, had the right expression; her hands and lips were rigidly folded. She gazed severely straight ahead of her, manifestly disassociating herself from the representatives of the modern Babylon on her right hand, and the lower menials on her left. Nigel restrained an impulse to tell them all to kneel down — though, if the inspector's suspicions were justified, there must be one person in the room who needed all their prayers.

"I suppose Lily has told you about Knott-Sloman," he said. Six heads nodded. "He is dead, I'm afraid. Took poison."

Everyone stirred. Nigel, his nerves screwed up to their most sensitive, could feel a wave of relief sweep through the room, feel it almost physically, like a cool wind after a scorching summer day. Was it just relief from the uncertainty that they had all been living in, the realisation that Knott-Sloman had made a tacit confession of his guilt? Or was there mixed with this somebody's far more passionate relief, because this time, at any rate, there was no question about suicide? Only Georgia Cavendish seemed untouched by the common emotion. She sat beside her brother, her sad mouth puckered up in some impenetrable perplexity and foreboding, her eyes still making reservations where all the others showed relief.

"The inspector has asked me to find out when Knott-Sloman was last seen," Nigel said. That did not take long. He had had tea with the rest in the drawing room. He had seemed then unusually silent and preoccupied. When tea was over he had asked Lucilla to come for a short walk. She had refused even to answer him. The inspector's wedge was evidently still firmly in place. Then he had gone out. That was at five minutes to five. About ten minutes later Lily Watkins had seen him open the back door quietly and look out. It was dark then, but not so dark that the figure of the constable stamping his feet in the yard was not visible. Knott-Sloman had muttered something to himself and gone back. He was not seen again. Nigel's questions were answered without any apparent hesitance or emotion. Cyril Knott-Sloman had been a menace to at least one of the party and a nuisance to the rest. That

172

was all the obituary he seemed likely to get; and the tawdry, stupid, overloud, over-brilliant and eternally dead excitement of the Fizz-and-Frolic Club would have to serve for his funeral games.

"I suppose no one heard any sound from his room?" Nigel asked. "He must have fallen to the floor pretty heavily."

"I certainly didn't," said Cavendish. "But I was in the morning room after tea, and that's not under his bedroom."

There was a short pause. Then Georgia seemed to remember something.

"Why, we heard a thump just overhead — about half-past five, wasn't it, Lucilla?"

"I don't remember it," Lucilla said indifferently.

"I was working in my bedroom for an hour after tea," said Starling. "It's next to his. I heard him enter it, about ten past five, I suppose it must have been, but nothing after that. Still, I was dealing with a damn-fool note on the aorist imperative by Watson in this month's *Classical,* so I wouldn't be likely to hear much."

"The aorist imperative in one room and death in the next," murmured Georgia.

Mrs Grant suddenly exclaimed, in her dourest tones: "The wages of sin is death."

Nell gave vent to an uncontrollable giggle, then clapped her hand to her mouth. It was clearly impossible to proceed with any inquiry, however tactful, after that. Before long Nigel saw the police car come up the drive. Movements were heard in the room overhead. Knowing what was happening, he was just as glad he was not there. More minutes passed. Then Bolter appeared and beckoned Nigel out. The inspector wanted to see him. As he went upstairs, he passed the sergeant on the staircase. "We shan't be keeping them much longer now," the sergeant said. "Just waiting for the police matron."

Doctor Wills was standing, with his usual air of saturnine detachment, by the washbasin, drying his hands on a towel. The inspector looked as excited as a bank manager could ever succeed in looking. Knott-Sloman's expression was fortunately not to be seen, as he was now covered over with a sheet.

"Hydrocyanic acid," the inspector said to Nigel. "The quickest killer there is. Dr Wills says he could not have taken the whole dose intended — there were some drops spilt on his clothing; also the froth on the mouth apparently indicates that death was not instantaneous."

"I can't give you much idea," said Dr Wills, "till we find the amount he took and in what form he took it. I suppose Bleakley will see the coroner about a post-mortem?"

When the doctor had gone, Nigel passed on to Blount the meagre information he had collected downstairs. Blount had searched three of the upstairs rooms and Bleakley was now engaged with the rest of them. Nothing had been found so far.

"It's my belief," Blount said, "the murderer may have hidden the evidence somewhere in the rest of the house — out-of-doors even, perhaps. The sergeant is going to make a start on the ground floor now. The fact that we can find no receptacle for poison in the room indicates

174

that it was not suicide. On the other hand, the murderer would want it to look like suicide, one supposes — and, if so, why should he trouble to remove the receptacle?"

"I still don't see how he pulled it off. Presumably he didn't go up to Knott-Sloman and say, 'Have a drink of this. It has a curious smell, but it's really quite wholesome.'"

"Presumably not. He must have put the stuff into something that Knott-Sloman would be bound to drink sooner or later, and then removed the thing when Sloman had taken it."

"Which implies that he had to keep on popping in and out of this room to see whether Knott-Sloman had taken his medicine yet. Rather unsettling for Knott-Sloman that would be."

"Well," said the inspector, a little nettled, "perhaps you can give a better explanation." Nigel moved restlessly about the room, picking up objects and putting them down.

"X might have wandered in with a couple of glasses or flasks or something, and asked Sloman to have a drink with him."

"Bringing in a branch of peach-blossom with him to account for the curious smell of one of the drinks," retorted Blount.

"By Jove," exclaimed Nigel, striding excitedly across the room. "I've got it! A cocktail. You expect a cocktail to smell like anything on earth. Damn these bits of shell! One keeps treading on them." He gathered them up and put them in the wastepaper basket.

"Yes," said Blount, "yes. That might have been it. And a couple of cocktail glasses are not so easy to dispose of. If he washed them and put them back in a cupboard, one of the servants may quite likely have seen him. I'll get on to that."

At this point the sergeant came in to announce that the ambulance had arrived, and with it the police matron. Blount went downstairs with him to break to the household that they would have to be searched. Men came into the room and removed the remains of Knott-Sloman, unwept, unhonoured and unsung. Then Nigel was left alone. He lit a cigarette, and as he did so became aware that the odour of bitter almonds, which had almost completely gone from the room, was suddenly much stronger again. He looked vaguely around. There seemed nothing to account for it. He put the cigarette to his lips again, and at once felt a slight chokiness in his throat. The smell was on the cigarette — and on his fingers, too, now. Had someone been poisoning his cigarettes? This was really too much like a shilling shocker. No, the stuff must have got on to his fingers first. What had he been touching lately? Certainly not the body. This was maddening. He must have had the instrument of death within his fingers a few minutes ago. He tried to remember what he had touched. Then his eyes lighted on the wastepaper basket. He went over and picked out of it the pieces of shell. Yes! That was it! They looked like walnut, but they smelt like bitter almonds.

Nigel's jubilation almost at once died down. The thing was fantastic. You might as well suggest that

Knott-Sloman had been killed by a mamba or a hamadryad as by a walnut. He laid the pieces out carefully on his handkerchief, as though they were a jigsaw and by putting them together he could solve the puzzle. One thing struck him at once: the shell was, for a walnut, curiously thin. This was obvious to the eye, apart from the unusual number of pieces into which it had cracked. Then he noticed another thing. The lower edges of some of the fragments were remarkably straight: they called attention to themselves like the border pieces of a jigsaw puzzle. Looking at these fragments through his magnifying lens, Nigel observed that their straight edges were coated with some substance. With a good deal of patience he contrived to build up a segment of the nut, and this made it quite evident that the nut had originally been sawn in half and its hemispheres joined together again with glue. Then he made a further discovery: a tiny hole had been drilled in the nut, and later filled in with putty.

Half the problem was now solved. The murderer had sawn the nut in half, presumably to remove the kernel and sandpaper its interior surface, so that the nut was almost eggshell thin in some places. Why had he done this? Possibly to lighten it; its weight, with poisonous liquid inside, might otherwise have roused Knott-Sloman's suspicion. The murderer, after scouring out the interior of the nut, had glued its halves together again, then bored a hole in the shell, injected the poison through a syringe, and filled up the hole again. So far, so good. But now Nigel came up against two mountainous obstacles. How could the murderer be certain that this particular nut would poison Knott-Sloman and not someone else? And how could it poison him, anyhow? When the nut was cracked, the liquid would presumably pour over one's fingers; unless one had a cut on them, it couldn't do any harm. The fumes of prussic acid were dangerous, of course, but surely not lethal in such a small quantity. Nigel thought and thought, but he couldn't get round the problem. He was on the point of giving it up, when a picture suddenly came unbidden into his mind. In the lounge before lunch Knott-Sloman, his head thrown a little back, cracking walnuts between his teeth. Eureka! All the other points now began to be illuminated. Nigel remembered now that, although Knott-Sloman sometimes used nutcrackers at dinner, he always used his teeth on informal occasions, so to speak. The murderer would know this, and be sure that no one else would attempt to crack a walnut in such a way, so that — if the poisoned nut did happen to get to the wrong person — no damage would be done. He had presumably put this particular nut on the plate beside Knott-Sloman's bed. After that, it was only a matter of time. This was another reason, too, for making the shell as thin as possible. If it was not very thin, the nut would be liable to split simply into its glued halves, and that might have called attention to it afterwards. Also, if it had been normally tough, it would not have shattered at one bite, and the bitter taste of the liquid would have made Knott-Sloman spit it out instantly. As it was, his strong jaws would crunch the weakened shell into fragments. His surprise at the lack of resistance would render him incapable of rejecting the liquid instantaneously, and the backward tilt of his head would send most of it down his throat. A very little of it, and the pieces of shell, he would then spit out. But that would be too late.

When Inspector Blount returned to the room, he found Nigel smoking a cigarette and playing idiotically with fragments of a nut. For a fearful moment Blount thought that the tragedy had turned his brain. But then Nigel said, with all the symptoms of sanity:

"You needn't go on with the search, Inspector. I've found the answer to the puzzle."

"The deuce you have!"

"Yes. It is one of those stories that are told in a nutshell."

Nigel told the story. The inspector looked polite, incredulous, absorbed, triumphant, and frankly horrified, by turns.

"Great Scott, Mr Strangeways, that's a grand piece of work of yours. But I don't like this; I don't like it at all. There's a sort of — what can you call it — deadly, cold precision about this crime. The sooner we get our hands on the fellow the better."

"Not much choice left now," said Nigel slowly.

"No. And it shouldn't take long, luckily. I wish Bellamy would come round. He's probably got the key to it all. The doctor says he has a good chance now, but he may be unconscious for days yet, and there's always the danger of loss of memory after a blow like that. We'll have to get on without him. I'm sending out descriptions of everyone here to the chemists. You can't

179

buy prussic acid like butter, but even if the murderer has managed to sign a false name in the register, which is most unlikely, we'll get him identified with luck. My chaps are going on with the search; but I imagine whoever fixed up that nut didn't do it here. Now, Mr Strangeways, if you're free for an hour or so, I'd like to clear up my ideas about —"

"No, no," interrupted Nigel firmly. "You professionals may be able to go for days without food; but it's now long after my dinner hour, and I propose to make a pretty large hole in the larder. You'd better join in. I'll get Lily to bring all the food there is in the house into the morning room."

Nigel ate steadily through a pound or so of cold beef, ten potatoes, half a loaf of bread, and the greater part of an apple pie, refusing any response to the inspector's professional gambits. At last he withdrew his head wistfully from an emptied jug of beer, wiped his mouth and said:

"Proceed. You have our ear."

"First, I take it there is no question now of suicide. Knott-Sloman would scarcely go to all that trouble with the nut for his own benefit."

"Dashed true and, if I may say so, very well put." Nigel was in that expansive, unanchored and vaguely drifting state of mind which anything over three pints of beer will induce.

"There's no point in our going into the whereabouts of everyone this afternoon, as the nut might have been placed there any time in the last few days. Mrs Grant says that the plate beside Knott-Sloman's bed was kept well supplied from the beginning of his stay. Now either this poisoning is connected with the two previous crimes, or it is not."

"A small point, but one worth making," murmured Nigel.

"If it is not, we should have to postulate two separate murderers in the house —"

"Two minds with but a single thought. Sorry. Pass on."

"We may be pretty certain that there *is* a connection. Very well, then. The obvious one is that Knott-Sloman had some knowledge which was vitally dangerous to the murderer. What could that be?"

"Knowledge about the murder of O'Brien, I should hazard." Nigel threw both legs over the arm of his armchair, lit a cigarette, and rumpled his hair in the manner of Stan Laurel.

"That's exactly what I had concluded. We know that Sloman was near the hut shortly before O'Brien's murder. Suppose he saw someone else enter the hut after O'Brien. The next day he finds murder has been committed. The natural reaction of his type would be not to expose this someone else to the police, but to cash in on his knowledge. He was killed because he was blackmailing the murderer of O'Brien."

"Why not sooner? Why did the murderer wait two days?"

"Ah, that's very significant to my mind. It was not till this afternoon that Knott-Sloman knew he was suspected. The only way he could get rid of this suspicion was to admit his having seen X enter the hut after O'Brien. He hesitated about doing this, because it involved killing the goose that was laying his golden eggs: also, perhaps, because such a statement would have been received by us with a certain lack of credulity. I suggest Sloman was keeping this statement as a last card, till he knew for certain whether we were bluffing or not. In the course of this afternoon the murderer discovers, either because Knott-Sloman tells him or from his demeanour, that Sloman is under suspicion. Fearing that Sloman's nerve will break and he will tell the police what he knows, the murderer at once lays the poison-trap for him."

"That's very sound up to a point. But it implies some pretty quick work with the preparation of the nut, doesn't it?"

"We should have still to assume that the murderer brought the nut with him. It might have been an alternative method of killing O'Brien, or perhaps just a safe way of carrying poison about with him against a possible emergency."

"Or, thirdly, there is this theory: X might have wanted to get rid of Knott-Sloman because he was blackmailing him, not over O'Brien's murder, but over something else. He brought the death-nut, as our American cousins would put it, on spec. Finding that Sloman was suspected of murder, he planted the nut in the expectation that it would flourish into a perfectly natural suicide. Note the beautifully constructed metaphor."

"Yes, that seems a very reasonable alternative, Mr Strangeways. Your theory would point to Cavendish. He has hinted himself that he was being blackmailed by Knott-Sloman, apart from the evidence we've got for it. He may quite well be the murderer of O'Brien, too. From what I've seen of him, I should say that his demeanour was highly suspicious. He looks nervous and worried, and everyone seems to have assumed rather too readily that this was due to his financial difficulties."

"Cavendish's demeanour is the oddest thing in this very *outré* case," murmured Nigel. The inspector took off his horn-rims with deliberation and, swinging them in his right hand, leant towards Nigel.

"Now then, sir, what exactly do you mean by that? You've got something on your mind."

"Sorry. I can't tell you — because I simply don't know. I've been watching Cavendish hard for two days, and his demeanour is more like that of a murderer on the point of losing his nerve than one could believe possible. He looks just too guilty to be true. It beats me."

Blount leant back, a bit disappointed. "I think you're being oversubtle. My experience is that the murderer — the educated type, not the thug, I mean — generally gives himself away in his behaviour. The poker-face fiend is a product of fiction."

"Well, I hope you're right."

Blount glanced sharply at Nigel. He was staring, with a glassy and hypnotised expression, apparently at the apex of the inspector's bald head.

"Funny," Nigel said, "I'd not noticed it before. A Picasso, isn't it?"

He got up and inspected a small framed drawing on the wall behind the inspector.

"You were saying, Mr Strangeways," Blount pressed relentlessly, "that you hoped I was right. Does that mean you suspect someone else?"

Nigel returned and slumped wearily into his chair. "In fairness to Edward Cavendish," he said, "one must admit that there are other possibilities. For instance, before lunch today there was a bit of a dust-up, featuring Knott-Sloman and Philip Starling. In the course of it Sloman blurted out that he knew a thing or two about Starling which would alter the attitude of the police to him. Mind you, I know Philip well. As far as murder goes, I should call him one hundred per cent pure. And —"

"The snag about him," Blount interrupted, "was that he couldn't have attacked Bellamy. Still, it is not inconceivable that this attack may not have been made by the murderer. I shall have to see Mrs Grant, though, to make sure that Bellamy really was about the place till two-thirty that afternoon."

"I shouldn't take that suggestion of mine too seriously. It was only made to show that Cavendish isn't the only pebble on the beach of the incarnadined sea. There's Lucilla, for instance. She'd just fallen out with Knott-Sloman: and when knaves fall out — Poison is a woman's weapon, they say. Knott-Sloman might have killed O'Brien with her complicity; then she sees he is on the point of losing his nerve and slips him the poison in self-protection. Or there's Mrs Grant — a woman, presumably, though she gives little evidence of it, and therefore a potential poisoner. Suppose that earlier in her life she had Sacrificed All for Love and Taken the Wrong Turning. She is left with a fatherless (fie!) cheeild, and spends the rest of her life working her fingers to the bone to put him through college. Knott-Sloman finds out her secret and blackmails her. "I had only one wish, to make a gentleman of him," sobs errant cook. No? You flout the suggestion? Well, I'm not sure I don't agree with you. I can't quite see Mrs Grant in the role of Another Poor Girl Gone Wrong. What about the gardener, then? Name of Jeremiah Pegrum: and a name like that should lead one into the worst excesses. Spends most of his time meditating in the outhouses, but you've only to read T. F. Powys to discover that murder is the chief winter sport amongst English rustics. The long winter evenings are coming. Buy a set of our guaranteed eversharp hatchets. It will keep young and old amused. Packed in fancy box, with directions, seven shillings and sixpence net. Packets of assorted hemlock, ratsbane, henbane and deadly nightshade, sixpence extra."

Inspector Blount rose deliberately. He exhibited that faint relaxation of the facial muscles by which a Scotsman indicates that a joke has been a roaring success. In his gravest official voice he said, "I will bear in mind your valuable suggestions, Mr Strangeways," and retired. Nigel went to bed soon, too. He did not, in spite of appearances, feel wildly hilarious. Indeed, he had scarcely laid his head on the pillow when he went off into a nightmare, in which Georgia Cavendish, her green parrot on her shoulder, smiled reproachfully at him and then the parrot turned into a loudspeaker that advanced gaping towards him, gaping and bellowing louder and louder, "Poison is a woman's weapon. POISON IS A WOMAN'S WEAPON!"

CHAPTER
ELEVEN

The Traveller's Tale

On the rare occasions afterwards when Nigel could be induced to talk about the fantastic and paradoxical case of the "Chatcombe Killings", as the newspapers once termed them, he was wont to say that it had been solved by a professor of Greek and a seventeenth-century dramatist. Whatever may be the truth of this dictum — and anyone who perseveres to the end of this book may incline to give Nigel Strangeways himself a considerable share of the credit — it provided a suitably cryptic opening to his account of this most cryptic of cases. When Nigel arose on the morning of the twenty-eighth of December, there were no indications that the end of the affair was in sight. It was one of those mornings when the world seems to be weeping hopelessly over man's first fall, and man himself, peering dismally and shamefacedly into his shaving mirror, wonders whether a sharp stroke over the left carotid artery would not really be best for all concerned. On Chatcombe Park a grey sky gloomed like the hangover of some Olympian debauch. Mists obscured the surrounding hills. And in the garden the leaves of evergreens were depressed and released spasmodically by raindrops from the trees overhead, like typewriter keys under invisible and inexpert fingers. Jeremiah Pegrum, feeling no doubt that the weather was sufficiently subnormal to justify an emergence from his usual outhouse, was pottering round the beds, a sack over his shoulders and an expression on his face that would have done credit to his Hebrew namesake. As Nigel shaved, the events of the last three days performed a sluggish and disordered dance round his mind. The conviction came upon him, more strongly than ever, that they would never set into a pattern until the central figure was clearly in position. O'Brien was the key, and until he knew a great deal more about O'Brien he would continue to fumble like a man trying to unlock an unfamiliar door in pitch darkness. Georgia was the person, surely, who could tell him most. If she would. The trouble was that, if one took each aspect of the crimes separately, one found it attaching itself most easily to some aspect of Georgia Cavendish. Yet the sum total of Georgia, so to speak, simply did not tally with the crimes as a whole. "By which ingenious nonsense," Nigel said to himself, "I really mean nothing more than that I like Georgia very much and prefer flying in the face of all probability to working out a case against her." A heart-to-heart with Georgia, anyway, must be the first thing in the programme. If she is innocent it will tell me a lot about O'Brien: if she is not, she will be bound to make hesitations and contradictions that will hint the worst about herself.

There was nobody in the dining room but Philip Starling. He was examining a piece of toast with the

188

expression of brisk animosity which he was wont to turn upon an untalented undergraduate's compositions.

"This toast," he declared, brandishing it in Nigel's face, "is a scandal. One expects this sort of thing in college; my colleagues are all so wrapped up in the Higher Criticism or Buchmanism or some other equally squalid form of intellectual suicide that they are quite blind to the importance of creature comforts. But in a private house, and one where the cooking otherwise reaches a very tolerable standard, one does expect one's toast to be crisp."

So saying, he piled marmalade on the offending piece and swallowed it with every appearance of relish.

"Possibly the recent contretemps have unsettled the kitchen staff," suggested Nigel.

"You refer to the murders? Do I detect a certain reproach beneath your words? We must preserve our sense of proportion, my dear Nigel. Your nonconformist conscience leads you to overestimate the importance of the next world at the expense of this. Now I maintain the opposite position. I hold that life is more important than death; and therefore that murder is no excuse for flabby toast. Though, apart from that, why Knott-Sloman's demise should unsettle anyone, I cannot conceive: it ought to have put the household staff on their best form. By the way, old boy, talking of murders, isn't it about time you solved these? Things are coming to a pretty pass. Yesterday I was searched, by a sergeant of police: a disagreeable experience, as I happen to be very ticklish. I can't go out of doors without being followed by a constable as though I were going to commit an offence in Hyde Park. My name will be mud in the common room when they find out I was staying at Chatcombe in the vac. And my digestion is suffering from the irregularity of the dinner hour."

"Dinner," said Nigel ruminatively: "dinner. It strikes a chord. There was something I meant to ask you. Now what the devil was it? Yes, I remember. You were going to tell me something O'Brien had done or said at dinner on Christmas night. You were saying, 'I suppose you noticed how O'Brien —' and then we were interrupted by that shindy over Arthur Bellamy."

Philip Starling looked puzzled. Then his brow cleared. "It was that passage he recited: 'Doth the silkworm expend her yellow labours.' He gave us to understand that it was Webster. Actually, it comes in one of Tourneur's plays. I didn't notice it at the time. It struck me later. Odd, because he seemed a well-read fellow."

Nigel was disappointed. He had expected some more valuable revelation. An hour later he went into the morning room and found Georgia Cavendish writing letters. She had on a suede leather coat and a bright red skirt, and her parrot was sitting on her shoulder.

"Will you come out for a walk?" he said. "I want to talk to you."

The parrot cocked an obscene eye at him, and enunciated brightly, "You naughty old b —!"

Georgia laughed. "I must apologise for Nestor. He had a nautical education. Yes, of course I will. Just wait

190

till I've finished this and put Nestor in his cage: he doesn't like rain."

A few minutes later Georgia came downstairs, enveloped in a huge cavalry sort of mackintosh, but with no hat. "Won't you get your hair very wet?" said Nigel, cramming on his own shapeless felt — an object so ancient that even the most uncritical bird would have thought twice before nesting in it.

"I like rain on my head, if you don't mind my looking like Medusa. How convenient it would be for a detective to wear a cap of darkness."

"I do. My hat is the sort of darkness that can be felt."

Georgia laughed delightedly. "I'm so glad to find somebody who still makes puns. It's the sign of a simple, childlike character — see Charles Lamb and savages passim."

"I'm afraid your belief in my simple, childlike nature will soon be shattered. My mind is really a tortuous sink of base suspicions."

"Well, it would be worth being disillusioned, if only to see what a tortuous sink looks like."

"It's what the pedagogues call a transferred epithet. But seriously, I've dragged you out of the house to extract information from you."

Georgia Cavendish made no comment. Nigel could not see the small fists in her big mackintosh pockets clench themselves. He was, as a matter of fact, giving Georgia full marks for having refrained from saying, "I thought you did not want me for my *beaux yeux* alone" — a temptation few women could have resisted. There was something a little intimidating about her

191

uncompromising silence, now that their preliminary verbal sparring was over. He took a deep breath, and said:

"I want you to tell me everything you can about O'Brien."

Georgia was silent for a moment. Then she said, "Are you asking me in your official capacity?"

"I have no official position here. On the other hand, I am bound to give the police any information that seems to me to have a bearing on the crimes."

"Well, that's honest at any rate," she said, looking down at the ground, her face puckered with indecision.

Nigel went on impulsively. "On paper I have worked it out that you are the person most likely to have committed both murders. In fact, I am quite convinced that you didn't." He broke off, wondering why he should be so breathless. It was an extraordinary beginning to a relationship which neither of them could possibly have foreseen — this academic accusation under the sombre and dripping oak trees. Georgia had halted, and was digging her foot into a wet mass of leaves. At last she looked up at Nigel with a small swift smile and said:

"Very well. I'll tell you. What do you want to know?"

Nigel was never to forget that walk through the melancholy park and the tale that it unfolded to him. It was not so much the contrast between the rainy downcast skies under which they walked and the blazing African vistas that her tale opened up to him. What he remembered most vividly was Georgia herself — the small, compact figure in the huge mackintosh;

her slouching yet somehow vital and characteristic gait; the rain streaming down her thin brown face, with its features resolute as a ship's figurehead and vivacious as the sea in a summer gale.

"I want you to tell me how you first met O'Brien, and everything that happened after it. Anything he said to you at any time about the people here. It's really important, or I wouldn't ask you. Perhaps it will be a good thing for you not to keep it bottled up any longer," he added with a flash of intuitive sympathy.

"It was last year. I was on an expedition into the Libyan Desert. Lieutenant Galton, a young cousin of mine — Henry Lewis — and myself. It was Henry's first expedition: he was highly strung, but a good youngster and dead keen. We were going to try to find the site of Zerzura, the lost oasis. People have tried before, and will go on trying. Nobody has found it yet. It's one of those alluring legends, like Atlantis. We took two Ford four-cylinders, rigged up for desert work. We had food for two months, and enough petrol and water to make the thing a joyride — or so we thought. Well, I won't bore you with a geography lesson: anyway, all that part of the desert looks alike: good hard sand as far as you can see, and nothing much else to look at except the sun and an occasional oasis till you get down to the Wadi Hawa in the south. A damn' fool sort of place to go motoring in, most people would think. I thought so too, before very long. On the twelfth day, I think it was, we had a hell of a sandstorm. They're quite harmless, you know, but apt to get on your nerves if you're not used to them. Henry wasn't. It left him pretty shaken, and after that he got a touch of the sun and began talking wildly about getting out of this infernal cauldron. It *is* a bit trying, if you're not used to it. It was my fault for bringing him. Anyway, one morning Galton and I were about twenty yards away from the cars taking observations — their magnetism affects compasses, you know, at close quarters — when we heard one of the cars starting up. Henry had cracked: he was going to drive straight home. Galton ran forward and got on to the car and stopped the engine. Then Henry shot him in the belly. After that Henry began to yell with laughter and take potshots with his revolver at the petrol and water tins on the other car. He holed five of them. There was nothing else for me to do. I had to shoot him. I shot him through the heart. He was lucky." Georgia added tonelessly, "Galton lived for three days more."

Nigel had that helpless, sickish feeling in the stomach that comes to the sedentary city-dweller when he hears at first hand of desperate actions such as these. He opened his mouth, but there seemed no comment on heaven or earth adequate to the situation, so he lit a cigarette, which was extinguished almost at once by the rain and disintegrated slowly in his mouth. Georgia went on:

"When it happened, we were between Uweinat and the Wadi Hawa, about a hundred and fifty miles away from the latter. I had the choice of going back to the rendezvous where we were expecting fresh supplies of water and petrol by camel transport from Selima, or pressing on across the Wadi Hawa to Kutum and

194

Fasher. We did not expect the camels for several days, and in any case the only hope for Galton seemed to be to get him to Kutum, whence he could be flown to Khartoum. So I made him as comfortable as I could in the body of one of the cars, and piled on it the few tins Henry had left us and set off. There wasn't much water left, anyway, and Galton needed a great deal, and we couldn't travel very fast, because it made his pain intolerable. Still, we got across the Wadi Hawa by nightfall, and I thought perhaps my luck might have turned. It hadn't. The next day we got into the subdesert, about the most hellish going for cars in the world — hard mounds of earth, tussocks of grass and innumerable dry rain channels. I reduced speed to seven miles an hour, but even that was too much for Galton, and I don't blame him. So I stopped. Galton wanted me to leave him and go on, but I felt it was my own fault it had all happened, and he was too weak to make much of a protest. The next day he died. I managed to bury him. It seemed the least I could do, though I didn't fancy it would be much use: the ground was too hard for me to get him in deep, and there are packs of wild dogs thereabouts — I had seen them in Wadi Hawa — also lions of a sort.

"Well, after that I went on for a bit. What with one thing and another, there was only half a tin of water and a tin of petrol left. Also the springs kept breaking. I say, I hope I'm not boring you. I'm afraid all this is rather off the point for your purpose."

Nigel cleared his dry throat and assured her that he was not finding the story tedious.

"I suppose I was getting a little anxious, with the water so low; anyway, I must have been driving too fast, because the back axle broke — and, say what you like about Fords, their axles don't break unless you maltreat them pretty outrageously. I was about a hundred miles from Kutum, but there are intervillage tracks nearer than that, so I swigged the rest of the water and began walking. You wouldn't believe that anyone could be accused of jaywalking in the desert. I must be the king of jaywalkers, because I hadn't gone more than half a mile when I trod on one of those blasted tussocks and sprained my ankle. I managed to crawl back to the car. If anyone *was* about the place, they'd be more likely to spot a car than a pedestrian. You can go a long time on one good bellyful of water, if you've trained yourself to it; but after three and a half days I was beginning to feel I'd gone long enough. I don't know if you've ever seen anyone who has died of thirst. It's an uncongenial spectacle, and I had no intention of letting it get as far as that. I always carry a dose of poison about with me when I'm travelling. Prussic acid. Nice quick stuff. I was toying with this when I heard an aeroplane engine. Of course, I didn't believe it at first. That sort of thing is generally one of the little sideshows that Providence puts up to amuse people in their last hours. But after a bit I managed to look up — and, sure enough, it *was* a real live aeroplane.

"I waved, rather feebly, I suppose, and the bloke in the aeroplane waved back. I calculated that it would take about ten hours for him to fly back and for a car to get across to me, and I thought I might just manage to hold out ten hours. But the bloke didn't go back. He circled about, only a hundred feet up, as though he was looking for a landing place. Damned silly waste of time, I called it. An archangel couldn't land in country like that. I flapped my hands at him, trying to make him go away, but I was too far gone to make a very forceful protest. And then the bloke did land. It was just the sort of bloody grand lunatic thing Fergus would do. When I saw he really meant to come down, I propped myself up and watched with my eyes popping out. One couldn't ask for a better entertainment in one's last hours, and if the fool was determined to break his neck and lose me my last chance, I didn't see why I shouldn't watch the sport. He put up his tail and started to float down. I shall never see anything like it if I live to be ninety. He handled that plane as if it was a piece of thistledown. He pancaked at the very last moment, but he must still have been going about fifty when he touched. The plane bounced along over the tussocks like a kangaroo, and stopped about twenty yards short of my radiator, with the undercarriage looking like a theater after Boat Race night. Then the bloke jumped out and came up to me with a hell of a grin on his face and said: 'Miss Cavendish, I presume.'"

"Believe me, I was a good deal more shaken up than he was, and that's saying a lot. In fact, as far as I remember, I burst out crying and was rather astonished to find I couldn't stop. Fergus was sweet. He fetched me water out of the aeroplane and made me drink it in teaspoonfuls with a dash of brandy, while he told me an

197

interminable and most improper story about a dowager on a picnic. After that I went to sleep, and when I woke up it was morning and Fergus was tinkering about with his plane. He made breakfast and told me who he was and how he had found me. The camel transport had gone to the rendezvous and waited about for us a bit. Then they had returned to Selima and given the alarm. Aeroplanes had been sent out, but they were searching too far north, of course. After a bit they found the other car and the remains of Henry Lewis. They could see the tracks of our car here and there going south, so they called it off, imagining that we were all right for the present. Fergus was at Khartoum when they returned, and suggested that he should go off in search for us round about the Wadi Hawa, to make sure that we were not in difficulties. That was how he had found me.

"Well, I was still pretty weak that day, so I lay about watching Fergus trying to mend the undercarriage. I had asked him, by the way, why he was such a blithering ass as to attempt a landing on such a surface. He answered, characteristically, that — except for a bishop's mitre — it was the only kind of thing he had not landed on so far and he wanted to see if it was possible. He said that now he would leave the bishop's mitre until he was tired of life and try it then, as it would ensure his dying in the odour of sanctity. I told him he surely needn't bother about repairing his plane, because they'd soon send out a search after him, and I was perfectly all right now, and anyway he'd never get the bus up into the air out of this. He said that (a) he liked repairing planes, (b) he had never been rescued before and he was not going to start now, (c) I was not perfectly all right, and the sooner I got back into a nursing home and began a rest cure the better, (d) that he hadn't enough water with him to last till some officious jack-in-office at Khartoum had recovered from the effects of his last official dinner and condescended to send out a search party, and (e) that if a crate could come down in this country it could get up off it again. So that was that.

"When he knocked off work he came and sat under the lean-to tent I had made against the side of the car, and asked me all sorts of questions about myself. He wanted to take my mind off the — er — recent events; and, besides, he was interested in everything — that was a part of his greatness. By nightfall that day he knew the whole story of my life. I hadn't realised before how interesting my life had been. He was the sort of person who makes you supremely interesting to yourself — only a great man can do that, or your lover, and he wasn't my lover yet — not by long chalks. Well, after the subject of me had been exhausted, he got me on to my family. I told him all about my parents and about Edward. Our parents died when I was quite young and there were only Edward and me, so I've always been rather soppy about him. Fergus saw that at once — he had extraordinarily keen intuition, and he made me tell him all about Edward, too. Edward used to go over to Ireland every summer before the war. We had relations there, so of course I made the usual dumb remark about whether Fergus had met him over there, as though Ireland was a small village or an educational conference or something. Fergus asked me where he'd stayed, and I told him it was at Meynart House, in County Wexford, and he said he knew that part of the country quite well.

"Then he said something about how lonely I should feel if my brother got married, and how I ought to get married myself anyway. And I told him that Edward was a confirmed bachelor by now, and how I had an idea he had fallen in love with some girl over in Ireland and she had chucked him. Fergus was very interested in that, but I couldn't tell him much, because it was the one thing that Edward had never opened up to me about. He said he would like to meet Edward some time, and I said he certainly should if we ever got out of this blasted desert. Then I asked him about himself. He told me a lot of Münchausen sort of stories about his adventures in the war and after; at least, if anyone else had told them they would have been pure Münchausen, but I had heard enough about him to know that they were probably true. Founded on fact, anyway — you know how an Irishman will garnish a true story with any number of picturesque falsehoods, just to make it more appetising. Fergus was a true artist in that. I asked him about his life before the war, but he rather put up the shutters over that. He did say, though, that he'd never known who his parents were and that he used to work on the land. And that's all I've ever found out about the prewar O'Brien. The next day Fergus got down to the undercarriage again. We managed to jack the plane up a bit, and he used pieces of the car and God knows what, and finally he'd rigged up a sort of Heath Robinson monstrosity that he said would get us off the ground all right. He was an absolute genius with his hands. I pointed out that it would fall to pieces as soon as it hit a bump, which meant before it had gone five yards, but he said we were going to make a runway. So the next day and most of the one after that we spent — I was all right by then physically — levelling out a hundred yards of those Godforsaken tussocks with spades and piling the stuff into the rain channels. We got off the ground, as it happened; but we hit something hardish at the far end, and that must have weakened the makeshift undercarriage, because when we landed at Cairo — Fergus insisted on going there instead of Khartoum, because he said the nursing homes there were better — we had a crack-up. Fergus got laid out properly and I was feeling I could do with a week in bed; so in the end we both went to the nursing home. Oh, I forgot to tell you that before we left Fergus pinned to the car a notice with *Per Ardua Ad Astra* written on one side, and a most offensive message to the Khartoum authorities on the other. The search party found it the next day. It caused some stir in official circles, I heard later."

"Well — er — thank you very much," said Nigel after a long pause. One comment seemed just about as adequate as any other.

"Not at all. A pleasure," Georgia replied with derisive banality. Then: "No, but it was, really. You must be very sympathetic. I've never told anyone else all that. I feel happier now than I've felt since Fergus was killed." Her voice spoke the phrase with a pathetic, careful, tentative control, like a convalescent taking his first walk. Nigel, staring in front of him, was seeing not a clump of wet beeches, but a young woman in the desert shooting her crazed companion with no more nor less compunction than she would have shot a mad dog: it was her life or his. Had it, in some mysterious way, been a question of her life or O'Brien's, too? He was seeing the same young woman toying with her dose of prussic acid. "Nice quick stuff." Jolly. Ripping. Makes the party go. He spoke with an unnatural harshness that quite startled Georgia.

"You did say prussic acid?"

"When? Oh, yes. Why?"

"Just a coincidence," answered Nigel unhappily. "That's what Knott-Sloman was poisoned with."

The so hardly gleaned happiness of the last hour was dashed from Georgia's face at a stroke. Nigel felt as if he had hit her on a wound just beginning to heal. However, he had to go on.

"What do you do with the stuff when you're not travelling?"

"I keep it locked up at home. Sometimes I pour it away."

"Should there be any at your home just now?"

Georgia hesitated. Then she whispered, as though in doubt, "Yes, there should be."

"I simply hate asking you all this. But, as you know, a poison of that sort can only be obtained legally through a doctor. I assume that you obtained it legally, and therefore it is only a matter of time before possession of it is traced to you. The police are bound to ask you about it before long; and it would simplify things for you and everyone else if you told them about it at once and gave them permission to fetch the poison from where you keep it — just to prove that it's not been used, I mean."

"No, no! I couldn't — I daren't do that," she exclaimed.

" 'Daren't'?"

"No. You see," she explained hurriedly, "last time I got it from a chemist — a great friend of mine. I forgot it till the last minute. He gave it to me without a doctor's prescription. It would get him into frightful trouble."

"How many people knew that you had — have the stuff?"

"Most of my friends, I expect. But you're wasting time. No one on earth knows where I keep it in the house." Georgia looked unbearably overstrained and wan. Nigel couldn't play the inquisitor any longer. He said:

"Please believe me. I've learnt that you are capable of shooting a man, and that you keep the same sort of poison that Knott-Sloman was killed with. But I believe still less than before that you killed him or O'Brien."

Georgia gave him a grateful smile, but her eyes were still preoccupied with some problem beyond the reach of any amateur detective's gallantry. Nigel felt a spasm of bitterness and disappointment. He had put himself out of the running as a detector of this crime by irrationally believing everything that Georgia told him;

yet his belief in her didn't seem of any use to her at all. She divined this, and put her hand on his arm.

"It does make the hell of a lot of difference, your being so good to me. But there are things I simply can't ask you to help me about. Now, what else do you want to know?"

"When did O'Brien first take up with Lucilla?"

"After he'd returned to England from Cairo early this year, as far as I know. He met her in our house. She was a flame of Edward's then."

"Why did he take up with her, do you think, really? She's not his sort, surely?"

"Well, he was a man, and Lucilla is very decidedly a woman. But I felt he was only amusing himself with her. He obviously had no tenderness for her. He was queer with women, though. Sometimes," she added in a low voice, "I felt that he didn't care even for me — not wholeheartedly, I mean. There was always a part of him elsewhere: it made him seem just a little inhuman, even to me. A demon lover. It sounds fantastic, but he was possessed sometimes. Something deeper than I could reach seemed to be driving him. The Greeks would have thought that the Eumenides were after him, I dare say."

"How did Knott-Sloman come into the picture? I should have thought he'd be the last person O'Brien would have any use for."

"Well, Lucilla was a sort of high-class decoy for his roadhouse. She'd taken Edward there a good deal, and one day she mentioned it to Fergus. Told him Knott-Sloman was running it. Fergus said he'd like to go and have a look at one of these latest blisters on the face of civilisation. They went there once or twice this summer. But I was certainly rather surprised to find Knott-Sloman down here."

"You don't happen to know where O'Brien got his money from, do you? He told me he was a rich man."

"That's funny. I asked him once. He said he'd got it by blackmailing an Indian maharajah. I expect it was one of his usual tales, with a nucleus of truth in the centre. He was in India after the war, and he probably did some potentate a service. They're stiff with gold and wouldn't think twice about giving Fergus a few chestfuls of it. He was careful about money, too — as careful about it as he was reckless of his own life. An odd trait."

"There's only one other thing I want to ask now. Do you think your brother knew that O'Brien was going to give up Lucilla?" Nigel caught a glimpse of the expression on Georgia's face and added hastily: "All right. I take that question back."

"Do you mind if we go back to the house now?" Georgia's voice was small and shaking a little. "I — my feet are getting so awfully wet."

Nigel took her arm. "Very well, my dear. You know, I don't believe you're tough at all," he said.

Georgia bit her trembling lip. She tried to say something. Then Nigel found her sobbing in his arms and himself whispering over her rain-wet hair:

"This case seems to have got quite out of my control now."

CHAPTER
TWELVE

Tales from the Past

That was not strictly true, Nigel said to himself later, reviewing recent events in the comparatively unemotional atmosphere of his bedroom. "It's not that the case is out of my control so much as that I've got to shift my grip on it. I am now, I suppose, what they call an interested party. Not that Georgia's breakdown can mean much, as far as she is concerned. The trouble is that it seems to mean the hell of a lot to me. Oh, my aunt! What an impossible detective I am, to go falling in love with my chief suspect. Or have I fallen in love with her? A question teeming with human interest; but we shall have to leave analysis till later. The point at the moment is that Georgia has to be kept out of Blount's claws. Funny thing, I hadn't realised before, but I don't think I really care for Blount. It must be his bald head. But it isn't Georgia only. There's that infernal brother of hers. She'd be heartbroken if anything happened to him. And if one thing is clear in this case, it is that she's deadly afraid he did the murders. She's been giving herself away over that from the very beginning. The way she looked at him in the hut that first morning; and pretending to have heard a thump overhead yesterday evening, when Edward had said he was in the morning room, so as to give him an alibi over Knott-Sloman; and letting it be known at once that she expected to benefit under the will, thus drawing suspicion off her brother and on to herself. Does she know something? Or does she just suspect?

"Well, that's an academic point. I've got to clear her brother, too. But that only leaves Lucilla. I can't go trying to pin everything on her, just because I don't want Georgia to be hurt. Not that there isn't a pretty good case against Lucilla. Still, I don't want to take part in a general *sauve-qui-peut*. It is not, now that I come to think of it, strictly accurate to say that Georgia has a face like a monkey — a damned attractive monkey, anyway. No, not a monkey at all. To hell with monkeys. They don't have noses that tilt agreeably upwards, or eyes that — Nigel's unprofessional rhapsodies were cut short by the entrance of Inspector Blount. His eyes sparkled briskly behind his horn-rimmed spectacles, and even his bald head seemed to give off a complacent glow — the ruddy bloodhound, thought Nigel with gross injustice.

"I saw you went for a walk with Miss Cavendish. Get anything out of her?" said Inspector Blount.

"Nothing relevant," answered Nigel coldly. "We were talking about O'Brien most of the time."

Blount cocked an inquisitive — and, to Nigel's eyes, distinctly offensive — glance over his horn-rims.

"I've been at Mrs Grant again. She swears black and blue that Bellamy was about the place till two-thirty on the day of the attack, so that lets Mr Starling out."

"It lets him out over the Bellamy incident," said Nigel grumpily.

"Uh-huh. I've also had a very interesting talk with Edward Cavendish. I made it pretty clear that he was in an awkward position, and it would be advisable for him to explain certain things as soon as possible. I hinted at the motives he might have had for both crimes, and so on. He blustered for a bit. Then he caved in. Said, very reluctantly, that the reason he had been so upset and nervous lately was that he was afraid his sister might know more about the crimes than he liked to admit to himself."

"Oh, he said that, did he?" exclaimed Nigel belligerently.

"Uh-huh. He said something about an incident that had been hushed up: Miss Cavendish shooting some relation of hers out in Africa — in self-defence, she had claimed. He also said that he had been most seriously disturbed about it all when he heard that Knott-Sloman had been poisoned, because he knew that his sister had some poison in her possession. I asked him what kind of poison, and he said prussic acid. I asked him what motive his sister could have had for killing a man she loved and another man who was a comparative stranger. At that point he stiffened up again. Said he had never meant to suggest that his sister had done the murders, but was just afraid that the discovery of certain facts about her by the police might lead them to connect her with the crimes. As to motive, he said, not too convincingly, it was quite ridiculous to suppose she could have had any reason for killing O'Brien and

Knott-Sloman; and, as the police had been so fertile in suggesting possible motives for himself, no doubt they could find an equal number for Georgia Cavendish without his assistance."

Had Edward Cavendish seen Nigel at that moment he would certainly have regretted the way he had caved in to the inspector. Nigel's tow-coloured hair had fallen over his right eye, there was an angry glow on his high cheekbones, and in his eyes a merciless and eager ferocity. Edward had put himself contemptibly beyond the pale. There was no reason now why Edward should be spared, except Georgia's own happiness; and it had now become a question of saving Georgia's life, brother or no brother. Nigel suddenly had a clear vision of Edward running out ahead of him to the hut that morning. There was something in it crying out for explanation. Yes! By heaven! That was it. And to think that he had never noticed such an obvious point before.

The inspector was saying, "After that little conversation with Cavendish I had another look at those notes you made on the case. In the light of what Cavendish has told us, your case against his sister is very convincing, Mr Strangeways. The point you made, that she was the only person intimate enough with O'Brien for him to trust her with him when he was expecting an attack — that's a very illuminating point indeed. Yes."

"I should have thought it would apply equally well to Lucilla Thrale. She had been intimate enough with him. And, by the way, Miss Cavendish told me about that poison this morning. She takes it with her on her expeditions, in case the worst comes to the worst. She was quite open about it."

Blount scratched his chin and looked at Nigel shrewdly. "You seem to have altered your mind recently. Well, there's no law against that. But I shall have to have a serious talk with Miss Cavendish. Perhaps she will tell me more than she told you," he added with ponderous irony. It fell rather flat on Nigel, whose mind was busy piecing together the rest of the evidence round that incredible glimpse of Edward running out ahead of him to the hut. More than ever now, it was necessary to dig out some more knowledge about O'Brien. He remembered the retired officer, Jimmy Hope, to whom Knott-Sloman had recommended him. Where did he live? Oh, yes, Staynton, near Bridgewest.

"I want to borrow that car of O'Brien's," he said. "Will it be all right?"

"Certainly. What's in your mind now?"

"I hope to be able to tell you a pretty staggering story when I get back. Hold yourself in till then. And for God's sake don't go arresting Georgia Cavendish. It'll only make you look silly when you have to release her again . . ."

An hour later Nigel was sitting in the untidy living room of a bungalow. Jimmy Hope was boiling water on a primus, hospitably insisting that he always made tea at four o'clock if any of the troops popped in. Jimmy Hope was a tall, bronzed man, active but nervous in his movements, and a little gone to seed. He was wearing a collarless shirt, a pullover, a pair of stained khaki riding

210

breeches and thick woollen socks. He gave Nigel tea and some stale scones, pouring out a whisky for himself.

"Rotguts," he said sardonically. "We had to take it in the War after a bit to get us off the ground, and now we've got the habit. The extraordinary thing about poor old Slip-Slop was that he never seemed to need it. Well, now, what d'you want to know? Whoever did him in deserves all that's coming to him — and a sight more. He was the sort of fellow you simply can't imagine dead. Though he did look pretty washed-out when I saw him last."

"Oh, you've met him lately, have you?"

"Rather. He asked me over last August, just after he'd settled in at Chatcombe. Looked like death, I thought, but he was in rare good form. Said he was just making a will and was giving half his money to the foundation of a fund for the painless extinction of staff officers. 'S a matter of fact, he asked me to witness the will."

"Did he really? There's been quite a to-do about that will. You and Bellamy were the witnesses, then?"

"No, not Bellamy. A sour-faced woman: his cook, I think she was."

Nigel digested this intractable morsel in silence. It eliminated the obvious reason for the attack on Bellamy: they should have realised before, though, that O'Brien would almost certainly leave him a legacy and therefore he would not witness the will. Then the murder of O'Brien very likely had nothing to do with the will either. Moreover, there was the singular fact that, although Bleakley had presumably asked her, Mrs Grant had not mentioned that she had been a witness.

"I suppose O'Brien didn't tell you what he was going to do with the will? Send it to his solicitors, or what?"

"No, he didn't. How are you fellows getting on? Hot on the trail? Or oughtn't one to ask?"

"Well, we're making progress of a sort. The trouble at the moment is that we can't find out anything about O'Brien before he joined up."

"You'll be lucky if you ever do. We never did. He and a young chap called Fear were posted to the flight I was in, late '15, if I remember right. Absolute David and Jonathan they were. I suspect they both joined up under age. Fear was an Irishman, too — came from Wexford — good family, and all that. Used to tell us all about his parents and the Big House, and so on. The only thing he wouldn't say a word about was O'Brien. We asked him often enough, because O'Brien never gave us any change, but he wasn't saying anything. In the end we gave up trying to find out. Someone started the usual rumour that O'Brien had had to leave the country in a hurry — taken a potshot at some bloke he didn't like from behind a hedge, in the good old Hibernian way, and we left it at that. Wouldn't be surprised myself if it was true, judging from the way he used to lay for the Huns. A holy terror he was — didn't care two hoots what happened to himself as long as he brought his man down."

"Was he like that from the beginning?" asked Nigel.

"Funny you should ask that. He wasn't. Mind you, he was a genius in the air from the beginning. But quite

212

reasonably careful at first. Then, after he'd been out a week or so, he suddenly asked for leave. Never seen anyone in such a stew. Moved heaven and earth to get it. But it was no good. Fritz was all over us in the air just then, and all leave had been stopped. O'Brien went about like a lost soul for a fortnight. Then one morning I came into the mess. He and young Fear were reading a letter. They both looked as if they had hit the side of a mountain. It was after this that O'Brien went crazy. He'd attack anything. Trying to get himself killed, none of us had the least doubt about it. But he was such a bloody wonder with a plane that he simply couldn't bring it off. It was the other fellow that went down every time. Honestly, we got a bit afraid of him. He went about with a look in his eyes like a ghost out of hell."

"What happened to Fear?"

"He was a damned good flyer, too. But he wouldn't have survived as long as he did without O'Brien. O'Brien used to look after him like a mother up in the air. Fear got quite peeved with him at times about it; said he could look after himself. But when they were separated he was killed soon enough."

"How was that?"

"They both got flights. I'd come home with a blighty by then, and only heard about it later. Fear was shot down leading his flight in a ground-strafe, late in 'seventeen, I think it was. O'Brien lost the whole of his flight the same week, in the same sector, I believe. Ruddy murder it was. They say that after Fear got his packet O'Brien spent all his spare time dropping out of the clouds on the wretched Huns. They thought he was possessed by seven devils."

"Well, I must be getting along. Thanks awfully for the information," Nigel said.

"Afraid I've not been much use. Once I get yarning away I can't stop. Have a spot before you go. No? Well, cheerio. Look me up some time when you've finished your sleuthing. A fellow gets pretty lonely with nothing but hens to talk to."

Nigel drove back very fast to Chatcombe. The interview with Jimmy Hope had thrown little new light on O'Brien, but it had cleared away most of the complications about the will. Nigel tried to fit in this discovery with the framework of the case that was slowly growing up in his mind. Yes, it unquestionably did fit. He pressed exultantly on the accelerator and scattered a flock of geese. Then the word "Wexford" came into his mind. O'Brien had joined up in company with a young man from Wexford — a young man whose parents lived in a Big House. Edward Cavendish had visited some big house in Wexford every summer before the War, Georgia had said. He had fallen in love, she thought, with a girl there. So there *was* a link between the prewar O'Brien and the prewar Cavendish. Was it purely a geographical one? Neither Cavendish nor O'Brien admitted having met each other before they were introduced by Georgia. He must go over to that place — what was it called? — Meynart House, at once. If it proved that Cavendish and O'Brien had not met there, it would be a wild-goose chase. If they *had* — well, he might get down to some rock-bottom motive for O'Brien's murder; and, even if he didn't, the fact that Cavendish had pretended not to have met O'Brien before would be suspicious enough.

Arrived back at Chatcombe, he found Inspector Blount and a telephone message awaiting him. The latter said that Lady Marlinworth would be glad if he would step over to the Towers as soon as he found it convenient, since she had an important piece of news for him. The inspector said that the post-mortem report had come in: Knott-Sloman had been killed by swallowing sixty grains of the anhydrous hydrocyanic acid. He had probably died in ten to fifteen minutes — but that had now become irrelevant. It was perhaps a little strange that so neat and tidy a murderer, Blount said grimly, should have apparently made no attempt to remove the pieces of the doctored nut. Still, the risk was probably not worth his while. Nigel told Blount what he had discovered about the will. Bleakley had just been having a conference with the inspector, so they routed him out and asked him had Mrs Grant ever been interrogated on this subject. She had, he said, and had told him she knew nothing whatever about the will. Blount at once went off to ginger up her memory. Nigel said he was going over to his uncle's house. Bleakley asked if he might go over with him. He was a shade disgruntled, because Blount had hinted that there might have been more interrogation of Lord and Lady Marlinworth, considering that they had been at dinner with O'Brien only a few hours before he was murdered. The superintendent took this amiss, not so much as an insinuation against his own efficiency as a lack of respect — amounting almost to blasphemy — for the landed gentry.

On their way out Nigel saw Georgia in the lounge. He lingered for a moment to ask her how she had got on with Inspector Blount. But, before he had time to open his mouth, she said, in tones that were doubly heart-rending because they held no trace of reproach or self-pity:

"I didn't think you would have to tell them about the poison."

It was said in a small, matter-of-fact voice, with just the faintest accentuation of the "you" to twist the blade round in the wound. Nigel had often rehearsed in fantasy a situation such as this. How often had his patience not been galled by books, plays and films in which hero and heroine protract an idiotic misunderstanding into chapters or acts or reels of wooden standoffishness, just for lack of the few words of obvious explanation at the beginning. If, he had said to himself dozens of times, I should ever find myself in such a theatrical situation, which God forbid, I should of course clear up the misunderstanding at once, like any other normal sensible person. It was therefore doubly aggravating to find now that his tongue simply couldn't form the correct words. "Go on, go on," whispered his enlightened self, "tell her you didn't give her away over the poison. There's no point being high horse and chivalrous, anyway — she'll find out the truth soon enough." But some unpredictable force had arisen in him, arguing with dull obstinacy. "I refuse to be the person to tell her that she was betrayed by her brother. It's no good. I refuse." Furious with this obstinate saboteur, Nigel yet found himself outside the room again without having said a word. Another triumph of savagery over civilised reason, he exclaimed to himself bitterly.

It was dark by the time he and Bleakley stood outside the front door of Chatcombe Towers. The butler let them in, nicely grading his reception to their respective social stations, Nigel being accorded the tepid affability due to a gentleman, while Bleakley, who was only a person, received a welcome without the chill off. They were then ushered into the drawing room, where Lord and Lady Marlinworth were sitting. This room was a veritable jungle of heirlooms, and an admirable setting for Lady Marlinworth, who, in spite of her age, had lost none of her agility in climbing up and down family trees. Here every development of aristocratic taste could be seen as clearly as strata on a geological section. Eighteenth-century pieces swooned elegantly, confronted by the brassy, assured stare of Victorian lumber. Layers of relatives, supercilious in gold frames or self-righteous in plush, made a commendable attempt to conceal totally the Edwardian wallpaper, whose scarlet and purple and orange writhings would have surprised even a veteran of delirium tremens. The visitor who, unnerved by the inhuman and popeyed glare of a platoon of bemedalled ancestors, sought to escape to another part of the room, would find himself hemmed in by archipelagoes of small tables crowded with the miscellaneous loot that these same military gentlemen had brought back from their foreign service. Lady Marlinworth was very proud of her room. Her husband by long practice had learnt to thread his way through its mazes. It was haunted by the faintest sandalwood and lavender perfume: also, perhaps, by the ghosts of generations of domestics, whose lives had been appreciably shortened by the dusting of it.

Lady Marlinworth received Nigel with composed pleasure. Superintendent Bleakley, whom she had instantly summed up as one of the lower orders but quite respectable, she addressed with cooing condescension. Her husband surveyed Bleakley, his well-bred but faded look giving him a marked resemblance to his great-grandfather's Derby winner, that hung on the wall behind him surrounded by a painted coat of arms, a heavily framed picture in oils which had originally represented the Relief of Lucknow, but now suggested a square of homemade toffee, a Whistler, and a photograph of some young women playing croquet — apparently at midnight in a churchyard.

"I understand," said Lord Marlinworth, tapping a rickety table that shuddered ecstatically under his fingers, "I understand there has been another fatality at the Dower House."

"We must have this sort of thing stopped, Mr. Bleakley," said Lady Marlinworth. "It is becoming quite a scandal in the county. I can't remember anything creating such a stir since that unfortunate De Lenthay gairl eloped with a chemist's assistant."

"Not quite a chemist's assistant, my dear. The young man was engaged in scientific research, if my memory serves me. Quite reputable. An undergraduate of Cambridge. I am profoundly distressed, though, by Knott-Sloman's sad end. A rough diamond, perhaps; but to one who has served his country so well in the field of battle much may be forgiven."

"Nonsense, Herbert," said the old lady with spirit. "I have no patience with such sentiments. He was a most disagreeable man. A good military record is no excuse for a man becoming the proprietor of a brothel."

Bleakley started convulsively, and Lord Marlinworth blew his nose in a deprecating manner.

"Oh, come, come, Elizabeth. Not a — ah, hum. It was a roadhouse, I believe the term is. No doubt the young people of today indulge themselves in pleasures which may seem a trifle bizarre to our generation. Petrol has wrought great changes. But we must not judge them too harshly. We, after all, were young once. *Et ego*, superintendent, *in Arcadia vixi* — what?"

"That is as may be, my lord," said Bleakley cautiously. "But what I came to — that is, I wonder if you could spare me a few minutes to talk over one or two points of the case, my lordship — er — your lordship?"

"By all means, my dear fellow, by all means," fluted Lord Marlinworth. "My wife will excuse us if we adjourn to my little sanctum — a poor thing but mine own, as the bard has it."

He piloted the bemused superintendent through the intricacies of the drawing room, and the door closed behind them.

"Now, Aunt Elizabeth," said Nigel, "you have some news for me."

"You asked me to try to remember when I had seen Mr O'Brien before —"

"Great Scott! Have you got it?" interrupted Nigel.

"Now, don't rush me, my dear Nigel," reproved Lady Marlinworth, clasping her slender fingers over a photograph album in front of her. "Remember, I am an old woman, and I will not be rushed. I happened to be going over some old photographs this morning, taken when I was much younger than I am now. I came to this volume, relics of a tour in Ireland, just before the war. Such a charming country. Such a pity it has got into the hands of a gang of desperadoes. Well, now, a cousin of my mother's, Viscount Ferns, had a place in the County Wexford. Burnt down now, I fear, like all those beautiful old houses. The year I am speaking of, your uncle and I stayed there for a week. The hospitality was quite embarrassing. I recollect your uncle saying that if our English politicians were invited for a fortnight to one of those country houses, the Irish Question would cease to exist. One day it was decided that we should pay a visit to our nearest neighbours — people called Fear — at Meynart House, seven miles away. We drove over there. Such a charming couple. And their daughter — what was her name now? — ah, yes, Judith. A delightful gairl — a tomboy, you know, but quite a ravishing little beauty. There was a son, too, I believe, but he was away from home just then. They said that we must have a picnic on the Blackstairs Mountains, just behind the house. So we all set out.

The ladies were accommodated on donkeys — asses, they call them out there — so old-world, I always thought. Now there's no use looking impatient, Nigel. I shall tell this story in my own way. Where was I? Oh, yes, on the donkey. Well, Mr Fear, who was the soul of kindness, saw that I was not used to such an animal. One had always connected donkeys with low people on Margate sands; but of course in Ireland it was quite different. At any rate he told one of his men to look after me. I have an idea he was an under-gardener. But, really, a most respectable young man, and so well spoken. Quite a wit, too. He and I got on famously together. I remember, after the expedition Herbert rallied me on the subject, and said I had lost my heart to the young man. Mr Fear took a photograph of us together. I dare say you would be interested to see it."

The old lady passed across the album. Nigel looked at the photograph she indicated. His aunt, swathed in furlongs of millinery, billowed over a long-suffering donkey. Holding the donkey by a short head-rope was a man in breeches, Norfolk jacket and a hat turned down all round. The man had no beard and no scar on his face; but the mobile, homely features, the impish expression that seemed about to break out any moment into some outrageous jest, the deep eyes — they were Fergus O'Brien.

"Well, I'm —" exclaimed Nigel. "This is brilliant of you, Aunt Elizabeth. You must have a marvellous memory for faces."

"Herbert always says that it is second only to that of our dear Royal Family. I didn't connect Mr O'Brien with the young man at Meynart House, though, until I came on this photograph. I'm sure his name wasn't O'Brien in those days."

"What happened to the family, do you know? I should like to go over there and have a talk with someone, if they're still living in the district. "

Lady Marlinworth sighed. "It is a very tragic story. My cousin, Viscount Ferns, told me something of it when he came to England in 1918. The son was killed in the war. That was the final blow. It broke his parents' hearts. They both died soon after. A most promising boy, I was told."

"The *final* blow?"

"Oh, yes. The daughter had been drowned. It must have been only a year after I met her. Her poor father found her one morning in the lake on the estate. So tragic. Such a lively girl, and really, sweetly pretty."

"I suppose you haven't photographs of any others of the party?"

"I'm afraid not. Herbert was going to take one of Judith Fear — he was quite captivated by her. But she was a shy, wilful thing. She just ran away laughing, on those long legs of hers."

The phrase called up an almost intolerably clear image of the girl in Nigel's mind. He felt as if he had known her, and her death was a personal loss.

"Well, thanks no end. I must be off to Ireland now. May I take this photograph ?"

Nigel hurried back to the Dower House and consulted a Bradshaw. If he drove to Bristol, he would be able to catch the eight fifty-five, and connect at

222

Newport with the Irish Mail to Fishguard. He ran upstairs and flung a few things into a suitcase. Now what else would he want? Photographs. He found Inspector Blount.

"Look here, Blount, I've got through to O'Brien's prewar existence at last. I'm going across to Ireland tonight — to the place where he was last heard of. I believe I'm on to something big. Can you hold your hand till I get back? And I want photographs of everyone in this house, alive or dead."

The inspector measured him in silence for a moment. Then he said, "They've got sets of photos at Taviston. You could call in for them on your way. But I'd like something more to go on if I am to postpone an arrest."

"Georgia Cavendish?"

Blount nodded. "Everything points to her. It's your own doing, Mr Strangeways, you know. You made out the case against her."

Nigel groaned inwardly. "Look here," he said, "what about Mrs Grant? How does she explain herself?"

"I hauled her over the coals about the will, but she just pinched up her lips and said that Bleakley had asked her if she knew anything about Mr O'Brien's will, and she had said no, because she didn't. She was ignorant of its contents, that is to say. He had not asked her if she had witnessed it, and therefore she had not given him the information. She was not going to be mixed up with all this sinful bloodshed more than she could help. A very difficult woman. Uh-huh."

"Hmm. Pretty outrageous sophistry on her part. She may find herself mixed up with it more than she likes, however. Now, look here. I must be off. I can just catch the train at Bristol if I take O'Brien's Lagonda. Keep your hands off Georgia till I come back. I believe I'll be able to give you a case then. Here's something to be going on with. The morning we found O'Brien's body there was a single track of footprints straight from the veranda to the hut. Now, neither Cavendish nor I, presumably, had the faintest idea he had been murdered. There was therefore no reason for us to take anything but the direct route to the hut, which would have been over the footprints. But Cavendish, who was just ahead of me, deliberately kept off them, and I followed suit unthinking. Now, why should Cavendish have so carefully avoided treading on those footprints unless he wanted them preserved? *And why should he want them preserved if it wasn't he who originally made them, in O'Brien's shoes, to conceal the fact that O'Brien had been murdered?* Laugh that one off! Well, cheerio! See you the day after tomorrow."

Nigel rushed out of the house, leaving Inspector Blount scratching his chin and thinking long thoughts.

CHAPTER
THIRTEEN

The Old Nurse's Tale

At seven thirty-nine the next morning Nigel stepped out of the train at Enniscorthy. He went into the station yard, where two ancient Fords were standing, buttressed up by two ragged and rather wild-looking young men. Nigel felt ridiculously a foreigner. He approached the driver of the less decrepit of the two cars and asked did he ply for hire.

"Where d'ye want to go, misther?"

"Well, I'm looking for a place called Meynart House. It's somewhere up by the Blackstairs Mountains. I don't know if there's a village there."

"That's a hell of a long way away. Why don't ye go up Vinegar Hill, now?" The young man jerked his head at a small hill above the town, crowned by what looked to Nigel — who had not seen round towers before — like a large inverted flowerpot. "Ye get a grand view up there, ye do, shure'." I'll drive you that way for half a crown." The young man produced a sudden and brilliant smile, and Nigel had the utmost difficulty in withstanding its hypnotic power. He cleared his throat and said with what firmness he could muster:

"No, I'm afraid I must go to Meynart. I've important business there."

The young man looked startled and incredulous. Then he said, "Well, I don't mind takin' ye there. How much will ye give me? Is five pounds too much for ye?"

The other driver, who had been an interested spectator of this colloquy, broke in huskily: "Don't you go in Flanagan's car, misther. Ye'd never get there at ahl. Now I'll take ye for four pound fifteen." He, too, released upon Nigel a smile of hypnotic brilliance.

"You keep outa this, Willie Noakes, or I'll give ye a crack. Don't listen to him, misther. He'd jaw the hide off an ass. Make it four pound ten."

Nigel hastily clinched the deal with him, fearing bloodshed. Then he asked if he could get some breakfast before they started. His driver spat and turned to the other competitor.

"Did ye hear that, Willie? The gentleman does be asking for breakfast, at half seven. Why, misther, everyone's asleep still, I declare to God Almighty."

"Ye might go and knock up Casey."

"Ah, he'd have the skin off me back, he would so. I'd be afeared to do ut."

Nigel insisted that he must have something to eat. Flanagan looked contemplative, then gave vent to a piercing screech:

"Jimmie! Jimmie Nolan! Come on outa that!"

A red-faced, fat man emerged yawning from the station. He wore a stationmaster's cap, but no other signs of officialdom.

226

"Come on till I tell ye what this gentleman does be wanting," yelled Flanagan at the top of his voice. "He's afther coming ahl the way from England without bite nor sup, and he perishing with starvation. Will ye give um some breakfast now or he'll be dying on us."

"Is ut breakfast?" wheezed the stationmaster amiably. "C'mon in, sir. Did y'ever eat soda bread? I'll bet ye they don't have that in England."

He led Nigel away, too dazed by all this unorthodoxy to make much protest. As he entered the station, Nigel turned and shouted to the driver — shouting seemed infectious hereabouts — "I'll be back in half an hour."

"Time enough, misther, time enough," yelled Flanagan. "You take yer bellyful, misther." He then lay down in the back of his car, threw his legs over the front seat and resumed his siesta.

A good hour later Nigel staggered out of the stationmaster's house. He had been plied so continuously with food and questions about "the big city" that his brain and stomach felt equally congested. He got into the car and they set off up the most precipitous streets, the Ford boiling and shuddering like a patient in high fever. Men and women came out of the doors of their houses and yelled encouragement. The children playing in the gutters were the most beautiful, the dirtiest and the healthiest that Nigel had ever seen. Now they were in open country, undulating, rich, vividly green, with the mountains blue in the distance. Nigel felt impatient and breathless and a little sick, as though he were going to meet a lover. At intervals of three miles the Ford stopped abruptly. Flanagan would get out, scratch his head, open the bonnet, and gingerly prod the interior. Every time, the car started up again. The process was, like the Roman Catholic Church, a triumphant blend of faith and ritual.

By half-past ten they had reached the little village of Meynart. Flanagan had without great difficulty wormed out of Nigel the nature of his business. Stronger men than Nigel have found it impossible to resist the impudence, the raffish charm, and the faintly sinister atmosphere of potential intimidation which Flanagan's sort turn upon the stranger. The young man entered into the situation with a wealth of suggestions and conspiratorial pantomime. Arrived at Meynart, he made straight for a whitewashed house in the window of which were set out clay pipes, jars of virulent-looking sweets and picture postcards. He could only have been in there a couple of minutes; but when he emerged he became the centre of a crowd which seemed to have materialised out of thin air rather than collected. A short meeting was then held, with Flanagan in the chair, in the course of which Nigel learnt (a) that Meynart House had been burnt down in the Troubles, (b) that the gentleman in the car was a decent quiet man and his overcoat must have cost a power of money, (c) that Patrick Creevy had seen one of his cows leppin' over a stile yesterday and consequently knew that a stranger would be arriving in the village before long, (d) that he, Nigel Strangeways, was a lawyer come from the big city to find out if any of the Fear family were living, because an uncle of theirs was just after dying in America, and he a millionaire — this was Flanagan's contribution to the debate, Flanagan having assured Nigel that it would go hard with him if he was discovered to have any connection with the police and (e) that if he wanted to know about the Fears he'd better ask Widow O'Brien.

The meeting then adjourned to a whitewashed cabin at the far end of the village. The crowd lifted up its voice and summoned the widow to come on out of that till she heard what this gentleman had to tell her, and he after coming all the way from America, God help him, with his pockets full of gold. At this point Flanagan turned ferociously upon the crowd and shooed them away like a pack of geese. He then seized Nigel's arm and hissed into his ear, in tones that would have done credit to a Lyceum melodrama: "Don't let on you're one of the police, now, or th' ould lady will folla ye with a hatchet."

Widow O'Brien showed no marked homicidal tendencies, however. She was a small, fat woman, with faded blue eyes, a face crinkled and mellow as a nut, and a red shawl over her head. She curtsied to Nigel and stepped aside for him to enter her cabin. It was reeking with peat smoke that seemed in no hurry to escape through the hole in the roof that served as a chimney. Nigel sat down on a three-legged stool, blinking and coughing, trying to accustom his eyes to the gloom. A hen attempted to roost on his lap, and a goat inspected him over the half-door in a deprecating manner. Widow O'Brien was fussing about somewhere in the darkness. Then she produced a teapot and began pouring out two cups.

"A cup of tea, sir, after your journey," she said with exquisite courtesy. "It's nice strong tea, so it is. Ye could trot a mouse on it."

Nigel felt an insane desire to be able to produce a live mouse out of his breast pocket, with the immortal Boy Scout alacrity of Harpo Marx. Instead, he took a gulp of the tea, and opened the conversation. It was difficult in these parts to feel any urgency, even when Georgia's peace of mind was at stake.

"I've come over to make enquiries about a family called Fear, who lived at Meynart House. They tell me that you are the best person to ask for the information."

"Is it the Fears?" said Mrs O'Brien comfortably, leaning back in her rocking-chair. "Indeed and I can tell ye about them. Didn't I live at the Big House from the day me husband died on me, God rest his soul, till it was burnt down by them blackguards the Tans? They was Quality, Mr Fear and his lady. The like you'll not find if you walked on your bare soles from here to Dublin."

"I suppose you were the housekeeper, Mrs O'Brien?"

"I was not," replied the old woman, highly flattered. "I went up to the Big House to be Miss Judith's nurse, when she was a baby. Ah, a dotey little love she was. And her brother Dermot. He was a right young gentleman, too. But bold!" Mrs O'Brien lifted her hands and rolled her eyes to heaven. "Manny's the time I've had him across me knee — and Miss Judith, too — and belted them with a slipper. Imps of mischuf they were, leadin' each other on and tormentin' the life out of every wan in the place. But ye couldn't be angry with them for long, shur'. They come and look up in yer face and smile at ye like two angels, and they just afther throwing stones through the greenhouse or painting the poony blue or some ijjut prank."

"It must have been fine for them, running wild in a place like this. I expect they were a credit to you when they grew up, Mrs O'Brien."

The old nurse sighed. "They were so, while they were spared. Master Dermot was a right young man. Shur ahl the young girls in Wexford and Wicklow was runnin' afther him. He was a grand lepper on a horse and won ahl the steeplechases in the sooutheast and a cup at the horse show up in Dublin. But he was a wild unaisy creature, and he wouldn't rest quiet till he'd gone traipsin' off to fight for the English. He and that young limb of Satan, Jack Lambert, just went off one day widout a word to annyone except maybe Miss Judith. His mother, poor soul, got a letter from him two days after — and she tearin' her hair out with anxiety — sayin' how he and Jack had joined the English army and they'd bring her back a lovely present from Berlin."

"Who was Jack Lambert?"

"He was under-gardener at the House. Viscount Ferns recommended him to Mr Fear, and he worked hard enough — I'll say that for him — except when he and Master Dermot went stravaguin' off on some wild spree or other. But he was only here for a year, when Master Dermot and he got it into their mad heads that they must go and join the English, as though they couldn't get ahl the excitement they wanted here. What happened to um after, I don't know at ahl. Master

Dermot was killed in France, the year of the Easter Rising. His da never overed it. A shtrong, shtern man he was, God help him, but that was the finish of him. He died in the next year, and poor Mrs Fear didn't live long after. She was the last of the Fears, and I'm thinkin' ye'll be hard set to find a more unlucky family."

"Miss Judith died, too?"

"She did. Before her brother, the darling. It was like having me own child taken away. What cut me heart was for the poor thing to be so unhappy when she died. She killed herself, ye see — and only a year before she'd been merry as a sunbeam the day long, the way ye'd think nothing would ever come nigh to harm her."

The old nurse fell silent. Nigel felt something pricking his eyes that wasn't peat smoke. Ridiculous to feel this way about a girl he had never set eyes on. Or hadn't he? Light began to flood into his brain, as two images made contact.

"Wait till I brew another pot of tea," Mrs O'Brien was saying, "and I'll tell ye the whole story."

She moved witchlike to and fro in front of the fire. Nigel got up to stretch himself, but collided with a side of bacon that hung from the rafters and sat down again hastily.

"Miss Judith grew up to be a lovely big girl — the apple of her da's eye, she was. Everyone loved her; the horses and cows would come gallopin' up when she called them; and she was so tender-hearted she'd give her shift to a beggar. A right madcap she was, too, like her brother. But sweet and innocent as the Mother of

God. Too innocent, I do be thinking, for this world. Well, now, there was a relative of the master, Mr Cavendish, that used to be staying at the house every summer. He came first when Miss Judith was a girleen, no more than thirteen years old. He used to play with her, and she called him Uncle Edward. He was a fine upstanding man, with grand clothes and a motor car and all, the like she'd seen few enough of round here, where the gentry was so poor, even in thim days, they'd bite the nobs off a hearse for hunger. After a few years the way it happened Miss Judith thought she was in love with him, and he old enough to be her father as the storybooks say. Mind ye, now, I'm not saying annything against him: he was a gentleman though a bit starchy in his ways for us Irish people. Miss Judith used to tease the life out of him and he took it very well. He fell in love with her, annyway. Ye'd not blame him if ye'd seen her; she'd a beauty that took the shine out of every girl in County Wexford. And, as I'm tellin' ye, she thought she'd fallen in love with him. Now her da was a stern man and had a temper like Satan, the way she was half afeared of him even though she had the spirit of nine. She knew he'd be in a powerful rage if he found out about her and this Mr Cavendish, she being so young and her da still thinkin' her only just out of the cradle. She was a great book-reader, too, and had romantic ideas the way young girls will. So what must she do but keep this precious love affair a secret. She'd write letters to Mr Cavendish and make me smuggle them out of the house to post them, her da having half a suspicion of the affair, I'm thinking. She ahlways could twist me round her pretty finger when she'd her heart set on something. And Mr Cavendish used to send letters to a girl friend of Judith's to send on to her, the way her da wouldn't find out by the handwriting.

"It was wonderful folly, and often enough I'd be tellin' Miss Judith no good would come of ut, but shur' it only made her mad. But that was nothing to what happened next. This Jack Lambert I'm telling ye about came along."

"What date was this, Mrs O'Brien?"

"Young Lambert went into service with Mr Fear in 1913. I remember he came the autumn after Mr Cavendish left. And it wasn't many months neither before he had Miss Judith bewitched entirely. Ah, he was a bold young devil; he had a tongue would make St Peter hand over his keys in a jiffy, and he'd look at ye with thim dark blue leprechaun's eyes of his the way ye'd be afther reaching out for a stoup of holy water against him. Well I remember the day — it was the next spring, and spring does be a fearful time for young maids — Miss Judith coming to me, half-laughing and half sobbing she was. 'Oh, nannie,' she says, 'I'm so happy. I love him. I don't know what to do at all, at all.'

"'Bide ye patient, my pretty lamb,' says I, 'sure he'll be coming back this summer and ye'll be eighteen then, and maybe your da will let ye be fiancied.'

"'Ah,' says she, 'it's not that one is in it. It's Jack Lambert I love,' says she, looking proud and haughty as an empress and half-frightened with it like a little girl afther finding a purse of money in a boreen.

234

"'Glory be to God,' says I, 'not that young spalpeen! Shur' he's only your da's gardener.'

"But divil a bit of good it was talkin' to her. Gardener or no gardener, she loved him and she'd marry him. She was frightened, though, that Mr Cavendish would find out ahl about ut when he came over in the summer, and she was so tender-hearted she didn't want him to be hurt. Mr Cavendish didn't come, after all, for the war broke out that time. But he went on writing to her, and she wrote to him, though not so often; but she couldn't quite bring herself to break it to him that she didn't love him anny more. And ahl the time she was slippin' off to Jack Lambert on the sly or ridin' with him about the country, her da having made Jack her groom. And when she wasn't with him she'd be dreamin' about him, the way annyone but a great gom like her da could see what was amiss.

"So it went on the rest of that year. But Miss Judith got so lovesick in the latter end she swore she must marry him, and she'd run away with him if her da didn't let her. I knew well enough he would not, he being a proud, austere man, would rather see her a tinker in a ditch, for all he loved her, than marrying into the common people. So I thought I'd best write to Mr Cavendish and ask him to come over and see if he couldn't win Miss Judith out of her madness. The day I wrote to him, she came to me and told me in secret that Master Dermot and Jack were going to join the English army, and everything would be ahl right now, because he'd be made an officer and come back with great renown, and her da couldn't deny her after that.

"It was almost the last time I ever saw her lookin' happy. It may have been that she couldn't really live widout Jack. She was spry enough at first. But the weeks went by and she got pale and silent and wouldn't take pleasure in annything. Her poor mother thought it was the green sickness, but I knew better. Miss Judith used to go walkin' by herself, like a ghost. Manny's the time I saw her starin' into the lake, still as a tree. She was so still and pale and sad, shur', ye'd be hard set to tell which was herself and which was the reflection. Mr Cavendish had written to her once or twice that time, but it didn't seem to do her anny good. One night I found her cryin' over a letter of his. She hid it away quick, but she'd not deceive me. 'Oh, nannie,' she said, 'what am I to do? It wasn't my fault. What did I do to him that he's so cruel. If Daddy finds out —'

" 'Holy Virgin,' says I, 'are ye tellin' me ye're going to have a baby, Miss Judith?'

"With that she burst out wildly, half laughing and half crying. 'Oh, you funny old dear! No, of course I'm not. I almost wish I was, though.' And she'd never tell a lie, God rest her. Then she turned very calm and quiet, the way I was frightened out of me skin lest her wits had gone. 'I'll never renege. I'll write to Jack. He'll know what to do. I'll ask him to come back. He must come back. Aren't I his beloved?' she said in the grave, serious, story-book way of hers. So she up and wrote to him, and for a few days she was like her old self, expecting him anny moment to be sailin' across the wather. But he never came, the heartless young devil. A week after that they took her up out of the lake. Her pretty cheeks were so wet ye'd think she was cryin' still, and she dead seven hours, maybe."

There was a long silence in the cabin. The old nurse was wiping her eyes on her sleeve, and Nigel trying to control the lump in his throat. He could see nothing but a girl looking into a lake, so sad and still and pale that she might have been her own reflection. After a bit he asked the nurse if she had a photograph of Judith Fear. Mrs O'Brien got up and fumbled about in a chest of drawers. Then she handed a photograph to Nigel. He took it to the door, to see more clearly — though it was only for confirmation of what was already a certainty in his mind. From the faded cardboard there looked out at him a dark-haired girl, a shy teasing smile on her lips, and in her eyes a sadness half guessed: a thin, elfish face, promising beauty and generosity and danger. It was the same girl, without shadow of doubt, whose photograph Nigel had seen in O'Brien's cubicle the day he had arrived at the Dower House. After that it seemed almost superfluous to produce the snapshot of his aunt on the donkey. The old nurse at once identified the young man as Jack Lambert. The circle was complete: a noose for someone.

Mrs O'Brien was astonished to hear that the wildcat young rogue, Jack Lambert, had borrowed her own name and become the great airman, Fergus O'Brien. His features had been altered quickly enough by wounds and whatever insatiable demon it was that drove him on, so when his photograph began to appear in the press, no one in this remote part of the world would have recognised it, even if they had seen it. It was strange, though, Nigel remarked to the old woman, that nobody ever seemed to have linked Fergus O'Brien with his early days in Ireland. Had he no relatives at all? No schoolfellows? What had he been doing before he turned up at Meynart House?

The nurse assumed that expression of shocked relish with which old ladies anticipate a nice bit of scandal.

"There can't be anny harm in telling ye, you being a friend of the family and everyone concerned in their graves. They did say around here that Jack Lambert was the natural son of Viscount Ferns. A girl over at Macmines, a farmer's daughter, went away suddenly to Dublin. There was rumours about it, the man being Viscount Ferns' tenant and he often visiting over that way. The girl was never heard of again and her da wouldn't so much as lay his tongue to her name. But when Jack Lambert came along, and his lordship afther using his influence with Mr Fear to get him taken on at the big house, people did be talking about ut and saying among themselves that Jack was the spit and image of the Viscount. Shur' I don't know if it was true; but his lordship was a lonely old man without childer of his own, the way he might have wanted the young man nigh to him, though he was a bastard, God help him. A poor weeshy old fella his lordship was at the latter end. After the Tans burnt down Meynart House, he took me into his service. A great one he was for his garden, though he would be calling all the flowers by heathenish names the like ye never heard of. Antirrhinums was his favourite, I do remember. Everyone around came to look at them. One time

238

during the Civil War, when his lordship was in England, the Staters and the Republicans had a battle in the garden, a right battle. After the battle was over, James Clancy — him that was the head gardener then — showed both armies round the garden, and he told me they particularly admired his lordship's antirrhinums."

Nigel reluctantly took leave of the old woman, promising he would send her a pound of the very best tea from London when he got back. He extracted Flanagan from a crowd of men who were staring over a wall in silent homage at an enormous black sow, and returned to Enniscorthy without mishap. When his train was just about due a terrific commotion arose in the station yard. An ass cart piled with mailbags shot in at the main entrance. It was driven by a postman, who rang a brass bell ecstatically and yelled salutations to everyone on the platform. The train was already appearing from the tunnel a hundred yards along the line when the cart hurled itself down the ramp, across the metals and up the far side. As the ass trotted along the platform, anyone who had letters to post threw them into the cart with encouraging shouts to its driver. It reached the far end of the platform a neck ahead of the mail van, and everyone congratulated themselves on the punctuality of the Irish Mail. Nigel felt that the country had given him a good send-off.

As the boat hung and swung on the huge channel swells, his mind was busy readjusting the shape of the case to fit these new and all-important revelations. Nigel was fortunate to possess an almost perfect verbal memory. He set himself, in the close confinement of his cabin, to recall everything that had been said from the first moment he had arrived at Chatcombe. Whenever he came to a remark that seemed of significance, he jotted it down in his notebook. So the outline of the case slowly filled in. Light filtered, like the dawn through his cabin ports, into places that had seemed irreclaimably dark. At last all but one of them were illuminated. There could be no doubt that Edward Cavendish had shot O'Brien. Everything went to confirm that. But the motives of the killings: these had to be altered and extended until they were almost unrecognisable from the point of view of his first dark gropings. Just one point remained outside the connecting lines he had drawn between all the others: an obstinate, stubborn point which irritated him disproportionately, partly because it did not seem really essential to the whole design and partly because it could so easily have been cleared up. An Irish packet-boat could scarcely be expected to carry as part of its fittings a copy of a rather obscure seventeenth-century playwright. But it was the lack of this, Nigel realised later, that — by holding him back from making a complete explanation of the case — led to the dizzy and melodramatic tragedy which finally terminated it.

CHAPTER
FOURTEEN

"As a Tale that is Told"

While Nigel Strangeways was dozing fitfully through South Wales, the occupants of the Dower House awoke to what the inspector had informed them would probably be their last day in it. There was a feeling of relief and irresponsibility in the air, as in a school on the last morning of the term. Even though they might not yet be free of the case, they would be glad to get away from the Dower House. It had become a prison, and there is a certain relief at walking out of a prison, even if one only entered it as a visitor — even, perhaps, if one is stepping out of it straight on to a scaffold.

No such speculations troubled the pretty head of Lily Watkins as she laid the breakfast table. She was thinking of a certain steady-going young farmer's lad, of springtime and her new Sunday frock. She was calculating, too, the amount of tips she would get from the ladies and gentlemen, and the amount of prestige that would be hers for ever as the finder of Knott-Sloman's body. What Mrs Grant was thinking was, as usual, clear to none but the recording angels. She bent over her frying rashers, if such a one could ever be said to bend, and eyed them with the thin-lipped and complacent regard which she would turn upon a pack of sinners sizzling in hell. Lucilla Thrale yawned and stretched her magnificent body — with a studied, practice-perfected languor, half asleep though she was. Then she came fully awake. Her muscles grew tense and her eyes on guard. Only a few more hours to keep it up. Philip Starling was stumping about his room, his shirt-tails hanging outside his trousers, his face sparkling with animation as he rolled round his tongue phrases that would finally demolish that charlatan editor of *Pindar*. When he had polished them to his satisfaction, he muttered, "Well, no one can say I don't see life." Edward Cavendish was trying to shave; but the razor shook uncontrollably in his hand and the look in his bloodshot eyes would have seriously discomposed a number of shareholders if they had been there to see it. The look in his sister's eyes was much less easy to read. Indignation, bitterness, fear, indecision, passed into some desperate resolve, and then softened beautifully into a quite different expression, as though a lover's hand had come over her face.

Georgia Cavendish was the first person, except for the policeman at the door, that Nigel met when he entered the house just before lunch.

"Tell me," she said. "Edward — is he —?" She could say no more.

"I'm afraid there's no doubt he shot O'Brien," said Nigel slowly, as though choosing his words to soften the blow. "He's in a tough place. I —"

"No, don't say any more. Nigel, the inspector told me about — about the poison, and Edward telling him I had it. I asked him. I couldn't really believe you had told him. I — it was damned decent of you."

She took Nigel's hand and quickly brushed her lips over it. Then she stared at him irresolutely for a second, her mouth trembling. Then she exclaimed, "Oh, hell and damnation!" and spun round and fled from the room. Nigel stared stupidly at the back of his hand, smiling vaguely. After a bit he collected himself and went to find Inspector Blount. The inspector was with Bleakley, routing about at the back of the house. The three adjourned to the morning room, and Nigel told them everything of significance he had learned in Ireland. Bleakley's eyes popped with excitement and his moustaches quivered like antennae. Blount took the news more calmly, but the eyes behind the big horn-rimmed spectacles registered every point with alert intelligence.

"Well, Mr Strangeways," he said when Nigel had finished, "that just about clinches it. I'm glad I held my hand, though after that point you made about Edward Cavendish and the footprints it was evident that the main suspicion must lie on him and not his sister. That was a very nice little piece of work of yours."

Nigel looked modestly down his nose. He drew out a packet of Player's and passed it round. Then he said:

"Before we start connecting up this new stuff with the rest of the case, I wonder would you mind if I set out all the other points which connect Edward Cavendish with the crimes. I put in some hard remembering last night on the boat and I've collected quite an imposing display. I don't want to seem to boss this little conclave," he added, "but there are several things which I know and you don't — only because I happened to be on the spot and you weren't. I didn't see their importance before, so I didn't mention them."

"You go right ahead, Mr Strangeways," said Blount.

"Well then, starting at the highly correct place, the beginning. The morning we found O'Brien. It is significant that when I got downstairs I found Cavendish on the veranda. Jaded businessman taking a breath of fresh country air. All proper and correct. But a nasty-minded, suspicious person might say that he was waiting there for someone to come out, so that he might tactfully keep this someone away from the footprints in the snow. Item, when I said that I was going out to the hut to see if O'Brien was awake yet, Cavendish slipped up badly, and quite failed to produce the correct reaction — any reaction at all, in fact."

Bleakley looked puzzled. The inspector did too: then he suddenly smacked his bald head in excitement.

"You mean, he should never have known that O'Brien was sleeping in the hut?"

"Exactly. He ought to have registered surprise. He should have assumed that O'Brien was in his bedroom in the house. The fact that he didn't suggests that he knew O'Brien was in the hut, and how would he know that unless he had seen him there that night? Point number two: not only did he keep me off the footprints, but also, when the rest of the party appeared on the veranda, Cavendish was very fussy about my seeing that

244

they shouldn't tread on the footprints either. Singular presence of mind in a layman who was still dithering under the spectacle of his host's corpse. Then there was the matter of the shoes. Cavendish was wearing an overcoat and therefore able to bring them out again to the hut underneath it. Moreover, he had far more time than the rest to plant them there. He was mopping his brow with a handkerchief and no doubt he used it to handle the shoes without leaving fingerprints. I suggest that he meant to plant them at once but couldn't find a favourable moment: I'm pretty sure they weren't in position when I had my look round. Then the others came out. My attention was concentrated on them to see how they were taking it and to make sure they didn't touch anything. He could easily have dumped the shoes then — probably when Lucilla threw her swooning act. That's all my contribution for the moment."

There was a short silence. Then the superintendent slapped his knee. "By gum, sir, I've just thought of something else. You talking about Cavendish puts me in mind of it. Do you remember Bellamy saying as how he had overslept that morning? He'd meant to go out the night before and watch the hut, but he felt so sleepy he dozed off and didn't even wake at his usual time in the morning? Well now, what was the evidence given by Miss Cavendish?" He licked his thumb and turned over the pages of a notebook. " 'I went into my brother's room,' " he recited in official monotone, " 'and asked for some sleeping draught: he'd packed it in his luggage. He was awake and got up to get it.' Now,

245

gentlemen" — he leant back triumphantly — "what does that suggest to your minds?"

"I think I can do that one," replied Blount dryly. "It suggests that Cavendish gave Bellamy some of the sleeping draught so that there should be no interference with what he proposed to do in the hut."

"He might have given me some too. I'd intended to stay on guard, but I dropped off and slept rather late. It might have been put in my coffee cup as they were passed along after dinner," said Nigel.

"That means he must have found out somehow that you were down here to investigate at O'Brien's request," said the inspector. "Will you lend me those notes a minute, sir?"

Bleakley handed the notebook over.

"I see that after this statement by Miss Cavendish, her brother deposed that he went to bed soon after twelve but couldn't get to sleep. He was still awake when Miss Cavendish went into his room at quarter to two. A man doesn't carry sleeping draught about with him for ornament. If he wasn't able to go to sleep, why didn't he take some of it? It suggests that he had not been back in his bedroom long before his sister came in."

All three sat back as if by common consent. The first stage of the case against Edward Cavendish seemed to be satisfactorily erected. Inspector Blount lit another cigarette and took up the tale.

"Those points of yours are very valuable to *us*, Mr Strangeways, but they will carry little weight in a court of law. Let us turn to the question of motive. It seems to me that, in the light of the fresh evidence you have given us, we shall have to discard Mr O'Brien's will as a factor of primary importance in the crime. We do not know whether Cavendish was a beneficiary under the will. If he knew he was, and committed murder to get the money, he would not be likely to pretend ignorance of the contents of the will, for, when it comes to light, the fact that he feigned ignorance would at once cast suspicion on him. On the other hand, he would surely never destroy the will if he had committed murder in order to profit by it. It may be, of course, that — knowing his sister to be a legatee, and knowing that she would give him as much money as he needed out of her share — he planned to kill O'Brien. But, however that may turn out, I think we will all agree it was a subsidiary motive, if one at all.

"Clearly Cavendish's chief motive was revenge. That fits both the tone of the threatening letters and what we now know about his earlier days in Ireland. He falls in love with this girl, Judith Fear. The strength of his attachment is proved by the way he, a man of substance and reputation, consented to the rather childish and undignified expedient of sending letters to her through a girlfriend of hers."

"His sister told me, too," Nigel put in, "that she thought he had been very hard hit by a love affair in Ireland, and that's why he had never married."

The inspector looked at Nigel with a kind of paternal severity. "That is further confirmation," he said dryly. "In due course Cavendish finds that Miss Fear's letters are becoming less and less affectionate, and in the end a letter comes from her old nurse to say that she has fallen in love with a gardener. That would be a severe blow, both to his affection and his pride. The nurse implores him to come over to Ireland and straighten things out, but he cannot get over, and has to content himself with writing to Judith Fear, urging her, no doubt, to cease from her madness and come back to her old lover. He presses his claims hard. Judith calls him 'cruel'; the weight of his pleading, added to the predicament she is in, is too much for a young, inexperienced girl."

"What do you mean, 'predicament'?" asked Nigel, breaking into the inspector's flowery discourse.

"Well, there can't be much doubt that she *was* going to have a baby. Her pallor, her change of manner, and what she finally did, all point to it. She told the nurse she wasn't maybe, but a sensitive girl like that might well be afraid to confess it even to her old nurse. At any rate, the next thing Cavendish hears is that she has drowned herself. Imagine his state of mind. This young scapegrace has not only taken the girl away from him but has deserted her when she most needed him and as good as killed her. Cavendish can do nothing. Jack Lambert has disappeared, and there is nothing to connect him with Fergus O'Brien. But the desire for revenge is not extinguished by twenty years. O'Brien is brought one day to the house by Georgia Cavendish. Somehow or other Cavendish learns that he is Jack Lambert. We shall have to establish that link before we can bring a really sound case into court, and it may be very difficult unless we can trap Cavendish into giving himself away over it. It is quite possible that, when he first heard of Judith's suicide, he asked for a detailed description of Jack Lambert, and he would be able to recognise him from that in spite of the changes time had made in his features.

"Then comes the final provocation. The man who has taken Judith Fear away from him twenty years ago now robs him again. Lucilla Thrale, who is his mistress, leaves him for O'Brien. His mind is made up now, if it wasn't before, that he will kill O'Brien. He writes the threatening letters. Very melodramatic, no doubt, but the whole case is melodramatic and the man is half mad with his hatred of O'Brien. He was a frequent visitor at Knott-Sloman's roadhouse, and wrote the notes on the typewriter there so that there could be no possibility of their being traced back to him. His opportunity comes when he is invited to the Christmas party down here. He sends off the third note and makes his preparations. He knows that his sister has some poison, and prepares the nut as a second line of attack. His first line is to shoot O'Brien and stage it as a suicide: it is partly with that end in view that he wrote the threatening letters, to ensure that O'Brien should be armed.

"When he arrives at Chatcombe he finds that the hut is the ideal place for a murder; away from the house, and soundproof. The next business is to get O'Brien there. No doubt he would have got him out into the hut on some other pretext, but it wasn't necessary, O'Brien having planned to sleep there already. Perhaps Cavendish had guessed he would do so for safety. He

249

dopes you and Bellamy to make sure there shall be no interference that night, should his opportunity arise. Then he watches."

"Where from?" interrupted Nigel.

"The veranda, most probably."

"Just on the off-chance that O'Brien would get out of bed and go for a stroll into the hut? Very sanguine of Cavendish."

"Well," said the inspector, rather nettled, "Cavendish may have made an appointment with O'Brien to meet him in the hut: or he may have discovered that Miss Thrale had asked O'Brien to meet her there. I can check up on that when we start asking Miss Thrale a few questions about one of the other developments of the case. The point is that O'Brien *did* go to the hut, and you've as good as proved that Cavendish did too. Surely you're not going back on that, are you, Mr Strangeways?"

"No, no. Certainly not. Pardon the interruption."

"Cavendish may have given O'Brien some very plausible reason for his coming to the hut, but I don't think O'Brien would have been right off his guard at first. They talk for a bit, and then Cavendish pounces on him, and there's a struggle in the course of which Cavendish turns the revolver against O'Brien and shoots him. The struggle was the first point at which his plans went wrong, because it left clues — the bruises on the wrist and the broken cufflink — which aroused your suspicions of the apparent suicide. Cavendish must have relied on lulling O'Brien's watchfulness to the extent of being able to get at his gun without a struggle. He failed in that, but he had a bit of luck in finding in O'Brien's pocket or on the table the note written by Miss Thrale asking O'Brien to meet her in the hut. He keeps it for future use, to draw suspicion on to Miss Thrale should the suicide fake be exposed. He tidies up the mess, and prepares to leave. Then he discovers to his horror that the ground is thick with snow. He sits down to find a way out of the trap. Finally he puts on O'Brien's shoes, walks backwards to the house, and everything is apparently OK."

"But Knott-Sloman has seen him enter the hut," put in the superintendent.

"Uh-huh. And he may have seen a lot more. Anyway, the next morning Cavendish gets the shoes back into the hut and thinks he's sitting pretty. He is soon disillusioned. The police suspect murder. He plants Lucilla Thrale's note in O'Brien's room for the police to find. But worse is to come. Knott-Sloman tells him he has seen him in the hut last night and demands a large sum for his silence. Cavendish is in desperation. His finances are in a precarious state and to buy off Knott-Sloman would ruin him. He temporises, but is determined that Knott-Sloman will have to go. So he puts the poisoned nut among the plateful by Sloman's bedside. His anxiety and distraction of manner were due to the uncertainty whether Knott-Sloman might not go to the police with his story before he came to the fatal nut. On top of all this Lucilla has weighed in with another piece of blackmail. She will tell the police what motives Cavendish had for murdering O'Brien, unless he buys her silence. It may have been after this that

Cavendish planted her note in O'Brien's room. At any rate, he is in a fearful predicament, and he very cleverly takes the first opportunity of spiking Lucilla's guns by admitting to the police the motives he had for killing O'Brien."

"What about the other note?" asked Nigel. "The one written by Knott-Sloman threatening action if O'Brien did not recompense Lucilla for deserting her?"

"I should say Sloman *did* find it in the hut, in spite of his denial, and sent it off in the package of letters to be rid of it."

"But why on earth not burn it at once? It wasn't of potential value, like Cavendish's letters. Now suppose Arthur Bellamy had found it."

Nigel's supposition made both police officers lift up their heads in surprise. He continued:

"Soon after I'd discovered O'Brien's body I asked Arthur to look round the hut to see if anything was missing. He might easily have found that note. Now he was absolutely devoted to his master and was quite capable of taking justice into his own hands. He finds the note and it arouses vague suspicions in his mind. Later in the morning he confronts Knott-Sloman with it. Sloman sees the danger of this note getting into the hands of the police, and plays for time. He plans with Lucilla to lay out Bellamy and take the note from him. After lunch Lucilla, sitting in the lounge, rings the bell. Bellamy comes. Meanwhile Sloman gets the poker, hides behind the swing-door. He cracks Bellamy on his way back to the kitchen, takes the note and hides the body and the poker."

"But your own argument still holds. Why didn't he burn the note?"

"Everything had to be done very quickly. He was supposed to have gone out of the billiard room to get the right time. He slipped the note back into his pocket. Now Lucilla told us that she handed over Cavendish's letters to Sloman after lunch on that day. He very likely had them in his pocket. It's surely not too imaginative to suppose that the note he had taken from Bellamy got slipped into one of the envelopes as he put it in his pocket. As soon as the game of billiards with Cavendish is over, he goes into the morning room and packs up these letters into a parcel and buzzes off to the village to post them. After that he finds that he's lost the note. Hard cheese on old Sloman."

"Yes, yes," said the inspector meditatively, "that might well have been it. But it's going to be the devil to prove."

"Don't you worry." Nigel was looking very grim. "Bleakley, will you ask Miss Thrale to step this way. The one advantage we amateurs have over you chaps is that there are no rules to stop us hitting below the belt." He added to Blount, "You'd better pretend afterwards that you didn't hear what is about to transpire."

Lucilla Thrale swayed in, beautiful and wary and sleek as a panther. Nigel took up a sheet of paper that lay in front of him.

"Before Knott-Sloman was so unfortunately taken from our midst," he said, "he left a confession. He says, amongst other things, that it was *you* who originated the plan for the attack on Arthur Bellamy. Is this —?"

He had no need to continue. Lucilla's lovely face flushed darkly. Her upper lip rose in a snarl.

"The swine!" she exclaimed shrilly. "It was his idea from beginning to —" She stopped suddenly and clapped her hand to her mouth. But it was too late by then. Blount rushed into the breach that Nigel had made, and Lucilla had to capitulate altogether. Before long they had a signed statement from her. Her part in the assault on Bellamy had been very much as Nigel had conjectured. Knott-Sloman had assured her, so she said, that they were both in danger as long as Bellamy had possession of the note: because the police would say, what Bellamy had already hinted to him earlier in the day, that they had conspired to kill O'Brien through fear of their blackmailing attempts being exposed by him. Bellamy, Knott-Sloman told her, had threatened in a very ugly way what he would do to him if he obtained further proof of his suspicions. But Knott-Sloman had assured her that he was only going to knock Bellamy out and get the note from him. After that it would be their word against his. She had been horrified to hear that the man had been nearly killed. Nigel and the inspector, however, came independently to the conclusion that Knott-Sloman had been so alarmed by Bellamy's threats of violence that he had determined to get in his blow first — and a decisive one. The one point over which Lucilla stood firm was that she had no notion the murderer of O'Brien was being blackmailed by Knott-Sloman.

After this Lucilla was dismissed. Blount wagged his head solemnly at Nigel and his left eyelid dropped the fraction of an inch. "Your methods are awful unconventional, Mr Strangeways," he said. "Well, it's a good thing we've got that Bellamy business cleared up. It was clever of Knott-Sloman to admit, when we confronted him with his note, that he had been looking for it in the hut and failed to find it. It took our attention away from the connection there might be between it and the attack on Bellamy. There can't be much question that Cavendish killed Knott-Sloman because he was threatening to tell us he'd seen him in the hut. I doubt Sloman wouldn't let Lucilla in on that; he wouldn't want to share the hush money with anyone else. Well now. Yes. We have motive and opportunity against Cavendish for both the crimes, though, of course, the motive for the second depends on his having committed the first. We shall have to do a good deal more inquiry and investigation, particularly at the Cavendishes' house in London. But we've got enough against him, I doubt, to ask for a warrant. What do you think, Mr Strangeways?"

Nigel started a little, and said dreamily, "Sorry; I've been lost in admiration of your narrative powers."

"Come now, Mr Strangeways. Are you trying to pull my leg?"

"Heaven forbid! No. I think you've made out your case admirably. But I believe I can get you certain evidence at once that will make any further investigation unnecessary. It's in a book, by the way. I expect O'Brien had a copy in the hut; if you'll just lend me the key I'll go and fetch it. The name of the book, you'll not be surprised to hear, is *The Revenger's Tragedy*."

Nigel levered himself to his feet. He was just taking the key from the inspector when a scream rang out, another scream, and then they heard something bumping down the staircase. Nigel was out of the door first. It was Georgia's voice they had heard. A pang of utter despair wrenched his heart. The three arrived at the foot of the staircase in a bunch. The constable who had been on guard at the front door was already there, bending over Georgia's body. Nigel thrust him away and knelt down beside her.

"Georgia! Darling! For God's sake! Are you all right? What's happened?"

The eyelid he could see fluttered in a movement absurdly like a wink. Then closed. Then her head turned and both eyes fluttered open.

"Oh dear," Georgia said dazedly, "I didn't half come down the hell of a crack."

It was at this moment that they heard through the open hall door the roar of a powerful engine accelerating away. Blount and Bleakley rushed out. They saw the back of O'Brien's Lagonda swaying down the curving drive. At the wheel was Edward Cavendish. Bleakley was blowing his whistle like mad. A police car swerved round out of the back yard. "Telephone!" Blount snapped to the superintendent. "Get the net out. You know the car's number."

Georgia gave Nigel's hand a squeeze. "Go along," she said. "Do what you can. I'm all right. I had to give him a chance."

256

Nigel bent down swiftly, kissed her, tweaked her smooth brown cheek, and ran out of the house, leaving Georgia sitting against the stair-foot, her legs spread out in an unladylike fashion, but smiling with peculiar contentment. Nigel just had time to swing himself into the back of the police car as it leapt forward. Blount leaned over from the front seat.

"Damned convenient for him his sister fell down the stairs just at that moment, blast her!" he said.

"Yes," said Nigel, looking down his nose. "I suppose he happened to be in the lavatory by the front door, and took the opportunity of the policeman leaving his post to slip out and do a bunk. A brilliant piece of opportunism by old Edward."

Blount looked at him irritably. "Well, he hasn't an earthly chance of getting away. A confession of guilt, that's all it is."

The tyres screamed. They were at the end of the drive and the gates were shut. Blount leapt out and shook them. They were locked too. The chauffeur blew Wagnerian blasts on his horn. The lodgekeeper emerged, in very slow motion.

"Unlock the gates! Get a move on! Police."

"Gennulman told me his lordship had given orders for the gates to be locked," mumbled the man uncertainly.

"If you don't open those — gates this instant I'll have you gaoled for obstruction. That's better. Which way did he go?"

The lodgekeeper pointed. They flung into motion again. A minute had been lost. That meant a mile, when one was chasing a Lagonda. The high, narrow hedges tearing past made Nigel feel as if he was being shot out of the mouth of a cannon. No, not a cannon, he thought as a sudden bend sent him sprawling into the other corner of the back seat, emphatically not a cannon; something more tortuous. One of those involved brass instruments that Thomas Hardy delighted in: a serpent!

> " 'There is a place provided in hell
> To sit upon a serpent's knee,' "

he sang dolefully. But was silenced by a branch that flicked out at him like a wet towel. Everything was blurred and rackety and disintegrating: it might have been a dream out of which he had just awoken. Only he was still in it. What were they doing, chasing a respectable financier down a Somerset lane? Wild West stuff! What's the hurry? He can't get away. We may only drive him into doing something desperate, and that would be a fatal error. Nigel became aware that his teeth were gritted together and his knees trembling. He was excited, enjoying the hunt. Blood sports in Somerset. Faugh!

They had stopped at a fork. Blount was out, scanning the road surface for tyre marks. He found what he wanted in a muddy patch a few yards down the left-hand road. They bucketed off again. "Keeping to the lanes," shouted Blount. "Looks as if he was making for Bridgewest." They were whirring like a swarm of hornets up a long incline. At the top the road fell away, and they swooped and swerved down the hillside for three miles. In the distance they could see the telegraph poles of a main road. Cavendish could twist and double in the lanes, but once he was on the main road he'd have to go straight for a bit, and the police patrols would be out. They took a blind corner at fifty. The main road was only a hundred yards ahead. Unfortunately there was a cow, too, and it was only twenty yards ahead. The chauffeur trod hard on his brake, but they were still doing thirty when they hit the cow. It was like hitting a man in the stomach with one's fist. The cow was carted up on to the radiator and dropped aside. They jumped out. There was glass everywhere. The headlights were twisted askew. The chauffeur opened the bonnet. One of the vanes of the fan had been broken clean off.

Blount set off running towards the main road, Nigel after him. They reached it. Almost opposite them, drawn up to the side of the road, was the Lagonda. But no sign of Edward Cavendish. Then they saw the placard, on a hoarding in a long broad meadow to their left.

AEROPLANE FLIGHTS.
FIVE SHILLINGS, FIVE MINUTES.

They ran into the meadow. There seemed to be nothing there but a hut, a windsleeve, and a small, brown-faced man in overalls. He was as laconic as the advertisement. When Blount asked had he seen a man get out of that Lagonda over there, he jerked his thumb at the sky. High and far away, Blount saw a little dot in the air. "Police," he panted: "we've got to get after him. Have you another plane? Or a telephone?"

"No telephone," said the brown-faced man, chewing expressionlessly on a piece of gum. "Here's Bert, though."

Another plane drifted silently over their heads, kissed the earth beyond, and ran down the field. They sprinted after it. Blount fired out orders like a machine-gun. Two passengers descended bemusedly from the plane. The mechanic was sent to ring up the nearest R.A.F. depot from the AA box and give them the number of the first plane.

"Got enough petrol?" snapped Blount.

The pilot jerked his head. They tumbled into the open cockpit. The plane taxied to the other end of the field, then turned into the wind and rushed at the horizon with a giant crescendo of engine. Would they never rise, thought Nigel, and looked down to find the earth already dropping and streaming away from them like green rapids. They banked steeply, with the lovely slow gesture of a dancer's hand. The speck in the sky was gone, but it was a cloudless day and they might pick it up again before long. What was happening out of sight up there? What would Cavendish do when his five shillings' worth was up? Or had he chartered the pilot for a longer journey? The sky gazed back at them blankly. The answer was not very important anyhow.

After ten minutes the speck was in sight again. They were heading for the sea. Perhaps Cavendish had hoped to escape to France or Spain.

" 'If to France or far-off Spain,
You'd cross the watery main,
To see your face again the seas I'd brave,' "

sang Nigel raucously. His voice was drowned by the
engine and torn away in tatters by the racing wind.
Blount bellowed in the pilot's ear:

"Are we gaining?"

The pilot nodded taciturnly. Blount fumed and
fidgeted. The whole of the heavens seemed to stretch
between them and that little black dot to the south. He
looked down. They were hardly moving at all. The
patchwork earth crawled past beneath reluctantly. He
gazed forward again. By Jove, they *were* catching them.
The speck was now a two-winged insect. Imperceptibly
and remorselessly as the minute hand pursues the hour
hand, they were creeping up on their quarry over the
blank white face of heaven. He turned and gesticulated
to Nigel. Cursing his short-sightedness, Nigel leant out
from the shelter of the cockpit. The wind fluttered his
eyelids madly, and he hastily drew in his head before
they were blown right off. The pilot, turning, shouted:

"Fred's seen us! He's holding her back!"

Yes, they were moving up fast now, high above the
other plane and to her right. But when they were within
quarter of a mile, their quarry seemed to lengthen her
stride again. They soon knew why. The pilot put down
his nose and dropped towards her, every wire
screaming. Now they were near enough to see the two
figures in the cockpit. Now nearer; so near that Blount
could see the revolver which Cavendish was pressing

into the back of his pilot. Their long dive brought their wheels within fifty feet of Cavendish's head. He looked up. Nigel was not to forget for a lifetime the look on his face. Then Nigel suddenly shouted words which the wind whirled away before Blount could catch them, and waved a handkerchief as though for a flag of truce. For Cavendish, still pointing the revolver at the pilot, was clambering desperately out of the cockpit. He stood, swayed, tilted, hung an eternity so, and then fell. He fell with arms and legs sprawling, like a dummy figure. Down and down and down. For years he seemed to be falling. They had lost sight of him altogether a few seconds before there appeared on the sea's face a tiny white splash, as though someone had thrown a very small pebble . . .

CHAPTER
FIFTEEN

The Tale Retold

"So she was avenged at last," said Nigel.

It was a week after Edward Cavendish had chartered the pilot for that long journey — a longer journey than he had anticipated. Nigel and his uncle and Philip Starling were sitting in Nigel's town flat. They were sipping sherry as an appetiser for the story which Nigel had promised to tell them. Philip knew nothing of the recent developments: Sir John Strangeways had received the documents and an outline of the case from Inspector Blount, but he hoped to have a number of points cleared up by his nephew this evening. Blount also had received an invitation but had pleaded an accumulation of business, and Nigel had not pressed him, which was unusual in one of his hospitable nature. Philip Starling was gazing with satisfaction into his glass of sherry: he tilted it, pursed his mouth and said, "A-ah. Some very tolerable liquor. Oxford taught you one thing at any rate, old boy." Sir John looked more like a wire-haired terrier than ever. He had the extraordinary faculty of sitting in a deep armchair and still looking alert. You expected him any minute to jump down and go trotting busily off, his ears cocked and his nose twitching. As Nigel spoke, Sir John was raising a glass to his lips. It stopped in mid-air. He cocked his head and said:

"'Avenged *at last'?* O'Brien was murdered a fortnight ago."

"Well, he had a long time to wait. Over twenty years. I should have thought 'at last' was in order," Nigel replied teasingly.

His uncle gave him a long, appraising stare. "No," he said finally, "you can't get away with that. You're just working up to one of those exhibitionist dramatic disclosures of yours. I know you. Showing off. Pah! Well, go ahead. Not bad sherry this."

"No," said Nigel, "nor is it meant to gargle with. Well, I suppose I'd better begin. You know the facts of the case; I've told Philip a certain amount and he is quite capable of making up the rest, especially if he goes on drinking my sherry at this rate. Besides, he gave me the solution. So you both start level."

"Gave you the solution? What the devil do you mean? Are you referring to that elementary point about Hercules and Cacus — a story which any —"

"Schoolboy would be able to tell you," interrupted Nigel. "No. I am not. What did you think of Blount's statement of the case, Uncle John?" he asked with apparent irrelevance.

"Me? Well, a bit fanciful in places, but there were some pretty big gaps in the evidence to bridge. Seemed the best possible explanation of all the facts. Cavendish's flight clinched it, anyway; and Blount's finding the poison gone from the place his sister had hidden it in, afterwards. Why do you ask?"

"Only that, academically speaking, of course, I thought Blount's interpretation was damned awful," said Nigel, staring dreamily at the ceiling. Sir John started up in his chair, exclaiming:

"But, good Lord, I thought you agreed with him. Now you've made me spill my sherry. All this infernal exhibitionism."

"I agree with him over a number of points: all the unessential ones, in fact. But the main outlines, the blood and bone of the case — far from it. I was just going to set up my own idea of its anatomy, so to speak, when Edward Cavendish did his ill-considered escaping trick."

"But, hang it all," said Sir John irritably, "Blount told me that you agreed with him about Cavendish having shot O'Brien."

"Oh, I did. I still do."

"I suppose," said his uncle with elaborate sarcasm, "that you are going to tell me that Cavendish shot O'Brien but was not the murderer."

"You are coming on very nicely," declared Nigel encouragingly, "that *is* just what I am going to tell you."

Philip Starling groaned. "Oh, God. Riddles. Just like our chaplain after a gaudy. I'm going."

He lay back and poured himself another glass of sherry. Sir John was staring at Nigel with painful intentness, as though his nephew were changing into a sea-serpent before his eyes.

"I'll just run through the weak points in Blount's case," said Nigel. "Now I never doubted that Cavendish went to the hut that night and made the footprints to bear out the suicide he had faked; after all, it was my idea. I'm also still quite prepared to believe that Knott-Sloman saw him enter the hut, and later blackmailed him, though there's no real evidence for that at all. But Cavendish as a murderer, or rather as capable of this particular kind of murder — no, I simply couldn't take it."

"You mean that Cavendish found O'Brien already dead when he entered the hut?" asked Sir John.

"In a sense," replied Nigel obliquely. "Now Blount, quite correctly, I thought, judged that O'Brien's will could only represent a secondary motive, if any at all. Revenge, he decided, must have been Cavendish's chief incentive; which fitted in with the tone of the threatening letters. That was his first error: a cardinal one. Philip, you knew Cavendish. An able, conventional, pompous, rather unhumorous business man. Can you for a moment imagine him composing these letters?"

Nigel handed them across, and prowled restlessly about the room while Philip Starling read them.

"No. Scarcely poor old Edward's style, are they? I can't imagine him indulging in all this melodrama. And the witticism about O'Brien going out on the Feast of Stephen, like King Wenceslas — that would be quite beyond the old boy's power. On internal evidence, Cavendish couldn't have written these, I agree."

"There you are," said Nigel triumphantly, "and Philip is an authority on stylistic evidence. But if

Cavendish *didn't* write them, he couldn't have planned the murder. It's altogether too much of a coincidence, for two separate people to have planned to kill O'Brien on the same day. Now for the psychological possibilities. Blount's theory was that Cavendish first put O'Brien on his guard by means of the threatening letters. Then followed him into the hut after midnight, knowing that O'Brien would be armed and quite apt to take a potshot at any intruder. He then held O'Brien in light conversation until he saw a chance to jump on him and turn the revolver against him in the struggle. Now I ask you, who on earth, knowing O'Brien's reputation as a fighter, would be crazy enough to make an attempt like that? Yet Blount had the nerve to suggest that Cavendish would. *Cavendish!* A man who was shivering with apprehension from the moment O'Brien's body was discovered: a man whose nerve cracked so badly that he began to make panicky and criminal insinuations against his sister as soon as Blount pressed him hard: a man who ran away before he had been accused. And the inspector had the almighty neck to claim that a jelly of a man like this would put his head right inside a lion's mouth — which was just about what he would have been doing if he'd carried out the murder plan as reconstructed by Blount. I must say, I was disappointed in old Blount over that."

"But the inspector was quite prepared to believe that Cavendish had got O'Brien out into the hut on some apparently innocent pretext: lulled his suspicions somehow or other," objected Sir John.

"Making an appointment with a bloke after midnight in a lonely hut is a damned curious way to lull his suspicions. After those letters, O'Brien was bound to be on the *qui vive* against everyone, and if Cavendish wrote them he'd know that. Anyway, if you really think Cavendish was capable of a plan of which the cornerstone was the snatching of a loaded revolver from a dangerous man, then I'll resign."

"I don't like your metaphor, but I think you've made out your case so far, Nigel."

"Good. Then there's the matter of the sleeping draught. Blount was right in deducing that Cavendish must have gone into his bedroom not long before Georgia came in to ask him for the stuff, and in pointing out that this strengthened the theory that he had been in the hut. One could understand him doping Bellamy. But why me? How could he have known that I was a danger to him? I've never allowed my name to get into the papers in connection with the cases I've worked on. Only my intimate friends know that I go in for this kind of thing."

"Still, he might have found out," said Philip. "It's difficult to touch blood and not be defiled with a certain measure of vulgar notoriety."

"Now, now, Philip, don't get truculent. Well, we'll pass over that and turn to a nut which is very much harder to crack, though Knott-Sloman didn't find it so. Blount's idea was that Cavendish brought the poisoned nut with him as an alternative should his first plan fall down. But O'Brien didn't crack nuts with his teeth. And if Cavendish used the nut simply as a receptacle, why go to all the bother of sandpapering it so thin that it would probably burst in his pocket, anyhow? It seemed clear to me at once that the nut couldn't have been intended for O'Brien. For Knott-Sloman, then? Now if Cavendish wanted to get rid of him because he was blackmailing him over O'Brien's murder, he would scarcely doctor up a nut days before he had done the murder, merely on the off-chance that somebody might butt in on him when he was doing it and blackmail him later. That means he must have been carrying the poison about with him, and carpentered the nut after Sloman threatened to expose him to the police. And Blount and I had agreed that would be difficult at the Dower House, with police strolling in and out all the time. Besides, if he intended to kill Knott-Sloman to prevent himself being exposed to the police, why adopt such a chancy delayed-action method? He couldn't possibly be certain that Knott-Sloman would eat that particular nut in time to prevent him giving his information to the authorities. The only possible solution on these lines was that Cavendish proposed to do away with Sloman because he was blackmailing him over Lucilla. Theoretically that was possible. But I've already shown that Cavendish was psychologically n.b.g. as the murderer of O'Brien. So it implied there were two murderers in our merry little house-party — 'you in your small corner, and I in mine,' as the hymn puts it — quite separate and unconnected. Well, I couldn't quite swallow that."

"A lucid and convincing piece of ratiocination," declared Philip Starling.

"The pleasure is mine," said Nigel. "There were other minor objections, too. For instance, Blount's theory necessitated Cavendish's having recognised O'Brien, though he had never set eyes on him before, from a twenty-year-old description of Jack Lambert. Pretty cute of him. Also, in a long talk I had with Georgia Cavendish she made no mention of her brother's having shown any particular interest in O'Brien. Of course she wouldn't, because she was deadly afraid her brother had killed him and she wouldn't care to give him away. But the impression I got from her was that O'Brien was interested in her brother and wanted to meet him. Now surely O'Brien wouldn't want to meet him if he had taken Judith away from him in the past and then deserted her? Judith must have told him about Cavendish after they'd fallen in love, and Georgia told him that her brother used to stay at Meynart House; so he must have identified Judith's first lover with Georgia's brother. That being so, if O'Brien had wronged Judith and Cavendish in the past, he would surely have been particularly on his guard against Edward."

Sir John Strangeways wrinkled his brows. "I see that. But are you going to make out that the Judith Fear business had nothing to do with the murder at all?"

"No, indeed. It had everything to do with it. Let's take that point next. Blount's theory was that Jack Lambert — O'Brien — had taken Judith from Cavendish, put the comether on her, given her a baby, left her, and by refusing to come back when she wrote to him for help, driven her to suicide. Now that gives

Cavendish a very good motive. But the facts are susceptible of an entirely different interpretation. In the first place, we knew O'Brien; and knowing him, one can be pretty sure he wouldn't treat a girl in that way: he was a wild enough spark in his young days, no doubt, but never what the feuilletons call a cad. Besides, there's good evidence that he deeply loved the girl."

"The nurse didn't seem to think so," said Sir John.

"She was biased, though. A dear old snob. Cavendish was 'quality' and Jack Lambert wasn't. But she placed the same false interpretation on what happened as Inspector Blount did, and even she believed Judith when she said she wasn't going to have a baby. Jack Lambert didn't 'desert' the girl: he went away to become an officer so that he'd have a better right to ask her father for her hand. The nurse said herself that Judith was 'spry enough' at first after he left. *Then* she got pale and silent and distracted. Not because she was going to have a baby: 'she'd never tell a lie', the old nurse said, and I believe her — she knew more about Judith Fear than Blount does: not because Lambert had deserted her — he hadn't. What was the one other thing we know happened between his departure and her death? *She received letters from Cavendish.* The nurse found her crying over one. 'What am I to do?' Judith said. 'It wasn't my fault. What did I do to him that he's so cruel. If daddy finds out —' The nurse thought she was talking about O'Brien. *I* am certain she was talking about Cavendish. The nurse had written to Cavendish, telling him what was going on. I submit that he wrote to Judith and said that if she didn't give up Jack Lambert and come back to him he'd expose her affair with Lambert to her father. I submit that such action would be entirely consonant with what we know of Cavendish's character, and that it explains perfectly Judith's outcry to the nurse. Her father was a stern man and she was a little frightened of him at the best of times. No wonder she cried, 'If daddy finds out —' And I'll go one further. We know that Judith wrote letters to Cavendish when she thought she was in love with him. She was an innocent, madcap, inexperienced, wildly romantic schoolgirl then. I wouldn't put it past Edward Cavendish to have threatened in addition that he would send those letters to her father if she didn't give up Jack Lambert."

"Yes," said Sir John slowly, "I think that's sound enough. But you haven't yet proved that O'Brien really did love this girl. Why didn't he come back to help her when she wrote to him?"

"Because he couldn't. Remember the evidence of Jimmy Hope, who was in the flight O'Brien got assigned to. A week after O'Brien arrived in France, he suddenly asked for leave — moved heaven and earth to get it — Hope said he was absolutely desperate. He couldn't get it; all leave had been stopped. Obviously he had received Judith's S.O.S. and was doing his best to go back and help her. A fortnight later Judith's brother receives a letter to say that she has drowned herself. It was after this that O'Brien went mad in the air — chucked his life away every day, only inscrutable Providence refused to accept it. And he kept on trying to kill himself for years. Do you still say he didn't really love her? — kept on until when?"

Sir John worried at his thick, sandy moustache. "Till when? I dunno. Till he gave up flying, I suppose. That was —"

"Yes," interrupted Nigel. "*O'Brien kept on trying to kill himself until he met Georgia Cavendish.*"

"Well. What then? He fell in love with her. Gave him a new interest: something to live for. Can't see it has much to do with the case."

"Yes. It certainly gave him a new interest in life," said Nigel, with a grimness that startled the other two. "But he didn't fall in love with Georgia. He was fond of her. They were lovers for a little. But it wasn't the same thing as with Judith Fear. Georgia said to me that time, 'I felt that he didn't care even for me — not wholeheartedly. There was always a part of him elsewhere.'" Nigel paused a moment. "Come along, Philip, you're fond of riddles. Why should meeting Georgia Cavendish alter O'Brien's whole manner of life?"

"Search me," the little don replied. "Perhaps she's a member of the Oxford Group."

Sir John Strangeways was sitting stone-still, his lips moving like the lips of a child trying to form some new and formidable word, almost comic expressions of bewilderment and incredulity and stupefaction passing over his face. Nigel glanced at him and went swiftly off at a tangent.

"Well then, Philip. As your excesses with my sherry seem to have obfuscated your usually brilliant

273

intelligence, I'll ask you a simpler one. At the Dower House on December the twenty-fifth, there were nine persons. O'Brien, Arthur Bellamy, Mrs Grant, Lucilla, Georgia, Edward Cavendish, Knott-Sloman, Philip Starling, Nigel Strangeways. Now which one of those fits best the following recipe for the murderer of O'Brien and Sloman? A person of steely courage and terrific ingenuity, possessing the type of humour that produced those threatening letters and daring enough to have carried out the threat; ingenious enough to have planned the nut-murder and with time enough to wait without showing any impatience till the nut took effect; a person with a very long memory, having access to Georgia's poison and to Knott-Sloman's typewriter; a person of sufficient literary attainments to be familiar with Tourneur's *Revenger's Tragedy*."

Philip Starling took a gulp of his sherry. His boyish, arrogant, appealing, brilliantly clever face wore an expression of unusual bewilderment and indecision. Finally he said:

"Well, old boy, I should say your conditions apply most accurately to myself."

Nigel moved swiftly over to the mantelpiece, and crammed a handful of salted almonds into his mouth. There was a short silence. Then Sir John Strangeways, articulating with the elaborate and unnatural caution of a drunken motorist before a police doctor, said:

"I think I am dreaming. But there's no shadow of doubt that your description, Nigel, applies to one and only one of those nine. I presume you have gone mad.

But the one person who answers that description accurately in every detail is Fergus O'Brien."

"Slow but sure," Nigel enunciated thickly through a barrage of salted almonds. "I was wondering when you'd get it."

Sir John spoke in quiet, humouring tones. "Your suggestion is, I take it, that O'Brien murdered himself?"

" 'Snot a suggestion. It's a fact."

"That, at the same time as he murdered himself, he was shot by Edward Cavendish?"

"Uh-huh, to quote Inspector Blount."

"And that, after he'd simultaneously murdered himself and been shot by Edward Cavendish, he poisoned Knott-Sloman?"

"Laboriously expressed, but true."

Sir John cast a pitying glance at his nephew, and said to Starling:

"Just ring up Colefax, will you? I believe he's the best alienist in London. You'd better send for two male attendants and an ambulance as well."

"I'll admit," Nigel continued imperturbably, "that it took me a little time to accustom myself to the idea. It's paradoxical, but, like all paradoxes, based on simplicity. I'll tell you the stages by which I arrived at it. First, there was Cavendish's demeanour. From the moment O'Brien's body was found I noticed that he looked, not merely nervous, but puzzled — bewildered, beat to the wide. Now if you've just murdered a chap, *pur et simple*, you don't look puzzled: there's no conundrum about it — merely a corpse. I called Blount's attention to Cavendish's demeanour, but it failed to ring the bell.

I couldn't understand myself why he looked so puzzled until that conversation I had with Georgia. The one thing which emerged clearly from it was that O'Brien seemed from the first peculiarly interested in her brother. There she was, in extremis, just rescued by him from certain death in the desert, and he starts plying her with questions about herself and her family. Later he went out of his way to cultivate Edward's acquaintance, although Edward was the last person you'd expect to be of any interest to him.

"Then I went over to Ireland. And it at once became apparent that, so far from Edward having reason to want O'Brien's blood, it was just the other way round. Cavendish had as good as forced Judith Fear into suicide, by threatening to expose her love affairs to her father. And she'd told O'Brien this in her last letter to him. Knowing O'Brien, that Irish temper which can remember wrongs for centuries — you yourself, uncle, said you thought he would have a long memory; knowing his ruthlessness, his grim humour, his passionate love for Judith Fear, I knew suddenly beyond all question that he was capable of waiting years for revenge, and then taking it.

"Once I'd got that clear I began to work out how the facts of the case fitted the theory of O'Brien as revenger. Somehow, evidently, he must have got Cavendish into a position in which Cavendish had to shoot him and then couldn't escape from the meshes. He wanted Cavendish to be tortured with the same agonies as Judith, the agonies of the trapped animal. His own life he didn't care two pins about — the doctors had said he was a dying man anyway. It seemed an insuperable problem — the mechanical side of it, I mean. I tried to imagine myself into the position of O'Brien, and start with the simplest point. How could he get Cavendish into the hut? Suddenly I remembered that note Lucilla wrote to O'Brien. 'I must see you tonight,' it ran. 'Can't we forget what has happened since — Meet me in the hut after the others have gone to bed,' etc. Now supposing O'Brien, after receiving it from her, had slipped it on to Cavendish's dressing table or somewhere. Lucilla had been Cavendish's mistress, so the second sentence would have a perfectly good meaning for him: O'Brien's name wasn't anywhere on the note, so Cavendish would have no reason to imagine it wasn't addressed to him. That was my first break. You see, the note was one way in which O'Brien could get Cavendish into the hut and be sure he wouldn't tell anyone else he was going.

"Well then, Cavendish and O'Brien are in the hut. In due course O'Brien suddenly threatens him with the revolver, acts as if he'd gone crazy-homicidal. He moves menacingly right up to Cavendish. But he doesn't mean to kill him — it would be letting him off too easily. He gets near enough to let Cavendish make a grab at the gun, struggles convincingly, presses Cavendish's finger on to the trigger as the revolver is pointing at him — and that was the end of Fergus O'Brien, and the beginning of his revenge. Of course, he was taking a risk. The risk that Cavendish would simply walk straight back to the house and tell everyone exactly what had happened. He was banking on Cavendish's psychological make-up — and he'd been studying that for months with all the deadly penetration of hate. He was banking on Cavendish's not having the nerve to tell the truth. And he won. Of course, he'd already taken steps to make it very difficult for Cavendish to tell the truth. He'd deliberately constructed two reasons why Cavendish should wish to murder him. He'd gone off with Lucilla; and he'd left Georgia a lot of money, knowing that Edward was financially in the soup. Those were the two motives, in fact, which made us first suspect Edward. The business of Judith Fear, I imagine, he did not want to be turned up; at any rate, he laid no train towards it: it's ironical that it was just this business which finally convinced the police that Cavendish was the murderer.

"I got so far in my imaginary reconstruction. There was nothing among the known facts that conflicted with this theory of O'Brien's getting Cavendish into the hut and trapping him into apparent murder. O'Brien had been helped by the snow, too, which he couldn't have counted on. But at this point old Edward put up a better fight than O'Brien had expected. He couldn't bring himself to tell what had actually happened: it would sound fantastic and would merely call attention to the very good reasons he had had for killing O'Brien. So he decided to fake a suicide. Except for the broken cufflink and the bruises on O'Brien's wrist, he left no clues behind him. The track in the snow was an improvisation of great brilliance. It's pretty gripping, when you come to think of it, this duel between a living man and a dead one."

The two listeners certainly were gripped. Philip Starling was following every point with alert and critical intelligence. Sir John's expression had passed from irritated incredulity, through scepticism, to a wary and qualified approval. Nigel went on.

"So far, so good for Edward Cavendish. But he couldn't keep it up. Whether Knott-Sloman had really seen him enter the hut and started to blackmail him, we shall never know. At any rate, Cavendish's morale — as O'Brien anticipated — began to collapse: he began to look exactly like a guilty man. But with a very important difference. He looked puzzled as well as nervous. Of course he looked puzzled. The fact that he did so clinched my bizarre theory. He was trying to puzzle out all the time why O'Brien had behaved in such an extraordinary way, why O'Brien had put him into such a precarious position. He had no reason to connect O'Brien with Jack Lambert. In fact, no other theory than mine could — as far as I could see — account for Cavendish looking both puzzled and apprehensive."

"Just a minute, Nigel. Surely O'Brien, if he had planned everything in this elaborate way, would have anticipated that Cavendish would fake a suicide?" asked Sir John.

"That was the very thing that next occurred to me. And it provided a reasonable explanation of four points that I didn't seem to be able to fit into any other theory. First, why should O'Brien have written those threatening letters and then shown them to us, except in order to make us suspicious of an appearance of

279

suicide when the time came? He made a mistake, though, in giving rein to his grim, impish sense of humour in those letters. He just couldn't deny himself a good joke. In fact, he said to me at dinner that first night, 'Y'know, if I was going to kill someone, I've a feeling I'd write to him just that way.' He couldn't resist a leg-pull. He ought to have written them in the character of Edward Cavendish. Second, the hints he let out about someone wanting to get hold of his aeroplane plans: I was puzzled almost from the beginning why he should load me up with a shilling-shocker tale of secret agents and the sinister Foreign Power and so on; it was just his flamboyant Irish imagination running away with him again. Third, the will. He told me he kept his will in the safe in the hut. Naturally, when we found his body, we looked in the safe, and the fact that it was empty seemed to prove that someone had murdered him to get hold of the will. He had, of course, taken it out of the safe — if it ever was there — and sent it in that sealed envelope to his solicitors long before. But he was a bit slipshod over his work here: didn't think it out far enough. Because it at once struck me as odd that any murderer should be able to open the safe. How could he know the combination? An intimate friend of his might know it, but surely not Cavendish. The fourth precaution he took against his death's being passed off as a suicide was to get me down. He hoped that I should be intelligent enough, with the aid of the hints he gave me, to see through a fake suicide: and he was convinced that I would not be intelligent enough to see right through to the real facts.

"When I had got that far, I was certain I held the true explanation of O'Brien's death. In no other way could I get round what was the biggest stumbling block — the question why O'Brien had allowed himself to be killed. From the beginning I could not really believe, you see, that a man like O'Brien, forewarned and forearmed against an attack as he was, would allow himself to be tricked and jumped on and then shot with his own revolver. It was fantastic. Then I looked around to see if other curious things I had noticed would fit in with my theory. Well, there was the photograph of Judith Fear in the hut. Why on earth should he remove and destroy it before the other guests arrived? The only sensible answer was that somebody might see it and recognise it, and that such a recognition would be fatal to his plans. But the only one of the guests who would recognise Judith Fear was Cavendish. Ergo, he destroyed it lest it should put Cavendish on his guard. All the time he was talking to me privately, too, I felt that there were dark undercurrents beneath what he was saying. After the other guests arrived, I was watching them like a stoat. I remember thinking on Christmas Day that the threats against O'Brien must be a hoax, because no one had seemed to be behaving less naturally to O'Brien than to the others, and I didn't believe you could plan a man's murder and yet act perfectly normally to him a few hours before it was scheduled. You may 'smile and smile, and be a villain,' but after the event, not before it. And, when I thought it over again, I realised that O'Brien was the only person there who was not behaving normally. He was just about to set in motion the events which were, slowly and surely, to murder Edward Cavendish. O'Brien hoped to give him a few weeks' hell with a noose at the end of them: even he could never have imagined the poetic justice of Cavendish's throwing himself from an aeroplane. Funny, I told Bleakley, long before I began to suspect, that I could imagine O'Brien killing a man for revenge."

Nigel paused. The other two were motionless. Then, as though by common consent, they raised their glasses to their lips. It might have been a toast, to Nigel; or perhaps to the remorseless, demon-driven spirit of Fergus O'Brien. Sir John said:

"I think perhaps we can postpone the visit of the alienist. That's a thundering good case you've made out, and I believe you're right. But what about Knott-Sloman? How did O'Brien kill him, and why?"

"Oh, compared with the rest of the case, that's fairly simple. The method pointed unerringly to O'Brien. Cavendish wouldn't have killed Knott-Sloman in that way, because if he wanted to get rid of him he'd want to get rid of him at once, before he could split to the police. If it were done when 'tis done, it were well it were done quickly. But O'Brien was in no hurry. He had eternity to wait, so a few days wouldn't matter. The nut was a delayed action shell and contained the kernel of the problem —"

Sir John groaned. "Didn't you teach him at Oxford that mixed metaphors are ungentlemanly, Starling?"

282

"On the contrary," said Nigel, "they are signs of a vivid and proleptic imagination. To proceed. If O'Brien had wished to kill Knott-Sloman after his own death, it was the *only* way he could do it. Delayed action. The revenging hand striking from Hades. O'Brien knew that Georgia had some poison and it wouldn't be very difficult for him to find where she kept it. He chose to kill Sloman in that post-mortem sort of way partly, I believe, in order to throw additional suspicion on Cavendish. He may have suspected that Sloman was blackmailing Cavendish, and of course Cavendish would be the obvious person to have pinched his sister's poison. O'Brien probably wrote the threatening letters on Knott-Sloman's typewriter with the same motive that a mischievous boy flings a stone at a church; it may hit a window or it may not. The threatening letters might hit Cavendish, a frequenter of the club, or Sloman its proprietor — or they might not. As it happened, they did. O'Brien took the poison, anyway, and prepared the nut and placed it at the bottom of the plateful by Knott-Sloman's bed. He had a funny womanish trait that made him like doing the household arrangements. It was he, I found, who put flowers in my bedroom and filled the biscuit tin. He knew Sloman's habit of cracking nuts in his teeth, and knew that he was the sort of greedy person who likes consuming his delicacies in private and is most unlikely to offer them to anyone else. But first he made sure at dinner that none of us could crack nuts with our teeth, and therefore would not be apt to do it in the ordinary course of events. It was taking a risk, of course. But

O'Brien had scant respect for human life, and the infinitesimal chance that the nut might get into the wrong person's mouth wouldn't worry him unduly. A bigger risk was that Georgia would be suspected of the murder. But he couldn't see any possible motive that might be attributed to her, I expect, and he didn't imagine for a moment that anyone could suspect her of killing himself. Everyone knew that she loved him.

"But the chief reason why Sloman had to be poisoned well after O'Brien himself died was that otherwise O'Brien might very easily have been suspected of it. You see, there was an obvious link between him and Knott-Sloman, and one would only have to pull on this sufficiently hard to draw up the real motive."

"I'll remember to use a link when I next go fishing," said Sir John sourly. "But what was the real motive? Blackmail?"

"No. Something much more colourful than that. The link was that they were both in the R.A.F. during the war. Sloman called O'Brien 'Slip-Slop' — a nickname that no one else of us used except Jimmy Hope, the chap in O'Brien's flight who lives near Bridgewest. It wasn't one of his nicknames that the press had familiarised us with — I was quite surprised when I first heard it. So it seemed a reasonable deduction that Knott-Sloman had served in the same unit as O'Brien. Now one of the first things that struck me about the house-party at Chatcombe was that it seemed really a very odd sort of party indeed. It was odd for a person like O'Brien, who ostensibly wanted to lead the life of a recluse, to have a party at all. It was still odder that he should invite at least three people who couldn't have been congenial to a man of his type — Cavendish, Lucilla and Knott-Sloman. He gave me the explanation that amongst the party were those he suspected as possible authors of the anonymous letters and that he wanted to have them under his eye. But that explanation only begged another question: Why had he ever taken up with a man like Knott-Sloman? Georgia told me that it was O'Brien's idea that he should go and visit Sloman's roadhouse. Yet O'Brien was the sort of person you'd think would avoid roadhouses like the plague."

"I must say I'd wondered myself what a bounder and a bore like Sloman was doing down here," said Philip Starling.

"Exactly. Now you remember telling me, uncle, that when O'Brien had become a flight commander some B.F. at headquarters ordered his flight to do a piece of ground strafing in impossible weather conditions, and all the flight were shot down except himself, and after that he became even more desperately daring than before. Now Jimmy Hope told me that, in the same week and the same sector, at the end of 1917 it was, Judith's brother had been shot down doing the same sort of work. He also told me how O'Brien and young Fear had been like David and Jonathan, how O'Brien looked after him in the air, and so on. Clearly, some of his love for Judith was transferred to young Fear: O'Brien tried to preserve her image in her brother. Now go over to a piece of Knott-Sloman's evidence. He said he had been a pilot in the R.A.F. and then got a staff job, and held command in O'Brien's sector from the summer of 1917. I hadn't begun to see light properly when I had that talk with Jimmy Hope. But after my day in Ireland I realised that O'Brien might very well have got it in for Knott-Sloman, *because Sloman had been the B.F. of a staff officer who sent young Fear to his death.* He held an Air Force command in that sector at that date. Last Tuesday I managed to dig up a bloke who was at H.Q. with Knott-Sloman, and he confirmed that Sloman did give the order. Cavendish was made to suffer the slow mental agonies of Judith, Knott-Sloman the swift annihilation of Judith's brother. It was poetical justice — poetical in more ways than one," Nigel added ruminatively.

"Is that, by any chance, a reference to *The Revenger's Tragedy?'* asked Philip Starling.

"You're waking up. Yes, it is. And that's what I meant by saying that you had given me the solution of the problem. You were the person who called my attention to the curious mistake O'Brien made at dinner when he quoted some lines from the play and attributed them to Webster. It was a kind of tryout — to see if anyone knew the play well enough to recognise the mistake. Not that he would have altered his plans if anyone had, I believe. But the fact is that both the murders and their motives had a most astonishing counterpart in that play of Tourneur's, as doubtless you realise now, Philip."

"Could you stop this literary chat, and tell me what you're driving at?" exclaimed Sir John Strangeways.

286

"If you would occasionally read something more high-class than seven-and-sixpenny bloods and gardening catalogues," retorted Nigel offensively, "you would not only improve your mind, but you would also render it unnecessary for me to give you elementary lessons in English literature. *The Revenger's Tragedy*, Tourneur, 1607, or thereabouts. A piece of really juicy Elizabethan carnage, interspersed with some divine bits of poetry. It opens very agreeably. A young man called Vendice enters with a skull in his hand. Then a Duke, whom Vendice addresses spiritedly but presumably *soatto voce*, 'Duke! Royal lecher! Go, grey-haired adultery!' He then warms to his work and calls the Duke a number of other things, including 'a parched and juiceless luxur'. It transpires presently that the skull Vendice holds is that of his dead mistress, whom the Duke has poisoned because she would not, in Vendice's admirably outspoken words, 'consent unto his palsied lust'. Cavendish was an old man compared with Judith, and she died because she would not consent to him.

"O'Brien must have been reading the play when he was contemplating his revenge, because both the situation and the action of Vendice correspond in a really uncanny way with O'Brien's. In the play, Vendice destroys the Duke by becoming his pander and then leading him into a pavilion at night with the promise of a new wench. He has rigged up a dummy behind a curtain, topped by the skull of his mistress, the lips of which he has smeared with a corrosive poison. The Duke rushes at this figure, kisses the skull before he realises that someone has made a terrible mistake, and

287

dies in acute discomfort. Now compare the Dower House version. O'Brien — Vendice: Cavendish — the Duke. O'Brien lures Cavendish into a pavilion at night, by pandering to his weakness, viz. Lucilla. It was really an amazing coincidence that Lucilla should have sent O'Brien that note just then, for by passing it on to Cavendish he was accurately re-enacting the business by which Vendice lured the Duke to his doom. It was the same with Knott-Sloman. He was killed through the instrument of his own appetite — he was excessively greedy over nuts: and that, too, was a murder of sheer, naked, flamboyant, rhetorical, Elizabethan revenge. Herbert Marlinworth was saying truer than he knew when he called O'Brien 'the last of the Elizabethans'.

"O'Brien must have had the play at his fingertips. You remember, Philip, the lines he quoted at dinner: 'Does the Silkworm expend her yellow labors For thee? For thee does she undo herself?' If only I'd remembered the three lines that come immediately before that passage, I'd have had the solution of everything in my hands. Listen to them —"

Nigel spoke the lines, his voice low and a little harsh as ever, but passionate with some profound emotion. Judith Fear, that sweet bewildered innocent whom he had never known, was as real to him at that moment as his two friends in the room:

"'And now methinks I could e'en chide myself
For doating on her beauty, though her death
Shall be revenged after no common action.'

288

"Yes, Judith Fear's death was revenged after no common action," Nigel went on after a long silence. "O'Brien had those lines on his lips as he went out to revenge her through his own death. The speeches of the remorseless, heartbroken Vendice must have been running through his head for months before. Why, the very first words he spoke to me were a phrase of Vendice's; and if only I'd been a bit quicker on the uptake I would have realised he had given me the first clue to the whole tortuous affair. I was snooping about in the hut; he caught me looking at that photograph of Judith Fear, and he came up behind me and said, 'My study's ornament'. I remember thinking vaguely it was rather an odd remark. The day Cavendish killed himself I read through *The Revenger's Tragedy,* and on the second page I came to this: Vendice is talking to the skull; he says:

"'My study's ornament, thou shell of death,
Once the bright face of my betrothed lady . . .'

"Thou shell of death. A shell contained O'Brien's vengeance on Knott-Sloman. And O'Brien's death was like a shell that held in secret the answer to the deaths of his two enemies. 'It is a piteous tale.' One could not help loving O'Brien. But for him love was buried in the grave of Judith. After she was dead, from the moment he brought down his first enemy plane to the moment he baited with his own body the trap for Cavendish, life for him was a revenger's tragedy, a shell of death."

There was a long, long silence in the room. The sound of traffic pulsed and ebbed along the streets below. Then Philip Starling rose to his feet and exclaimed briskly:

"Well, Nigel, old boy, you're a credit to my pedagogy. The only redeeming feature I can see in this case is the extinction of Knott-Sloman. A squalid fellow."

"Oh, I wouldn't quite say that," Nigel said softly. "Not the *only* redeeming feature."

Judith Fear's lovely, sad, elfish face was fading from his mind's eye. And the face of Georgia Cavendish seemed to smile at him out of the shadowy future.

Also available in ISIS Large Print:

Sidney Chambers and the
Shadow of Death

James Runcie

Sidney Chambers, the Vicar of Grantchester, is a 32-year-old bachelor. Tall, with eyes the colour of hazelnuts, he is both an unconventional clergyman and a reluctant detective. Working in association with his friend, Inspector Geordie Keating, Sidney is able to go where the Police cannot, eliciting surprise revelations and confessions from his parishioners; whether it involves the apparent suicide of a local solicitor, a scandalous jewellery theft at a New Year's Eve dinner party, or the unexplained death of a jazz promoter's daughter. Alongside his inquiries, Sidney also manages to find time to enjoy cricket, warm beer, hot jazz, and the company of an attractive, lively young woman called Amanda.

ISBN 978-0-7531-9044-9 (hb)
ISBN 978-0-7531-9045-6 (pb)

The Blind Side

Patricia Wentworth

Craddock House was so full of squabblers, gossips, feuding family and eavesdroppers that Ross Craddock's killer must have felt quite at home. There was Lee Fenton, Ross's first cousin, heard calling Ross "a swine" and subsequently sleepwalking (so she claimed) into the victim's flat. There was the loveable spinster aunt whom Ross was cruelly evicting and who just happened to enter the house at 2a.m. — in time to see a figure fleeing. And there was the beautiful blood-smudged Mavis Grey, quite capable of looking after herself; and Bobby Foster, Mavis's enraged suitor, who managed to leave his fingerprints all through the house. Indeed, with so many clues and suspects throwing themselves at Inspector Lamb, how could he possibly notice the deadliest one of all?

ISBN 978-0-7531-9040-1 (hb)
ISBN 978-0-7531-9041-8 (pb)